Stitching a Dream

by

Ellen Parker

The Wild Rose Press, Inc.
PO Box 708
Adams Basin, NY 14410-0708
Visit us at www.thewildrosepress.com

Publishing History
First Edition, 2024
Trade Paperback ISBN 978-1-5092-5632-7
Digital ISBN 978-1-5092-5633-4

Published in the United States of America

Dedication

To Roy,
for his patience and participation in research trips
disguised as vacation.

Praise for Ellen Parker

"STITCHING A DREAM is a masterful glimpse of German immigrants settling into American culture. This story highlights the difficulties of overcoming language barriers and social morays to earn respect and acceptance as part of a community. Wonderfully crafted. Highly recommend you read this."

~Linda Gilman, author

~*~

"The book was So Good! Felt like I was right there as everything was happening."

~Barbara Bettis, author of The Right Knight

~*~

"STITCHNG A DREAM is a sweet historical romance about a woman building a new life for herself and her son. Her principles are tested but she sticks to them even when it causes hardship. If you love slow burn romance and found family, this book is for you."

~Wendy Blanton, author

Chapter One

Elm Ridge, Illinois, September 26, 1851

Polly Black lifted her gaze from the plain wood coffin. Similar to the other two dozen mourners gathered in the cemetery, she stood stiff and silent. *Respectful. Childbirth is hazardous.* She held her breath as four men lowered the late Jane Rush and her infant son into the deep grave.

Pastor Harter, leader of Elm Ridge's American Christian Church, launched into a rambling prayer.

Shifting her weight without moving her feet, Polly glanced to the far side of the wagon track. More than a dozen stone markers of various sizes marked graves in the German Lutheran portion of the town cemetery. In a blink, the pleasant September afternoon vanished, and memories of a spring sky before rain overwhelmed her.

A little more than two weeks after arriving in Elm Ridge from St. Louis, she had stood over there, near the elm. She stayed separate from the other mourners and grieved baker Bernard Keil in private. Pleased to see many friends gathered, she recognized only the new widow and the young bakery assistant. She blinked back tears, remembering the ladies' kindness during her first visit to the shop. Listening carefully, she managed to pick out the words *Gott, Himmel, und Engle* from the pastor's final prayer. "God, heaven, and angel," she whispered.

A steamboat whistled on the Mississippi River.

Polly jerked into the present. Dipping her head, she studied the green, gathered shirt of her best dress for a long moment. She lifted her handkerchief, blotted stray tears, and backed one step. *I must not act foolish.* She recalled two brief conversations after church services with the shy Mrs. Rush. With one hand, she stilled the end of her bonnet ribbon before shifting her gaze toward the immediate family at the end of the grave. *Husband, young daughter, sister with husband and three sons,* she mouthed. *I will keep them in my prayers.*

"Shall we go?" Abigail Clark—owner of the town's sole dress shop, Polly's employer, and true friend—touched her arm.

"Certainly." She cast a final glance toward the *Deutsch* portion of the cemetery and stepped toward the wagon track.

"'Tis a sadness when a young wife is taken." Mrs. Clark, a widow of many years, half-stumbled on the uneven ground.

Polly grasped the older woman's elbow. Half her employer's age and four inches taller, she supplied a strong, guiding arm. She swallowed thoughts of similar grief evident on so many faces when a kind, vigorous man died unexpectedly. "Easy now. No good will come if you are lame when we re-open for business tomorrow."

"No fear." She patted Polly's hand when they reached level ground near the gate. "I've gotten my feet on the path now."

Polly matched her step to Abigail's. Tipping her

head, she tucked a wayward, light-brown curl into place and gazed at the clear, bright-blue sky. Strolling in companionable silence, she listened to their footsteps on the plank sidewalk and admired the mixture of buildings constructed with brick and others of wood along Fruit Street. "Tonight, I will finish hemming the drape to separate the shop and living quarters. We make a good team, you and I."

Abigail chuckled without breaking her stride.

"I speak the truth. Your skill at organizing a shop, designing a dress, and cutting without waste is unmatched. My strength is limited to the mundane work of stitching the pieces together."

"Pshaw. You have a good eye for color. At your tender age, I struggled to select fabric flattering to a customer's complexion."

Tender age? I'm five and twenty. I have a child old enough to begin school.

"After our summer disaster, you lifted my spirits. When you suggested we offer mending while the new building was under construction, the work enabled me to keep a clear mind. I did not place an unnecessary burden on my sister and her family." She halted a dozen steps from Third Street. "We might have received a blessing in disguise."

Blessing? Polly shivered in the mild air. Months later, memories of her carelessness with the kindling and the resulting disaster haunted her dreams. "The fire destroyed all our supplies and my living quarters. Joseph's life depended on a near stranger. "I do not understand how you see a blessing."

Abigail shook her head before launching into an explanation. "During your weeks with *Frau* Keil, you

3

increased your language skills and developed friendships in the *Deutsch* community. Perhaps some of the immigrants will become our customers."

"You would have done similar." She glanced toward the wooden sidewalk and felt a flush climb her neck.

Abigail adjusted her shawl and resumed walking. "Go and fetch your son from the bakery. Do not hurry home. You have earned a nice visit with your *Deutsch* friends."

"The unpacking?" Polly recalled the bright bolts of cloth waiting to be arranged on the new shelves.

"Half a barrel of goods is easy to manage." Mrs. Clark swished her hands, urging Polly to go. "Reward me with a few of the delicious ginger cookies the *Fraulein* bakes—if any remain."

A few minutes later, Polly stepped into Keil's Bakery and drew a deep breath. Scents of fresh bread, cut apples, and warm cinnamon wafted in the air. She peered through the nearly empty shelves and glimpsed her son's bright-copper hair beside *Fraulein* Mueller's elbow. *He is growing. I want to keep him close.* Good sense returned and she sighed. Next month, the school term began. The time was proper for him to learn from an actual schoolmaster. She also hoped he would make a friend or two. *"Guten Abend, Frau* Keil. Was Joseph obedient?"

"Your boy was good as gold." The tall, slender woman handed change to a customer with a round basket. "You arrived at a good time. Soon, I will close for the day. Can you stay for tea?"

"Mama." The boy turned and smiled. Setting a small, white bowl and bleached, linen towel on the sturdy worktable, he hurried toward her in his unique, limping gait. "*Fraulein* Mueller let me dry the spoons…and…other things."

Polly pulled her son close and ruffled his hair. *The only inheritance from his father.* "I am glad to hear a good report. Yes, I will stay for tea and a short chat."

"Come to the garden." Louisa Mueller, the young, fair-haired baker, paused at the doorless workroom entrance while drying her hands on her apron. "I want you to see how large the cabbages have grown. Thanks to your diligent work at keeping the weeds pulled, we will have many crocks of kraut this winter."

A short time later, wearing a borrowed apron over her church dress, Polly leaned over one of the raised beds in the bakery's garden and pulled a shriveled potato vine. "Careful now," she addressed Joseph, "let me dig with the fork, and together, we will find the treasure for supper."

"One…two…three." Joseph counted potatoes and placed them in a bucket. "We wash. We eat."

"After the washing, we cook before we eat." Polly lifted the container and stepped toward the garden gate.

"Did you go to a burial today?"

She caught her balance after the unexpected question. Delaying a response until she set the bucket under the pump spout, she faced her son. "Yes. Pastor Harter led a funeral service for a woman and her baby."

"Like when Papa died?" He leaned toward his stronger leg until his right foot was barely on the ground.

Fighting against the second wave of memories on the topic in one afternoon, she grasped the pump handle. *Dreams of Joseph meeting his father were crushed under a wagon on a mild, May afternoon.* Details insisted on returning. Honest, reliable men, construction workers near the accident site, stated the wagon bore the symbol of her brother, Leo's, grist mill. *Was he involved?* She shook the idea away. *Leo disliked the victim, but he is a swindler, not a violent man.* She gave silent thanks her brother moved from Elm Ridge last month.

"Mama?"

"Yes, Joseph." She focused on her son's question. "Today's service was in English. Pastor Harter said the prayers. For your Papa, the prayers and readings were in *Deutsch.*"

"Papa spoke *Deutsch?*" He widened his eyes.

She nodded. *Soon...I must find a suitable time to tell my son more of his father.*

****

Ignoring the noise of roustabouts moving freight into the levee warehouse, Kurt Tafel slid a pin into the bracket to secure the wagon's rear board. "*Ende.*" He slapped the smooth wood with one hand and smiled at the young driver. "We make good use of today's final light. Do you know the wheelwright's place—where Apple and Third Streets meet?"

Hans Hoffmann continued along the wagon's side and touched the brake linkage. "*Ja*, easy to find."

"*Gute.*" Kurt set one foot on the left, front wheel hub and hoisted himself onto the high seat. Settling his large frame into position, he sighed. He removed his flat, leather cap and pushed fingers through thick hair in need of a trim. *Elm Ridge, Illinois—my new home.* He reviewed the most important events since arriving on yesterday's northbound packet steamboat. The newspaper articles which drew him to this town were correct in saying the *Deutsch* immigrant portion of the village was growing. He held a little skepticism regarding the price the land agent required to rent a shop with attached living quarters. However, during his stroll around town last evening, he did not see much competition to his cobbler trade. A moment later, Hans perched on the wagon seat. Without a word to his passenger, he unwrapped the reins, released the brake, and ordered the team into motion. The horses, a pair of Percheron geldings, climbed the slope from levee to the main portion of the town at a steady rate.

"Tell me, young man, have you lived long in Illinois?" Kurt studied the driver without turning his head. *Young for a teamster. Holds his body stiff. Handles the team well.*

"Arrived in April…this year. The town is a good place. I plan to stay. Kind people—for the most part."

At the final phrase, Kurt sealed his lips. Yes, every village or city, no matter where or when the people immigrated from, contained a few residents determined to make life difficult for their neighbors. "Much like Pennsylvania then."

"Tell me of Pennsylvania. On the ship, I viewed a map, but I do not remember all the places. You travelled from east, no?" Hans guided the team past shops with both English and *Deutsch* signs.

For the next several minutes, Kurt talked of his family and glanced at the activity on the street and sidewalks. "*Grossvater* brought his bride to America and earned his living as a shoemaker. The trade is a family tradition, going back to my grandfather's grandfather and beyond. My father and brothers also both make and repair shoes. However, Pikeland is not large enough to support five Tafel brothers in the same business. So I read of Illinois in the newspaper and set out on an adventure. If all goes well, I will encourage my youngest brother to join me."

Hans nodded understanding. "An honest man with a trade does well here."

Kurt paused his gaze on the driver's sturdy, wooden shoes. *Appear new.* In the next instant, he glanced over his shoulder to check all his worldly goods remained secure. "*Ja.* Tell me, have you driven wagons long?"

Laughing, Hans turned his head for only a moment. "My usual duties at Bergmann's Livery are mucking stalls, preparing rations, and cleaning harness. But the horses and I grow fond of each other. Today, when *Herr* Weiss returned from his morning assignment too ill to sit upright, *Herr* Bergmann allowed me to take this short, simple chore."

"Your employer shows much trust." Kurt moved his gaze from one side of the street to the other as the team plodded steady toward the foundry's chimney, the tallest structure in the village. He noticed two women in dark bonnets carrying baskets draped with checkered cloths. A man in a cloth workman's cap crossed the street and a well-dressed man exited a shop. A moment later, he sighted a woman in a green dress and black shawl guiding a small, red-haired boy into a new building.

Hans pulled the team to a halt at the corner. Pointing toward a long, low, vacant building across the diagonal, he half-stood. "Is this the place?"

"*Ja.* Pull to the side. I will open a double-wide

door and make the unloading easy. No?" Moments later, Kurt unlocked the front door to the rented shop and stepped into air laden with traces of hardwood shavings and stale tobacco. He hurried through the work area and unbarred a pair of wide doors. "We make quick work."

Hans lowered the wagon tailgate and climbed into the bed.

For the next twenty minutes, Kurt and Hans transferred chests and barrels of household goods, tools, and leather into the building.

Kurt set one hand on the largest chest. He skimmed his fingers over the dark wood scarred from much handling through the years since it held all his grandfather's possessions during the journey from Westphalia to Pennsylvania. "*Danke, danke.* How much to settle my bill for a day of storage and delivery?"

"*Herr* Bergmann." Hans removed his dark, wool cap and wiped his brow. "*Herr* Bergmann will figure the cost. Do you want a ride to the stable?"

"*Gute.*" Kurt became aware of a warm flush on his neck. Only a fool would expect a temporary driver to know the fees and handle money. The employer's trust was shown by putting the horses into the young man's care. "One minute, I lock the building against the town thief before I go with you and clear my account."

Hans retreated to the team and checked the harness.

Shrugging, Kurt tended to his own tasks. In a few moments, he approached the wagon, stepped on the hub, and settled beside Hans. "We go now. I noticed a tavern near the stables. Do they serve an evening meal?"

"*Ja,* decent stew and beer at modest price. I eat

under their roof many a night."

"And the other days—when you do not dine at the tavern?"

The driver blushed. "*Mein Schatz.* Pretty girl. Baker."

"A sweetheart. *Danke.*" Kurt chuckled. "Now I will not embarrass myself or flirt with pretty girl at the bakery."

An hour later, Kurt scooped the last bite from a bowl of ham and vegetable stew. *Best meal since...guest of* Herr *and* Frau *Heilmann in St. Louis.* He sipped beer and studied the other tavern patrons. Always quick to glance at a stranger's shoes, he watched a man arrive and place his wooden clogs in the line of footwear against the wall. The brogans and boots worn by the tavern patrons varied from new to tattered. *Business will be good—if I can persuade them to come to my shop.*

A loud laugh from a nearby table jerked Kurt out of his musing. He lifted his stein and smiled at a pair of men starting a card game. Glancing toward the ceiling, he remembered he needed to introduce himself and talk of his trade at more than the levee and stable. He pressed his lips as the novice teamster, Hans Hoffmann, joined two other young men in another part of the room. He studied the man and recognized a twinge of jealousy. *Two full years have passed since Irish Kathleen abandoned me for a railroad worker—Irish and Catholic.* Downing the last of his beer, he forced his thoughts to practical matters—preparing and opening his shop. He pushed dreams of wife and family into the future.

Chapter Two

Midmorning the next day, Polly listened for a moment before opening the drape between the dress shop workroom and sales area. *Our first official day of business since the July fire.* She pushed the thick fabric aside and fastened the loop to hold the divider open.

"We have a nice supply of fine, white cotton. Have you considered a new collar to freshen your Sunday dress?" Abigail enticed a customer to make a modest purchase.

"I'm not certain. Actually, I came to ask you about a repair." Mrs. Fox, their neighbor, lifted a christening gown from her basket. "I want to gift this gown to my daughter. However, it is damaged. Can you reset the sleeves?"

"Hmmm. It will be a tricky business." Abigail held the garment to take full advantage of the sunlight through the window. "We can do it. Let me spread the gown onto the counter for a closer inspection."

In silence, Polly stepped to the worktable and threaded a needle. She slid one of a pair of new, deep-rose undersleeves toward her and prepared to place the first basting stitch.

"Mama."

Polly shifted her attention from the conversation and gave it to her son. "What do you need, Joseph?"

"May I play outside?" He stood with wide,

pleading eyes and the divider curtain resting against his shoulder.

She turned her head and checked the sky through the window. Noting a fine, clear day, she sealed her lips while her protective nature debated common sense. This summer, during their weeks sharing the bakery apartment with *Frau* Keil, her son matured in front of her eyes. Unlike scant months ago, he showed great interest in the world around him and asked many questions about how and why to do everyday tasks. "Did you carry in wood for the stove?" She waited for his nod. "Stay close. Come straight home when the noon foundry whistle blows."

"Yes, Mama. Thank you, Mama." He turned toward the back door.

"Bid farewell to Mrs. Clark."

"Yes, Mama." He brushed tiny bits of dirt and bark from his shirt before he stepped forward. A moment later, he addressed Abigail in a rush. "Good day, Mrs. Clark and…Mrs. Fox. I go to explore."

"Be careful in the street," Mrs. Clark advised.

Mrs. Fox cleared her throat. "Will you visit the new neighbor?"

"New neighbor?" Polly tucked her needle for the next large stitch. She'd heard nothing of a newcomer to this corner during her last round of errands.

"Across the street…my Charles noticed a light at the front window late last evening." Mrs. Fox fussed with the blue cloth in her shopping basket.

Polly glanced toward Joseph.

He stilled with one hand on the shop's door knob.

"If you visit, mind your manners." She intersected his gaze. He nodded, rotated the knob, and slipped outside amid the bell's tinkle.

"A family?" Polly directed her question to Mrs. Fox. If a new neighbor had children, perhaps Joseph could make a friend.

The cooper's wife shrugged. "I observed the land agent talking with a stranger on the lot yesterday—a tall man."

"I suspect our little scout will be full of information when he returns for lunch." Mrs. Clark focused on the christening gown draped across the counter.

Little scout. Polly stifled a laugh, bobbed her head to Mrs. Fox, and returned her attention to the new undersleeves for Mrs. Hill, an order placed early in the week, before the shop officially re-opened. Placing large basting stitches, Polly make quick progress. Each time she removed a pin and placed it into the green, velvet pincushion, she drew a deep breath. The scent of fresh plaster faded a little each day. However, she remained determined to keep her sparse furniture from touching the walls until well into next week. She took another stitch. As she worked, she recalled a description of the shop across the street—a building with a large apartment—two bedrooms—plenty of room for a family. Dare she wish for Joseph to make a playmate or she a friend?

****

After eleven the same morning, Kurt hummed "*Grossvatertanz,* Grandfather Dance" and cleaned his new workshop. He turned the broom and coaxed dirt from the corner behind the front door. *Ein gute Tag.* A good day. He swished the accumulated dirt into a small mound with brisk strokes. In the next moment, he held a piece of bent tin against the floor and collected the debris. Straightening, he glanced around the tidied space. The cobwebs were gone and the floor clean, but not to his mother's high standards. He sighed and blinked away a memory of the spotless kitchen in the tidy, six-room Tafel home. "*Vater,*" he whispered, "you maintained the shop in an equally neat condition." He shook his head. A man, or a boy, soon lost count of the number of times *Herr* Tafel admonished his sons to return expensive tools and the important carved, hardwood lasts which shaped the shoes, to their proper places.

Kurt ambled through a narrow doorway into the apartment. Dumping the debris from the shop floor into a bucket, he surveyed the living quarters. The dust laid thick on every surface, too much for the building to have been empty only one month. He set one hand on the scarred table, the only furniture in the room, and the piece wobbled. *First, I sweep—then, I find proper shims for the table's short leg.*

Working steadily, Kurt muttered lists of all the things to do before he could open for business. "I must check the chimneys for both stoves—shop and kitchen. I will inquire about an honest wood dealer. Purchase a cot or proper bed—today. Explore the shed for materials to install more pegs and shelves in the shop. Introduce myself at every store I enter. I cannot be shy—people in Elm Ridge do not know the Tafel reputation in shoemaking." Lost in the rhythm of the light, physical work, he started to sing. "The moon has risen…"

"The little golden stars…"

Kurt spun toward the origin of the high, clear voice. Closing his lips to hide his surprise, he discovered a small, red-haired boy standing at the open kitchen door. In an instant, he estimated the child's age as four, no more than five. "*Wer? Welcher?*"

"*Mein...mein...*"

Holding his mouth steady in a hint of a smile, Kurt studied the child with wide, brown eyes and clasped hands. "*Wei heissen Sie?*"

"I go. No trouble." The boy retreated two awkward steps.

"*Nein.* Don't go. I speak English. Better?" Kurt held his breath until the boy nodded. "My name is *Herr* Tafel. What are you called?"

Pursing his lips, the boy blinked. "Joseph."

"A good name—from the Bible." He raised his gaze to the street where a single horse pulled a cart piled high with firewood. "Tell me, Joseph"—he squatted to be nearer in height—"do you live near?"

The boy nodded, swallowed, and edged forward. "I live with Mama at the dress shop."

Kurt failed to recall mention of a dressmaker in the land agent's ramblings about the neighbors. Remembering the view through the dirty shop window, he ventured a guess. "Across the street...in the new building?"

"The loft smells like fresh wood. I pretend I sleep in a tree. Very pleasant. Unless I dream of the fire. Then I get scared and wish to be at the bakery again."

"Ahh." Kurt stood and recalled several of the comments overheard at the tavern during last evening's supper. According to one man, the plasterer finished last week. Another worker claimed to have completed installing a counter and shelves three days ago. Kurt shifted his thinking to the present situation. "Is your mother a dressmaker?"

"Mama sews. Mrs. Clark owns the shop. She smells like peppermints. Sometimes, she rewards me with one."

"A good smell—peppermints." Kurt added a few of the candies to his mental list of basic pantry items.

Joseph inched across the threshold. "What work do you do?"

"I am a cobbler. I repair shoes…and make new ones." He glanced toward the boy's bare feet. *Summer is near an end. I hope he has shoes for winter.*

"Our neighbor, Mr. Fox, makes barrels. One day, he let me watch."

"It is good to watch—and learn."

A loud whistle shattered the conversation.

Joseph clapped his hands over his ears until the sound faded. "Foundry whistle—I must go home. Good-bye, *Herr* Tafel."

"Come visit again." Kurt wished to call back his words as soon as they left his lips. An invitation was polite. However, children caused him unease. From the doorway, he watched the boy scamper in an uneven gait around the end of his workshop. He hurried to the front window and spied the child as he stepped onto the wood sidewalk. In the next moment, the boy continued along the side of the new building and out of sight. *Mama sews. No mention of Papa.*

For a long moment, he stared toward the front of the dress shop. New and unpainted, the structure was narrow to the street and included two steps from sidewalk to door. He observed a stout woman in a dark shawl and black bonnet exit the building and cross Third Street. "The shop owner, Mrs. Clark? The same building a woman with a green dress and black shawl entered with a boy yesterday. I must call on my neighbors," he whispered into the still air. "I start with…Mr. Fox, the cooper…like a proper newcomer."

Chapter Three

Sunday morning, Polly stood in front of the shop's long mirror. Brushing final specks of lint from narrow, dark-green pleats on her bodice, she sighed. The mirror revealed pale cheeks and tired eyes. She settled her green bonnet over russet hair confined in a simple bun. She suppressed a yawn and concentrated on tying the wide, black ribbons. *Vanity is a sin.* During a slow blink, she gave thanks for eyes which functioned well, regardless of size or set. "Joseph, are you ready?"

"Yes, Mama." He eased past the tan drape separating living quarters from the business area.

She inspected his face. "Good, no crumbs." She adjusted one of his suspenders a fraction of an inch before giving one more glance toward her mirror image. "Come, it is time to walk to church."

"May I sit by the window today?"

"Perhaps." *To count birds during the sermon?* She draped a black shawl across her shoulders and tied a neat knot. A moment later, she handed Joseph his new, flat wool cap and followed him out the front door. Pivoting on the top step, she locked the shop.

"Good morning, *Herr* Tafel."

Eager to see the man Joseph chattered about during yesterday's lunch, she curved her lips into a small smile before turning. The man crossing the street was large, near to six feet tall, with wide shoulders. He wore a well-cut, dark suit over a white, linen shirt. His face was round, his cheeks ruddy, and his mouth open as if to speak. "God has given us a fine, autumn day, has He not?" He doffed a flat, leather cap and exposed abundant, pale hair.

She swallowed sudden moisture gathering in her mouth and forced her gaze to abandon the handsome man. His favored address of *Herr* implied immigrant. She reminded herself to be both polite and cautious. "Indeed. Good morning—I am Polly Black. I believe you have already met my son."

"Correct." He gave a brief nod toward Joseph before he looked directly at her face. "I walk this morning to the German Lutheran Church on Sixth Street. Are you going the same direction? May I escort you?"

She managed to hide her smile at his good English with a definite *Deutsch* accent. "My son and I attend the American Christian Church on the same street. You are welcome to accompany us today. I believe your destination is a few blocks farther."

"Excellent. *Danke.*" He replaced his hat and matched her step as the trio started on the sidewalk. "It is good to meet you. A person does well to become acquainted with their neighbors. Friendship can be born from simple introductions. No?"

She pressed her lips to smother building laughter. *Deutsch* question and sentence structure continued to humor her, even after years of acquaintance with the immigrant seamstresses in St. Louis and recent weeks living with *Frau* Keil. "Friends is good. Tell me, *Herr* Tafel, have you lived in America many years?"

"All my life." He offered a hand to steady her

elbow as she stepped into the street. "Until I started my journey this summer, I live in Pennsylvania. *Mein Grossvater's* generation settled in a fine town one day's journey from Philadelphia. In recent years, many Irish and Americans arrive and become neighbors to the *Deutsch*. Many new customs among the residents—the little community sounds like a babble in the marketplace."

"Well said." She glanced to his dark-brown, polished boots. "Joseph reported you are a cobbler."

"*Ja,* six generations the trade goes back in my family. Four brothers and I learn from *Vater und Grossvater.* The newspapers are full of reports from Illinois...speaking much of opportunity. I decide one-and-thirty years under my parents' roof is long enough. I begin an adventure. Elm Ridge"—he gestured at a new addition to a building—"grows. I pray business follows."

"I wish you well." She raised her gaze to the modest, red-brick building across the street and halted. "Since Joseph and I arrived in mid-May, we have met many kind people—American and immigrant."

Turning his head, he nodded at the structure with a double-wide, white door and painted window frames. "Church? We part here?"

"Do you know the rest of the way?"

"*Ja.* I see white cross on steeple." He pointed south before he removed his cap and faced her.

Joseph tugged on Kurt's sleeve. "May I come and watch you make shoes?"

"Ask your mother."

"May I?" Joseph tipped his head and stared with wide eyes.

When you ask so politely, I want to give you the entire world. She moistened her lips. "Not today. We will talk later. Now is time for worship."

"Mrs. Black, Joseph, I wish you a fine day." Kurt half-bowed, pivoted, and strode along Sixth Street.

Standing still, Polly held her breath as he walked away. The jingle of harness, as a buggy pulled to a stop in front of the church, snapped her attention away from the new neighbor and the questions swirling in her mind.

Half an hour later, Polly sat straight and pretended to listen to every word of the sermon. Inside her brain, words unrelated to the pastor's message circled. She marveled at the idea a new acquaintance was born and raised to adulthood while under the same roof. In silence, she counted different states, towns, and houses where she'd lived. Her first memories were of three towns and five houses in Ohio. *Mama said I was born in Virginia, in a little settlement a mile from the Ohio River.* She hid her fingers in her skirt folds and recalled two villages and three houses in Illinois. Blinking slowly, she remembered burying her mother in Vandalia. *Papa, Leo, and I moved to St. Louis before a week passed.*

"Thus saith the Lord." Pastor Harter thumped one hand onto the sturdy lectern.

"Amen," Polly replied within the congregation's chorus. A few minutes later, she stood and bowed her head for prayer. Unbidden, her thoughts drifted to the past. She shivered at the memory of loading the wagon late one night during her twelfth summer, the first time she realized why Papa moved the family so often— always west. Walking beside the horse on the road to

Vandalia, she finally understood Papa swindled people and fled ahead of the law. She clasped her hands tightly and pondered the actions of her brother, Leo, a man continuing his father's sly business practices. Her inquiries in St. Louis indicated Leo threatened Bernard's life and drove him from the city to prevent her marriage to the baker. She clenched her hands until they hurt, knowing the excuse he would give—immigrant.

"Mama," Joseph whispered. "Does pastor pray for every person in the world by name?"

Holding one upright finger against her lips, she suppressed a smile. After a final hymn and a blessing, Polly guided Joseph out of the building into warm, midday sunshine. She greeted several women with a nod and a smile before she paused on the trampled grass. Adjusting her shawl, she gathered courage and approached a group of four men, including George Rush, the recent widower. "Sunday greetings." She paused two paces from the tall man. "I am truly saddened by the loss of your wife and infant. How are you faring? Do you need someone to furnish a hot meal?"

George turned and leaned toward her. "Black—have I got the name right?"

"Yes, I am Polly Black, seamstress at Mrs. Clark's dress shop." She skimmed her gaze over limp strands of dark-brown hair visible from the edge of his low-crown hat. Studying his face, she noted deep creases near his mouth, which gave him a frown.. She reminded herself of his recent tragedy. *I doubt he sleeps well or finds joy in life this past week.* Without turning her head, she glimpsed a small figure running toward them.

"I appreciate your words. I'm not in need of food." He scooped a young girl with chestnut curls into his arms. "My darling Hannah at my side is all I lack."

"I understand." She recalled clinging tight to Joseph when she learned of Bernard's death. Nodding to each of the other men in the group, she retreated and strode toward a clump of women.

"Good day, Mrs. Black…have you news from the shop?" Mrs. Cook, the hardware dealer's wife, spoke with her usual kindness.

Polly greeted each of the ladies in turn. "Good news…we are open regular hours. Every few days, more fabric and trims arrive. Our shelves are filling with lawns, flannel, and chintzes."

"Buttons?" Mrs. Franklin asked. "My girls manage to lose and break enough buttons for an entire gown in a week."

Polly halted the words on her tongue. *Six girls—yes, you need to keep a large button box.* "A selection of both bone and wood arrived Friday."

"Have you wool for winter frocks?" Mrs. Cook glanced toward the skirt of her plain gown.

She surveyed their interested expressions and relaxed. "We expect an order to arrive this week. Mrs. Clark requested a wide variety of colors."

Mrs. Franklin shifted an infant to the opposite shoulder. "I favor the browns."

"Did you have a good potato crop?" Mrs. Cook asked Mrs. Franklin.

Polly listened much, spoke little, and maintained a watchful eye on Joseph. Twice, she observed him approach another child, exchange a few words, and stand in place when the other youngster scampered away. *My son needs a friend.* She blinked twice to banish the image of Joseph standing beside a tall man with a cherub face. *Impossible. Within a week, Joseph will pester the man with questions and exhaust the cobbler's patience.*

****

"One beer and one dinner plate." Kurt set a coin onto the counter. Each breath of spicy-sausage-and-kraut scented air from the kitchen made his mouth water. *Althoff's Beer Garden—a busy place after church services.* He nodded to a few men he recognized from either the recently dismissed worship service or his evenings at First Street Tavern.

On the main portion of the property, families gathered at scattered tables or spread picnic blankets. Children called to each other and started impromptu games. Two boys tossed a ball near the small stage where the musicians would play later in the day.

Kurt lifted his stein and yielded to the next customer in the growing line.

"*Guten Tag.* I see you found Althoff's."

"*Ja,* I listen and learn directions from men at church." Kurt smiled at Hans Hoffmann, the young stable hand. He glanced toward Hans's feet and noted worn brogans with signs of repairs.

"Allow me to introduce my friend, Fredrick Mueller, who owns a fine farm east of town."

Kurt assessed the farmer with genuine interest before he clasped hands and introduced himself. "I am new to Elm Ridge…a cobbler by trade." He swept his hand downward to direct their attention to his Wellingtons. "Yes, I wear my craft as an advertisement. I offer repairs also." Herr *Mueller's shoes appear in*

24

good repair. "Tell me"—he gestured to a half-completed structure to the side of the present building—"what is under construction."

"You see a business expansion—a proper dance hall and assembly room. In another month, or certainly by St. Nicholas Day, Sunday music will not be at the weather's whim." Fredrick shifted his gaze toward Hans.

Scowling, the younger man edged toward the counter.

Kurt sipped tart lager from his full stein and alternated his gaze between the two men. Noting Fredrick's smiling eyes in contrast to Hans's sour expression, he concluded the friends disagreed about music. "*Gute.* Judging by the size of today's crowd, I understand the need for a proper building for lectures and dancing."

"Would you join us?" Fredrick pointed toward the picnic area. "The music will not begin for some time. On fine days like this, *mein Frau* brings nice food basket."

"*Danke. Ein Minute.*" Kurt turned toward the counter in the same instant the serving girl extended his plate of food. He smiled at the worker and sighed with pleasure when he lowered his gaze to generous portions of veal sausage, steaming kraut, and buttered potatoes. Carrying his plate in one hand and stein in the other, he followed his new friends through the gathering crowd.

An hour later, with lively music added to the voices in the air, Kurt visited with Fredrick and his wife while their son, a toddler, eyed him cautiously. "I understand now why Hans called his *Schatz* the pretty girl in the bakery."

"*Ja.* My cousin is a charming young woman." Fredrick coaxed his son to his lap. "At first, I doubted if Hans was steady. But *Herr* Bergmann is satisfied with his work at the livery. I have seen a change in him since spring…like watching a boy stumble into manhood."

Kurt nodded. During his two short, business conversations with the stable owner, he sensed an approval of the young man. *Trusted him to drive my goods from levee to shop.* He closed his eyes for a moment and allowed the sounds of accordion, violin, and tuba to envelope his senses. A moment later, he scanned the dance spectators and pushed to his feet. "I cannot sit any longer. I think I will ask the dark-haired girl in the rust dress for the next dance."

While the band played sets of polkas, waltzes, and schottisches, Kurt danced with several women. Young girls, mature matrons, or energic widows, he did not discriminate. Energy flowed into him from the music. With the familiar melodies in the air, the cares and worries of all the tasks necessary to start a business on his own slipped from his shoulders and vanished.

"*Danke. Danke.* You dance like you were born to it." Louisa Mueller panted as the musicians announced a break.

He laughed and followed her to the picnic blanket where Hans guarded the dozing child. "You are a talented dance partner. I will stop at the bakery tomorrow and discover if Hans's boast is true."

"What have I been bragging about?" Hans patted a space beside him for Louisa to sit.

"Baking. I have checked my chimneys and feel confident about lighting a stove. Therefore, I will prepare one or two meals this week. I danced with a woman named *Frau* Hebing, and she bragged of her husband's sausages."

"*Ja. Herr* Hebing and his sons operate a fine butcher shop—next to bakery. Convenient? No?" Louisa gestured Kurt to sit. "Good bacon—best I taste in America."

Leaning back on his elbows, Kurt relaxed and scanned the crowd. Fredrick and his wife, Anna, weaved through the beer garden guests and paused often to exchange bits of conversation with acquaintances. He closed his eyes for a moment and listened with pleasure to the familiar cadence of *Deutsch.* Within moments, he picked out at least three dialects. Smiling, he drifted into memories of this morning's conversation with Mrs. Black. He realized speaking in English with her flowed easy—smoother than any other American in Elm Ridge. *She neither scowled nor laughed at my words in* Deutsch *order. Not a word of her son's father—is the man dead?*

The tuba sounded the introduction to a popular march.

Kurt stood.

"You dance more?" Hans tucked his knees close to his chest.

"Keeps me limber," Kurt replied. "*Frau* Mueller, will you do me the honor?"

Anna chuckled. "Ignore Hans when the topic is music. Our brown milk cow keeps better rhythm."

A few minutes later, guiding Anna among the dancers, Kurt's thoughts drifted again to Mrs. Black. As he led her in a waltz and held her close, he imagined her delicate smile.

Chapter Four

A few days later, Kurt sat at his long, narrow worktable and dribbled clear oil across his whetstone. Setting aside the container, he rubbed an expanding circle with two fingers. "*Gute, gute.*" He breathed in the scent of linseed and smiled. He considered the sweet smell the best part of sharpening knives, different from the satisfaction of testing a good blade.

A steamboat whistled from the river.

He glanced at the clock on a shelf in easy sight of both front door and worktable. *Past three, I believe I hear the afternoon packet.* He mouthed the observation into the quiet air.

Each day, two scheduled steamboats, one from the north and the other from the south, added their arrival and departure blasts to the tempo of life in Elm Ridge. The foundry, the largest business in the village, signaled the beginning of the workday with a single, short whistle. The same powerful whistle dismissed workers at noon and called them back an hour later. Two, short bursts toward evening signaled the end of the workday. The other businesses within hearing followed the same whistles with minor adjustments for the type of work.

He glanced out the shop's large, clean window at high clouds. Estimating at least two hours of good daylight remained, he shook his head and recalled the layers of fine sawdust, wood smoke, and street grime he washed from the glass. During his first day in the building, the sunlight arrived through a man-made fog. Now, the light in his work area stayed similar to the day in the street.

Humming one of his favorite hymns, he stroked the first knife's curved blade against the prepared stone. *One verse, then turn and sharpen the blade's other edge.* At each switch of sides, he checked on his sleeping guest.

Joseph sat slumped against the workroom side of the short sales counter. Forehead resting on knees, the boy made a compact bundle of human.

Kurt reviewed the boy's daily afternoon visits. The first few days, he continued with his own work and spoke little to the youngster. Then, after Joseph had twice swept up wood and leather scraps without direction, he spoke with him as a craftsman to an untrained helper. Today, for example, Kurt showed him the sizes etched into each last. Then he supervised the hanging of the lasts by men's, women's, child, and higher heel, beside the rows of pinchers and awls. All the while, Kurt organized tools and inspected blades.

After sweeping the floor, Joseph had asked to rest for a minute. Sitting hidden from anyone entering the shop, the boy promptly fell asleep.

Creak. Bump.

Kurt snapped his attention from the blade in his hand to the door. As the visitor became visible, he skipped a breath. "Good afternoon, Mrs. Black."

"Have you seen Joseph? He was due home an hour ago." Polly, tiny lines near her eyes deepening, remained standing in the open doorway and clutched the ends of her black shawl tight to her chest.

"*Ja.*" He stood and beckoned her forward. "He served as cobbler's helper, then"—Kurt pointed.

The boy lifted his head and rubbed sleep from his eyes. "Mama?"

"I've been looking for you." She stood in front of him and crossed her arms.

Joseph staggered to his feet and addressed the floor. "I'm sorry. I only meant to sit for a minute. My friend and I hung lasts, brought in water, and swept the floor. I did not count the clock…"

Tick…tock…tick…

"My fault." Kurt interrupted the creeping silence. Glancing at the half-sharpened knife on the table, he brushed debris from his shirt. "I did not ask how soon he needed to return home. I kept finding little chores."

She spun and glared at Kurt. "Do not take the blame for him. Joseph knows my rules. He failed to pay attention to the time. I expected to find him in our own yard. He spends much time watching beetles in the wood pile or searching for smooth stones in the rubble pit."

Kurt studied her posture when she again faced Joseph. He failed to find the sternness of an exacting parent in her stance. Lifting one hand to his face, he hid his building mirth.

She tapped one foot and stared at her son.

I sense more kindness and warmth than exasperation. He recalled the fierceness in his mother's voice when he, or one of his brothers, found mischief. "Joseph was a welcome visitor." He stopped his tongue against his teeth, puzzled at his own statement. "Will the situation lessen his punishment?"

"Doubtful." She glanced toward Kurt before again directing her full attention to Joseph. Reaching out, she cupped his chin and directed his gaze. "Listen to me. You must follow the rules. Tell me where you are going and pay attention to the time."

"Yes, Mama." The universal defeat of little boys caught misbehaving coated his words.

"We will go home now. You will do your chores—no complaints. Not a word out of place when *Frau* Keil visits."

"Yes, Mama." He tipped his face toward the floor.

"No treats for you—no matter what she brings from the bakery. Do you understand?"

Joseph nodded.

"You are acquainted with the ladies at Keil's Bakery?" Kurt spoke without pausing to think. He thought of the final bit of a rye loaf waiting in his kitchen and moistened his lips.

"We are friends. After the fire, *Frau* Keil offered shelter. She and *Fraulein* Mueller are fine people. Have you met?" She turned her face toward him.

"*Ja.* I dance a little with *Fraulein* Mueller at beer garden Sunday afternoon. Monday, I make purchases at both butcher and baker." He studied the way she tightened her lips at his words.

"I expect you will become acquainted with many of our *Deutsch* residents from church and…after."

Uncertain if her tone on the final word indicated disapproval of dancing, beer, or all *Deutsch* entertainments, he cleared his throat and steadied his gaze on her delicate, agile hands. "A fire—I hear whispers at the tavern and a word from Mr. Fox. Will you tell me the true story?"

"Another time." She sighed. "We must go home. *Frau* Keil promised to cut Joseph's hair proper for school—the term begins Monday."

Forcing his gaze from Polly toward her son, he silently agreed the boy's hair was indeed longer than the fashion for schoolboys. "We shall speak again. Perhaps you will allow me to escort you once more to your American church."

"Perhaps." She extended one hand toward Joseph.

"We are neighbors—across the street. Good to be friends? No?" He sealed his lips and failed to slow racing thoughts of establishing a warm friendship. She was American, he was—not a true immigrant—but *Deutsch*—with different customs, religion, and language.

She smiled small with her mouth and bright with her hazel eyes.

Kurt, aware of a skipped heartbeat, led them to the front door. "You will pardon if I forget and mix *Deutsch* with my English?"

She nodded and broadened her smile. "I understand your speech well enough. I do not see language as a barrier to friendship between neighboring businesses."

"*Gute.*" He opened the door and stood, touching his back to the plain, wood wall. He held his words until she paused on the final step. "Joseph is welcome to visit—with your permission."

She nodded. "In a few days, *Herr* Tafel—not tomorrow."

A moment later, he stood with one shoulder against the doorframe and watched the pair cross the street. *She is more lovely each time we speak.* He continued to gaze into the street long after Polly and Joseph were out of sight within the dress shop. He lifted his hand in a friendly greeting to the driver of a coal wagon. In silence, he moved his lips. *Mrs. Black adores her son. She is not afraid to have* Deutsch *friends. Still no mention of the boy's father. Dare I ask? I do not wish to cause her pain.*

****

After Monday breakfast, Polly wiped the final bowl and nested the dish in the cupboard. She glanced around her living space and released a contented sigh. The apartment was tidy and vegetables simmered with beef bones for soup. One peek out the window confirmed a pleasant, clear day.

"All done, Mama." Joseph entered from the back porch and set the empty slops bucket at the end of the washstand.

"Are you ready for your first day of school?" Aware of school's necessity, she forced cheer into her voice.

He plunged his hands into the basin before he reached for the hard soap. "I want you to teach me."

"School is good for boys." She untied her apron and hung it on a peg. "Mr. Hopewell can teach you a great many new things. You will have classmates—perhaps make a friend." She resisted the urge to ruffle his hair. *I must loosen my hold and give him some independence if he is to grow into a proper boy—and man.*

He shook his hands over the basin and grabbed the towel. "I know my letters. You can teach me how they make words."

"No argument—today, you will begin in Mr. Hopewell's classroom." She settled her green bonnet over her smooth bun.

"Next term? Can...may I wait for next term?" Tipping his face toward her, he clasped his hands and lifted them to his chin.

She shook her head. "No...final...the fee is paid." Giving him an inspection, she curved her lips into a small smile.

Joseph wore a clean shirt today. Pale, canvas trousers, the pair without patches, were free from stains and his suspenders were adjusted properly. "Wear your hat." She pointed to the child-sized, dark-brown, flat cap on a peg. As long as the weather remained mild, no one would comment on his lack of a coat. She knotted her shawl and reminded herself only one or two nights' work remained to finish his wool coat. *Lack of shoes remains a problem.* Friday, when she found a pair of boy's shoes at Mr. Clemons' shop, she was refused the one dollar credit she needed. The merchant even declined to accept partial payment to reserve the brogans. *Fussy old man. Does he intend to raise the price when the weather turns cold?* She led the way and opened the shop door.

Joseph paused at the bottom of the steps. "I will do extra chores without complaining."

Clamping her jaw to prevent a laugh, she checked if Abigail approached on Apple Street before she locked the door. "You are the proper age for school. Come, today we walk together. I want to have a quick word with Mr. Hopewell before he rings the bell."

During the three blocks to school, Polly took care not to hold Joseph's hand. Glancing at his bare feet, unequal in size and the right foot refusing to point straight ahead, she tucked one hand into her pocket and crossed her fingers. In silence, she made a wish for the other children to understand and not be cruel. She would have the cash for shoes in one week—two at the most.

"Mama."

She shifted her attention to Joseph.

"How soon will I be able to read? Will I need to go to school long?"

"The Elm Ridge school teaches two terms a year—second term ends in spring." She paused for a wagon to complete a turn before she guided them across Fifth Street.

"And then I finish?"

"Not exactly." She failed to find words to explain multiple school years to a boy who lacked the concept of time beyond today. Perhaps she should be thankful Joseph lived in the moment. Unless asked a direct question, he did not speak of St. Louis, the steamboat trip, or events before the fire.

"Is that Mr. Hopewell?" Joseph halted beside her and stared toward a plump man in a black waistcoat.

Two girls, both with dark hair in neat braids, dashed across the dirt street, up the wide steps, and through the open schoolhouse door. "Yes. I will introduce you." She read doubt and hesitation in his narrowed eyes and scrunched brow. "Then you go inside while he and I have a conversation on the front step."

Four hours later, Polly measured and marked buttonholes on a bodice. She visualized the fabric and color flattering Mrs. Cook's complexion and allowed a brief smile.

Jingle-jingle.

"One minute." She laid measure and chalk on the table and stepped toward the sales area. Expecting to see Abigail returning, Polly froze.

"*Guten*...good day." Kurt removed his flat, leather cap and roamed his gaze over the merchandise shelves. "Neat...organized."

"Thank you." *Tidy is easy when the goods are sparse.* Since their recent shipments were incomplete, Mrs. Clark was at the levee, checking for misplaced barrels or crates at the local warehouse. "We like the customer to see the goods well...to make satisfactory selection. And you—what do you seek in a dress shop?"

The tips of his ears reddened. "I...do you have linen thread...thick...strong?"

She studied his large hand resting beside a dish of shell buttons. She noted long fingers, with few rough calluses. Raising her gaze, she encountered curved lips below ruddy cheeks. Lest her face show too much attraction, she pivoted toward the shelves behind the counter. Reaching for a tin box on the top shelf, she pressed her lips. *Please, may this warmth on my neck not be a flush.* "We have several linen threads." She set the box on the counter and eased off the lid. "Are any of these suitable?"

He inserted two fingers among the threads and tipped each spool in turn to view the stamped gauge.

Resisting the sudden urge to fan her face, Polly gripped the counter's edge. *What if? No, 'tis dangerous to imagine his fingers against my skin.*

****

"Beeswax," Kurt muttered the single word as his fingers closed around a spool of dark, sturdy thread.

"Pardon?" Polly whispered.

He glanced at her face, drew a quick breath, and averted his gaze. *She draws my attention like iron seeks the magnet.* Blinking, he banished an image of guiding her in a waltz. "Do you have beeswax?"

"One moment, I will check." Polly squatted behind the counter.

From his suddenly increased height advantage, he admired the perfectly straight part in her light-brown hair. As he listened to her shift objects on a shelf, he became aware how each faint sound raised his heart rate. Sealing his lips, he thought of a dozen reasons to keep an American woman at a formal distance.

She stood and set a round, flat tin on the counter. "Let me check the wax. The tin appears scorched and might be rescued from the fire."

He nodded and held his breath. Without a conscious decision, he settled his gaze on her delicate, agile hands. He swallowed and lowered his hand out of sight. *Do not assist unless she asks. I fear if I touch her once I will not want to stop.* "I don't often visit dress shops."

"Perhaps we can change your habits. Mrs. Clark and I are both clever with a needle—if your clothes should need mending." She gave the tin's lid a quarter turn, pushed with her thumb, and popped the cover free. "Dark—appears to have melted and hardened again. Useable?"

He extended one hand. "May I?" In the next instant, he swiped his little finger across the wax's surface. Lifting the digit near his nose, he sniffed the familiar scent of extinguished church candles. "*Ja, gute.* How much?"

After consulting a thin booklet, she stated a price for thread and wax. "Only Mrs. Clark can give a discount for damaged goods."

"Not important—the wax will serve well for my purpose." He tapped the tin. An instant later, he withdrew several coins from his pocket and picked out the payment. Intersecting her gaze, he cleared his throat. "Will you tell me of the fire?"

Her features stiffened into a mask. "I-I…it is not a story to tell across a dress shop counter."

"Another day?" He lifted one shoulder. "Perhaps on a fine evening we might share a stoop." An image—him smoking his evening pipe, Polly sitting beside him, and Joseph playing nearby—rushed in.

"You extend a charming invitation." She held her lips into a small, straight line.

Studying her face, he wondered if a quiet, evening conversation on an exposed step would ruin her reputation. Did she have a jealous, absent husband? Was a gentleman courting her? He tucked his purchases into a coat pocket.

"Get up now." *Snap.*

Kurt whirled toward the window in time to see a tall man, driving a low-sided wagon, flick a whip.

The tip missed contact with the near horse by mere inches.

"Who?" He stepped closer to the window and searched for a business name on the wagon's side.

Polly stepped from behind the counter and peered into the street. "The wagon is from Franklin and Rush lumber—see the two pine trees painted on the back board. I'm not certain of the driver."

He memorized the symbol and business name. *Best*

not to judge. I did not see the team's behavior before the whip cracked. "Is Joseph here?"

"School—first day—a reluctant student." She concealed her hands in abundant skirt gathers.

Memories of he and his brothers, all unwilling schoolboys, swept into his mind, and he smiled. Between them, the Tafel brothers managed to find dozens of ways to frustrate their mother on the first day of a new term. "Your son is bright. When he visits my shop, he asks many questions. In addition, he remembers the answers I give."

She tipped her head.

"I do not wish to embarrass you. I would like to give Joseph a gift."

"A present?" She lifted her head and narrowed her gaze. "We are not well acquainted."

Ignoring her comment, he focused on the shelf behind her. "When I inspected the shed on my lot, I discovered a cat with three kittens. For the last few days, I have left them a dish of bread soaked in milk. I believe soon the mother will abandon them to fend for themselves. Would a kitten be useful in a dress shop?"

She circled her index finger on the counter, but the action did nothing to hide the smile in her eyes. "I need to speak with Mrs. Clark. But I'm inclined to accept. Mice can do much damage to our fabrics. Will you be keeping the others?"

"*Ja.* A mouse or two can do much harm to a leather supply. I find such pests small but persistent. Nearly every business in our Pennsylvania town kept a cat or two—except the saddler." He closed his eyes for a long moment and shivered. "The man preferred to keep a large, black snake."

She swallowed and raised one hand in front of her mouth. "A kitten is more suitable to our business. A cat is less likely to startle our customers."

Nodding, he took a step toward the door. "Discuss the topic with Mrs. Clark. I believe dusk will be the best time to catch kittens." He opened the door, paused, and turned his head toward her. "Bring a basket with a good lid."

Fifteen minutes later, after a quick lunch of flavorful rye bread with sweet, dark honey, Kurt removed two pieces of leather from the shallow soaking pan. Transferring the future soles and heels to the press, he hummed a folk tune. *Repairs to the brogans will not be difficult. I will add six stitches to the uppers as a bonus, and the shoes will be good for many months.*

Lifting his gaze to the street, he observed a woman enter the dress shop. Speaking lower than a murmur, he whittled sole pegs. "Elm Ridge is a fine place—good *Deutsch* shops, Americans friendly, for the most part, and many poor shoes to repair or replace." He dropped a smooth peg into the tray. "Charming, and pretty, dressmaker neighbor."

Chapter Five

Friday afternoon, the low sun cast long, narrow shadows across Elm Ridge. Employees tidied workspaces, and businessmen served final customers after the foundry's dismissal whistle.

Polly glanced toward Joseph and adjusted her steps to match his smaller ones. "Mind your manners, son."

"Yes, Mama." He scurried the final yards to Kurt's apartment door.

Tap-tap-tap.

"Ein Minute." Kurt's deep voice sounded before the final knock faded.

Polly adjusted her lips into a small smile. She carried a basket loaned by Mrs. Clark's sister. A hinged lid and sturdy clasp made the container ideal for carrying a small animal. *I suspect the kitten will be unhappy, no matter the transport method.* She reviewed the preparations at the dress shop. Today, she had prepared a shallow box of sand and selected one small, chipped bowl for bread and milk. She recalled the delight on Mrs. Clark's face and the excitement in her voice at the prospect of a shop kitten.

"Good evening, *Herr* Tafel." Joseph began speaking the instant the door hinges creaked. "Mama tells me you have kittens in your shed."

Kurt nodded to the boy before steadying his gaze on her face. *"Ja.* Three kittens are too many for one cobbler." He winked at Polly. "Do you know of anyone who would accept one as a gift?"

She swallowed twice. Men didn't wink at her—she was neither pretty nor witty—aside from Leo when he wanted her to hold her tongue against his string of lies. Squeezing both hands against the basket handle, she moistened her lips. "Is this a good time? We don't want to disturb your supper."

"Good time, yes. I will turn the sign in my shop window and join you."

A few moments later, Polly stood inside the shed and blinked to adjust her eyes. With the door closed, the only light entered through a small, high window. At the smells of long-ago chickens, she wrinkled her nose. Much dust, a scattering of wood shavings, and a few feathers in the corner came into clearer focus with each blink. Small piles of lumber were scattered in an area smaller than the dress shop workroom. One deep shelf held a few crumpled, canvas sacks and a dented, tin pail. She squatted, peered under the shelf, and spotted a straw nest.

"Are they hiding?" Joseph whispered.

"They are shy," Kurt replied in an equally low voice. "Wait and watch for a few minutes before you decide which one should live at the dress shop."

Setting the basket beside the door, Polly followed Kurt's advice.

A black-and-white kitten, sitting on a low pile of boards, clarified first in the dim light.

A moment later, she noticed a gray, with a white patch on her back, stalking a calico's tail. *I've seen an adult calico prowling in Mrs. Fox's garden. The mother?* "Do you see them?"

"Uh-uh." Joseph accompanied the sound with an exaggerated nod.

"We are in luck. Mama cat is gone hunting." Kurt crouched and took small, waddle-steps until he was under the window.

Joseph inched forward and extended one hand toward the calico.

Zip—the kitten darted into the near darkness under the shelf.

"Fast." Joseph gulped.

Polly stifled a laugh.

"I want to pet the one with three colors," Joseph whispered.

Clearing his throat, Kurt sent the three kittens into motion. "We will wait, work together, and catch her."

"A girl cat?" The boy tipped his head.

Kurt nodded once. "They are all girls—I checked yesterday."

"Stay quiet and look into the far corner. They are huddled together. Remember they can scratch." Polly advanced with small, awkward steps. Glancing right, she noticed Kurt mimicking her actions.

"Ah-choo."

The kittens fled in three different directions.

"Bless you," Polly whispered.

"Gesundheit," Kurt added.

Joseph sniffed. "I'm sorry. Now we need to start over."

Easing to her full height, Polly searched for kittens. She spied little Miss Black-and-White in the shadow of some lumber.

The gray crouched, ready to pounce at Kurt's heel.

She turned her face toward the door to search for

the calico. Swallowing a laugh not to startle the felines again, she smiled at the kitten perched on the basket lid.

In the next blink, Kurt lunged and captured the calico with both hands. "Quick. Open the basket."

Joseph fumbled with the simple latch while the kitten hissed and twisted within Kurt's grasp.

Polly held her breath and lingered her gaze on Kurt's large, strong hands, which demonstrated a gentleness with small boys and frightened kittens. She managed two steps forward before man and boy had the calico secure in the basket.

"Done." Kurt rested one hand on the closed lid.

"What happens to the others?" Joseph pushed to his feet. "Do you want help to catch them? No school tomorrow—I can help."

Polly reached behind Joseph, raised the latch, and opened the door.

"I will entice them into my shop by moving a dish of food closer each day." Kurt lifted the basket, checked the pin in the hasp, and presented the container.

"He has a plan, Joseph. You need to pay heed to your own kitten. Let *Herr* Tafel deal with the two others."

"Can she sleep with me?" He followed his mother into the final light of the day and tipped up his face. "I have room on my cot."

Kurt chuckled and set the shed door open a few inches. "A cat picks her own bed. Give her a few days to become acquainted with her new home. Then tell me where she likes best."

"Home is behind the dress shop." Joseph held his face close to the basket and spoke to the kitten. "We have both downstairs and a loft. You will have much to explore tonight."

Polly glanced toward the darkening sky. Touching her son on the shoulder, she sent him a silent caution to stop speaking. "Thank you for the adventure, *Herr* Tafel. We will watch close and keep our kitten inside for a few days, until she learns home. I expect Joseph will cross the street and give you regular reports."

"I enjoy his visits."

"Don't let my son become a pest." She pressed her lips and sorted her next words with care. "One day soon, when young ears are at school, you and I will discuss our eventful summer." She glanced toward the ground and wished him not to ask too many questions about her complicated relationship with *Frau* Keil.

"I understand." He accompanied them across his yard to the corner.

"Come for lunch—Tuesday. I will attempt to answer your many questions." She slipped one hand into a pocket and crossed her fingers. Thinking a wish for Abigail's presence in the workroom sufficient to halt potential rumors and gossip, she sighed. *My reputation is a fragile cloak on the best of days. Was I wrong to let others assume I am a widow?*

He rubbed his chin with three fingers. "Tuesday—I take my meal after the second whistle calls the laborers for their afternoon tasks."

"Excellent. Mrs. Clark takes the workers' lunch hour. Customers allowing, join me when she returns. Come, Joseph, we must go and introduce Miss Calico to her new home." After quick farewells, she shepherded her son across the street.

"I don't want to call her Miss Calico." He formed a

brief pout and shook his head.

"Do you have a name in mind?" She reviewed the few names of pet cats she'd known.

Outside the shop's back door, Joseph paused and rubbed his chin. "Not yet. Let me think on it until morning. I want the name to fit."

Surprised at his mimic of Kurt's recent action, she unlatched the door to the back porch. "Morning—after your chores—you can tell me what you decide." Entering the main room, she prayed for no regrets for inviting a man into her home. She set the basket on the floor and checked that the doors and windows were secure. "Open the lid, Joseph."

A blur of kitten exited the basket and dashed under the lowest loft step.

During the next few hours, Polly served supper, did routine chores, and sewed the final buttons on Joseph's new, winter coat. "I must guard against impulse," she whispered into the quiet air after Joseph had gone to bed in the loft. "My tongue—and heart—turn unreliable when *Herr* Tafel is near."

****

Monday morning, Polly entered Clemons' Dry Goods. After a glance toward a small display of tin cookware and a blue-and-white china platter, she stepped left, toward the men's and boy's clothing display. Shirts in three sizes lay neatly folded on a shelf. Suspenders and a fine gray-and-black waistcoat occupied pride of place at the end. Two sidesteps later, she paused in front of the shoes. She searched the shelf but failed to see the boy's pair.

"Buying for your son, Mrs. Black?" The spry, white-haired proprietor rounded the end of the central

46

sales counter.

A tiny spot glowed warm in her chest at his use of the title. Before moving to Elm Ridge, she decided letting people assume she was a widow gave her and Joseph the best possible reputation. Fortunately, during the ten weeks both she and her brother, Leo, lived in the town, he did not contradict her story—to her knowledge. What could Leo have gained—especially after the phrase "Joseph's father died" became true? She faced the merchant. "Two weeks ago, I looked at brogans in a smaller size. Do you still have them?" She lifted the smallest shoe on the shelf and inspected the stitching. She recognized the moderate quality of a shoe too large for Joseph's bigger foot—even with a bit of soft wool in the toe. She kept a modest, friendly expression.

"Sold last week." He clipped the words.

She set the shoe beside its partner on the shelf, certain her disappointment showed. "I see. Do you have more ordered—in the smaller size?"

"You could do a special order. Cost an extra fifty cents." He shifted his weight and intersected her gaze.

Swallowing, she steadied her expression. If he required the entire cost, plus the extra fee, in advance, her remaining coins would purchase only the minimum of eggs and bread this week. Remembering a small patch of frost near her woodpile yesterday morning, she was aware the weather would soon turn cold. "How long?"

"Last order of shoes took a month to arrive." He set one hand on a hip.

A chill rose from her toes to chest. "Winter approaches."

"Don't dally." Mr. Clemons pulled a blanket from a shelf and fussed with folding the thick, tan cloth. "I send my orders on the Saturday packet."

Polly studied the merchant's scarred fingers against the heavy cloth and recalled another person folding a dull-red blanket. *Madam Robineau never purchased shoes.* Gripping her fingers tight against her shopping basket's handle, she turned toward the door. "If I want a special order, I'll return before end of business today."

"Fair enough." He tipped his head toward the houseware display. "Received some fine tea sets in the last shipment."

"Perhaps another day." She tossed the words and a tiny smile over her shoulder an instant before she crossed the shop's threshold.

An hour later, Polly exited the fourth and final dry goods store in Elm Ridge. Random *Deutsch* words, absent when attempting to state her business to the merchant, spun a slow circle in her mind. She lifted one hand to her forehead, as if checking for a fever. None of the stores stocked a suitable pair of shoes for her son. *The final merchant, Herr* Meile, *showed no patience for my poor* Deutsch. *I must ask* Frau *Keil to help me practice.*

After a quick stop to purchase a ham hock from *Herr* Hebing, she entered the bakery. One step inside, she paused to allow the delightful scents of fresh bread and cinnamon buns to fill her lungs.

"*Guten Morgan.* Have you come for your usual loaf of wheat bread?" *Frau* Keil beckoned her toward the counter.

"*Ja.*" As her headache threatened, she blinked slowly. Glancing at the bakery clock, she sighed.

Errands which should have taken an hour already kept her from the dress shop twice longer. She forced a smile, aware no blame for the delay rested with the bakery. No, these women, especially *Frau* Keil, tended to lift her spirits. During her weeks as a guest, the conversations in the garden or while mending in the evening, enabled both the widow and herself to accept Bernard Keil's sudden death. "A sweet also—one which keeps well."

"Fresh *Kuchen*—apple?" Charlotte pointed toward a round dessert topped with apple slices and fragrant cinnamon.

"Excellent." She set her basket on the counter, stepped to the workroom entrance, and greeted Louisa. "I must not linger. Too many errands this morning without much to show in my basket. I want to thank you again, *Fraulein,* for Joseph's new stockings."

"Knitting is one of my joys—music is another." Louisa rotated thick cookie dough before rolling it into a larger, thinner circle.

After paying for her baked goods, and bidding her friends a good day, Polly exited the shop. She pictured Madam Robineau, her favorite St. Louis landlady. The half-breed widow of a Frenchman, the woman's authoritative posture, gray braid, and fringed moccasins set her apart from both *Deutsch* and American boarders. Pleased with the specifics of the memory, Polly determined to propose an idea at tomorrow's lunch.

"Mrs. Black."

She jerked her attention toward the sharp male voice. Turning right, she hesitated while a horse and rider clopped past, then nodded at the tall man crossing the street. "Good day, Mr. Rush."

"What a pleasure to cross paths today." He halted three feet away and removed his low-crowned hat.

"Is that your wagon in front of the hardware? I do hope you have not interrupted important business to give me greetings." She held her covered basket close to her body.

"Today's trade with Mr. Cook is complete." He tipped his head and studied the bakery sign. "Are you finished with errands? I have a topic I'd like to discuss."

She paused her gaze on the deep, serious lines around his mouth. Skimming other portions of his face, she noted the same mixture of charm and cunning often present in her brother's eyes. Urging her tongue to caution, she moistened her lips. "My shopping used most of the morning today. I must return to the dress shop without delay."

"Come"—he gestured toward the waiting team across the street. "I will give you a ride, and we can talk along the way."

"Walking the few blocks to the shop is not a problem." She tightened her grip on the basket handle.

"I insist." He slapped his hat over mussed brown hair and advanced one step.

She pressed her lips tight. Glancing toward the sky, she exhaled when a cloud drifted east to expose bright sunshine. *Daylight. A few blocks. What is the harm?* She gathered her thin, invisible cloak of respectability close. "We will go direct to Mrs. Clark's dress shop?"

"Certainly." He paced beside her and jutted his elbow.

Without touching him, she strode to the wide, low-sided wagon. Gathering her skirts with one hand, she placed a foot on the front wheel hub and climbed to the seat. She fussed with the gingham cloth over her purchases until he settled on the bench, gathered the reins, and released the wagon brake. She stared at the ears of the near horse, moistened her lips, and broke the silence. "Did you have something specific to tell me?"

Ordering the team into motion, he turned his face toward her. "I miss my daughter, Hannah."

"She appears a sweet child. However, I do not know her well."

"Jane's sister lives too far away. I only see my daughter on Sundays—not enough."

Polly nodded. A moment later, she lifted a hand to wave at an acquaintance walking along the street. "Have you considered hiring a housekeeper?" With a reputation as one of the richest men in town, she did not see cost as an obstacle. "Perhaps one of the boarders at Mrs. Bender's would like a position."

"I don't want some dried-up, old woman tending my Hannah." He spat into the street.

Rough manners for a successful businessman. "Have you spoken with Pastor Harter? He would know if one of the farm girls is looking for work." She visualized the unmarried women in the modest congregation and could name girls on the cusp of womanhood or ladies ten or more years older than herself.

Guiding the team around the corner, he pulled the sorrels to a halt in front of the dress shop. "What I need, Mrs. Black, is a wife. Gal your age would be right."

Swallowing a word ladies didn't utter in public, she gathered her skirts in one hand in preparation to step down from the wagon. Once both feet were on solid ground, she tilted her head and looked straight into his face. "You shock me, Mr. Rush. Your wife is less than a month in her grave."

"Jane ain't coming back. Don't see any sense in dallying."

She blinked at both his bluntness and timing. "My answer is *no*—a firm decline." She adjusted her grip on the basket and backed from the wagon. Pausing for a moment, she steadied her knees and prayed for a firm voice. "Good day, Mr. Rush. I thank you kindly for the ride."

"Mrs. Black." He spoke with an air of command.

Half-turned toward the shop door, she hesitated. *What does the man want? I gave him a clear, polite answer. He's a near stranger—with a trace of unpleasant disposition.*

"I suggest you think careful on my offer." He swiped the back of his hand across his mouth. "Not many men will consider bringing an unknown man's son into a marriage."

She lifted her gaze to his face and studied his narrowed eyes and firmed mouth. Questions of what her brother, Leo, had shared with the man raced through her mind. Did Leo brag to the lumber dealer of preventing her marriage to an immigrant? Both of them, Mr. Rush and Leo, made no secret of their dislike for the *Deutsch*. In the next instant, she blinked, pivoted, and rested a hand on the short rail at the side of the steps. She remained still and listened to the slap of reins and creak of wheels starting to move. *Good Lord, did he expect me to agree?*

Chapter Six

Late Tuesday morning, a brisk, northwest breeze reminded Kurt the season would soon change. He suppressed a shiver under his shirt and joined *Herr* Knapp, the sign maker, on the sidewalk.

"Not enough room above the door." *Herr* Knapp looked at the wooden gutter attached to the roof's edge.

"I agree." Kurt extended one arm high above his head and tapped the siding. "Can you hang the sign here, between front door and large window? Will the panel have enough clearance?"

The short, slender man jotted another word on an already full scrap of paper and moved his ladder to the left. "*Ja,* I take one more measure to be certain."

Kurt steadied the smooth wood rail.

Standing on the fourth rung, *Herr* Knapp extended his measuring stick and nodded. "Sign three feet, bracket adds six inches, all will be high enough for a man with one of those stovepipe hats to walk past. Good?"

The foundry whistle screamed over the town, dismissing the daytime workers for lunch.

Kurt nodded his reply.

A moment later, the sign maker stood on the sidewalk and scribbled on his paper. "Let me review. The finished sign will be two feet wide and three feet high—double sided. I'm to paint one figure, a brown shoe, on the lower portion. On the top you want *Tafel* in dark blue letters. I will color the background white, and I will use same style brace as sign at Hebing's butcher shop. I mount midway between door and window."

"Ja. Gute." Kurt finished his business with *Herr* Knapp while observing Mrs. Clark exiting the dress shop. He smiled internally, pleased the shop owner left promptly. The plan to join Mrs. Black at the next foundry whistle was on schedule.

Folding his measuring stick into a tidy bundle, the sign maker tucked the tool into his work apron and surveyed the street. "Good corner for business. I wish you success. Sign will be ready in one week."

"I will pay the rest of the money the day you install." Kurt lowered the ladder.

"Gute. Now I go eat fine lunch with my wife and select choice lumber for your sign." He hooked one arm through the ladder at the balance point and took a step toward the river. "Take care, *Herr* Tafel."

For a long moment, Kurt remained on his front step and gazed at the dress shop. *She is American, widow by appearance. I am* Deutsch *and not trustworthy to guard children.* Once he entered his shop, Kurt concentrated on preparing new soles for *Herr* Hebing's boots. He removed the damp, pliable leather from the press and traced a pattern. Exchanging his pencil for a sharp, curved knife, he cut a smooth, rounded shape. He clamped two layers of thick leather together. A moment later, he selected the medium awl and moved the ash pegs within easy reach. Humming a folk tune, he breathed the familiar scents of damp leather and neat's-foot oil.

Whuuu. The shrill foundry whistle summoned the

workers for the afternoon hours.

Kurt lifted his head and surveyed his work. With every third peg in place, holding the sole secure, he knew this was a suitable place to pause. He slid his sharp awl and light hammer into their leather pouches and untied his work apron. After brushing bits of dust and debris from his clothes, he pushed his fingers through his hair. Aware his heart was galloping with excitement, he forced a few slow, even breaths. *I go to visit a neighbor—learn facts to replace rumor.* He mouthed the words as he shrugged into his coat, settled his cap, and tucked a gift into his pocket.

A pair of minutes later, the dress shop bell tinkled in the still air as Kurt stepped inside, removed his cap, and closed the door. "Good day, Mrs. Black."

"You are prompt—a good thing." She smiled and set a spool of wide ribbon onto a shelf.

Mrs. Clark, emitting an aura of peppermint, nodded from her position near the dress form. "Greetings, *Herr* Tafel. Does business go well at the cobbler's?"

"A few customers are beginning to find me." He hid a sigh. Speaking with one or two new people at the tavern each evening proved a slow way to make a business known. "Go"—she gestured toward a drape over a narrow opening—"enjoy your lunch and conversation."

"This way." Polly held the tan curtain aside and gestured him to enter.

One breath of the delicious smell radiating from the stove and Kurt felt his stomach rumble. *Onion, ham, and sweet—delicious.* Walking farther into the apartment, he noted the stove with a large cooking surface. In his next glance, he spotted a rectangular table under a window. Two simple wooden chairs and place settings of mismatched dishes were ready. A simple washstand and a corner cupboard completed the furnishings on this side of the room. Shifting his gaze, he found a view of Third Street through a square window. A small, round table sat under the glass. A lamp, a book, and a pincushion occupied the scarred surface. A plain chair held a large sewing basket. A set of open steps to the loft occupied a fair amount of space on that side of the central support beam. "Cozy."

"The sleeping quarters are upstairs. The new building is taller—I am able to stand upright one step to each side of the peak. Also new"—she gestured toward a door near the washstand—"a proper, enclosed, back porch."

"Good storage place." He blinked away images of the porch with coats on pegs and shoes lined against the wall in the Pennsylvania home. Reaching high, he fingered the joint between support post and main beam. "Good workmanship— built to last many years."

"Barring tragedy." She tipped her face toward the floor. "Take a place at the table. Today, we dine on beans with a little ham."

He swallowed the sudden moisture in his mouth. "A favorite—the meal makes your home smell warm and welcoming."

"You flatter me before you take the first bite."

He stood behind the chair on the table's far side. With a pause to smile at the view of bread on a round board beside pots of butter and jam, he reached into his pocket. "My garden, or rather, the weed patch within a broken fence, does not have flowers—so I brought you a different sort of token."

She paused the ladle above the open Dutch oven.

He set the gift at the rounded tip of her table knife. Glancing, he observed her expression change from wide, surprised eyes to quiet curiosity.

She carried his meal to the table. "What did you bring?" She wiped her fingers on her apron before touching the smooth wood. "A darning egg?"

"A simple gesture—to a neighbor."

She lifted the gift and rotated the oval in her palm. "'Tis beautiful, smooth as dress silk. The size, smaller than a duck egg, will be perfect when stitching the tight spaces on girls' dresses. I will treasure it. Thank you. *Danke*."

"It is a small item. I am pleased you will find the gift useful." Kurt tipped his gaze to the table top as heat crept over his neck. *No gift from my hands will match your charms.*

****

A few moments later, Polly folded her hands, bowed her head, and whispered a short prayer of thanks for food—and the company. Lifting her gaze, she encountered Kurt's alert blue eyes.

"Similar to our family table prayer—I think." He dipped his spoon into his bowl of ham and beans. Blowing to cool the first bite, he hesitated. "I did not see the kitten when I arrived. How is she settling?"

She lowered her spoon into her bowl and relaxed. "Joseph has named the kitten Swifty…because she runs fast. I think she is learning *home*. This morning, she followed Joseph to the pump. But with a little coaxing…and a bit of moistened bread crust…she returned inside."

"Sunday afternoon, the black kitten crossed my

threshold." He swallowed. "A moment later, the clock chimed, and she scampered away."

Smiling at the picture his words painted, she met his gaze. "I think the kitten is upstairs. I often find her napping on Joseph's cot."

"Sounds as if they are starting to be friends." He cut a slice of bread, offered it, and cut another for himself. "Will you tell me of the fire? I hear unreliable snatches of conversation in the tavern. Or is it less painful to speak of other things?"

She transferred one small spoonful of blackberry jam onto her bread. "I was careless—and foolish." Over and over, last evening, and until he walked through the door, she rehearsed phrases to tell him of the terrible summer day. But now the words clogged in her throat. *I almost lost the most precious thing in my life. I doubt I could continue without my son.* She glanced toward the ceiling. "The fire happened the third of July...in the afternoon...while Mrs. Clark was gone on errands."

He nodded and chewed buttered bread.

"The kindling was in a flimsy basket, instead of a proper tin pail. I'm not sure when, but the basket ended up too close to the stove and caught fire. Good sense fled from my brain. I grabbed a rug to smother the flames, but the fabric flared in my hands. Joseph napped in the loft...I called and called for him." She paused, swallowed remembered panic, and gestured toward the shop wall beyond the stairs. "The steps were different, narrow, steep...between a ladder and proper stairs. I think I fainted from the smoke."

"Who found you?" Kurt inched one hand forward, paused beside her bread plate, and withdrew it past the table's center.

"Two men entered the shop…crashed in the door. One…a *Deutsch* physician who has since moved from town…carried me to safety. The other…Hans Hoffmann…climbed into the loft and rescued Joseph. They were trapped by the flames and Hans…he…" She shifted her gaze toward the window and blinked. "Hans jumped from the window with my son clinging to his chest." She fumbled for a handkerchief and dabbed her eyes. "I'm sorry. I have not told the story since a few days after. The memories…"

"You love your son—a good thing—no?"

She smiled, despite the spilling tears. Even after years of listening to *Deutsch* people pose questions, the word order amused her.

"Enough of the fire. I have upset you. I thank you for enough information to sort truth from rumor and exaggeration the next time the topic makes the rounds."

Drawing a deep breath, she blinked away a few final tears. "*Frau* Keil—we already had a fragile friendship—offered shelter to Joseph and I. We lived with her above the bakery until this building was finished. I will forever be grateful to my *Deutsch* friends."

He pushed his chair from the table and stood. "I will return to work. I apologize for stirring strong memories. I ask to learn the truth."

She pressed her fingertips against the table's edge and rose. "The gossips embellish many stories. My heart is easier after telling you the truth. Rather like…con—" She snapped tight her lips. She told her new neighbor neither a confession nor a confidence. "Others—including *Herr* Hoffmann—could tell the story as well."

He retrieved his cap. "The meal was delicious."

"Wait, one minute…I want to ask you something special." She hurried to her sewing basket and pulled out the thick, wool stockings Louisa had knit for Joseph. "The weather is growing colder, and the Elm Ridge shops do not have any boys' shoes. I wonder—is it possible to make a soft, leather sole for these stockings? Give his feet protection like a moccasin?"

"You know moccasins?" He raised his brows.

She nodded. "A long story from my years in St. Louis—a landlady." In the next moment, her heart warmed with memories of Madam Robineau working in the kitchen while wearing a faded calico gown.

"I believe you must tell your St. Louis story on another day—or evening." He fingered the small, knit stitches. "Send Joseph to my shop with his stockings. I will measure his feet and figure a solution to the problem."

"I will pay." She forced her gaze away from his enticing fingers.

"Half the price of shoes from the store?" He tipped his head a few degrees.

She smiled and allowed relief to flood her limbs. "Yes, a fair price, I think. I'm sure Joseph will be glad to come to your shop after school tomorrow."

"I look forward to solving your problem." He strode toward the shop entrance.

A few minutes later, Polly stood beside Abigail at the counter. She watched Kurt enter his shop and turn the small sign in his window.

"A good man—I think." Mrs. Clark straightened narrow, black lace.

"A friend," Polly sent a short, silent prayer to avoid

foolishness with a male, *Deutsch* friend toward the ceiling. Blinking, she banished the memory of another *Deutsch*-speaking man. Bernard started as a friend, became a lover, and was driven from St. Louis before vows could be said. She returned to the living quarters and tidied the kitchen. *No. I'm not a naïve girl anymore. I will take great care with my delicate cloak of respectability.*

****

Kurt worked the repaired boot off the jointed, maple last. Humming a lively folk tune, he smiled. Each time he recalled yesterday's lunch with Polly, his heart wanted to dance. He collected a rag and the small container of polish from a shelf and reviewed today's highlights. "*Herr* Hebing's boots are now tight against rain and snow. A sunny day following a frosty morning quickens my step. Many tasks to finish before the weather turns to hard winter." He held one boot and rubbed a growing circle on the dark leather. "Best of all, today I receive a letter from my family."

Snort...snort.

Noise from the street prompted him to lift his gaze in time to see a man lead a reluctant horse down the street. He glanced toward the shop entrance. A new, brass bell hung near the door's top. After an early morning visit to the hardware, and a few minutes to mount the signal, he would no longer be startled by a customer while he worked with his back to the door. In the next instant, he refreshed the polish on his rag and resumed work.

"*Ein Tochter auf mein Bruder.* My brother has a daughter." He repeated the most important portion of the letter to the quiet workshop. "Greta Marie Tafel,

61

born the first day of September, I pray you grow to be a bright, healthy child." He rotated the boot, continued to polish, and frowned at the memory of another girl with the same name. His sister, forever aged three years, was the youngest child and only girl in the Tafel household. *A simple task and I failed—with tragic results.* He squeezed shut his eyes for a long moment and recalled his mother's instructions. *Watch your sister while I return the mending to the neighbor. All started well— Father and my brothers were in the shop. I searched the lumber beside the barn for a piece to repair a gate. Greta played near the wood pile.*

"One minute"—he set down the first boot and lifted the other—"one minute for Greta to reach between the wrong logs, disturb the rattlesnake, and receive the fatal bite." Her scream repeated in his mind, and he shivered. Memories of the next frantic minutes, including a failed attempt to remove the poison, overwhelmed Kurt. Ever since, he knew others should not trust him with a child's safety. He struggled to breathe. Breaking out of his trance-like state, he gulped air laced with cold ashes and stale tobacco. "I deserve eternity in hell. I as good as killed her."

Jingle-jingle.

Kurt snapped closed his lips and shifted his attention toward the door.

"*Guten Tag, Herr* Tafel." Joseph advanced around the counter, clutching a wad of gray, knit material.

"Good day, young man. Did you learn new things at school today?"

Joseph shrugged and tilted his head. "Mama said you will made shoes out of socks. I don't understand."

Kurt set aside the boot, polish, and rag, before he

beckoned the boy closer. "Soon, the weather will be cold all day, not only frost in the early morning. Your mother and I discussed a way to help keep your feet warm. She wants my help to send you to school in moccasins."

"Indian shoes?" Joseph scrunched his face until his eyebrows almost touched.

"May I see the stockings?" He extended one hand. A moment later, he unfolded the material and inspected the close, even stitches. "Excellent workmanship. Did your mother knit these?"

Joseph shook his head. "*Fraulein* Mueller."

Sealing his lips, Kurt added another item to the list which made Hans Hoffmann a lucky man to have *Fraulein* Mueller for a *Schatz.* He blinked and focused on the task at hand. After setting the stockings onto the worktable, he addressed his guest. "Are you ready to have your feet measured?"

"My feet don't match." He tipped his face and stared at his dirt-smudged bare toes against the smooth, wide floorboards. "I'm not like other people."

"I see. Did you know your feet make you special? Not one other red-haired boy in Elm Ridge, or even all of Illinois, is exactly like you."

"I met another boy with red hair." He raised one hand and lifted a strand.

Kurt widened his eyes and shaped his mouth into a circle. "In Elm Ridge?"

"No." Joseph shook his head and frowned. "Where we lived before—St. Lo…St. Louis."

"I believe you." Kurt stood, stepped to his display of tools, and selected a wide board with a sturdy rim attached to one end and one side. Next, he opened a drawer and chose a piece of chalk and a pencil. "Has anyone measured your feet before?"

"I don't think so." He displayed both hands with palms forward. "Will it hurt? Or tickle like Mama's measuring tape against my skin?"

Kurt walked to where the light was best and set the measure on the floor. "No pain. Step close to this special board, and I will show you how a Tafel cobbler measures feet for a good fit."

Joseph joined Kurt near the window and alternated his gaze between the board and the shoemaker.

"We will start with your larger foot. Stand on the wood with your heel and little toe touching the edge."

"Like this?" The boy placed his left foot on the board.

Kurt squatted, adjusted the measure a portion of an inch, and looked at Joseph's face. "Now, stand on one foot." He paused for the boy to find his balance. With one smooth stroke, he drew a chalk mark along the side of the foot. In the next instant, he pulled the chalk across the slant of the toes until the two lines intersected. "Done with the first foot. You may step off the board."

Squinting at the lines, Joseph shook his head. "It doesn't look like a foot. Do you make square shoes?"

Kurt contained his chuckle. "No—I mark the largest places. Then I cut the leather like a regular foot. Understand?" He waited for a nod. "Now, we mark your right foot."

"Because it's different?"

"Exactly. Step on the measure and set your heel and the bump where your big toe begins against the board's rim."

Joseph trembled as he stood on his weaker leg. "This foot isn't as strong."

"I work quick." Kurt drew two lines with his pencil. "Done. Now, you may stand on both feet."

Sighing, the boy stepped off the special board. "Are we done measuring? How long to turn stockings and lines into moccasins? May I come and watch?"

"We will measure one more thing." Kurt set the board on the table, stepped to the shelves, and returned with several thin strips of wood. "I want you to walk for me—to the far end of the table."

"Why?" Joseph met the tall man's gaze.

Kurt sent what he intended as a stern look toward the boy. "Since I talked with your mother, an idea grew in my head." He squatted and gestured for the boy to begin moving. "Walk in a straight line, turn around, and take a few steps toward me."

After a shrug, the child faced the far wall and followed directions.

"Very good. Can you stand still as a stone with your hands on your hips—like this?" He demonstrated arms akimbo.

"Like this?" Joseph straightened and puffed his chest.

"Excellent." Kurt pressed his lips to contain a laugh at the imitation of an important man ready to give his opinion to a passerby. He knelt in front of the boy and worked one shim under the smaller heel. Leaning back, he compared the elbows. "Hold still, not done yet." He worked a second, thicker shim into place. After inserting a third strip of wood, he inspected the result and nodded. "Good. We are done. You may move your arms and legs."

"Now, you make moccasins? Can…may I watch." Joseph's eyes sparkled.

Picking up the shims, Kurt pressed them tight with his fingers and held them against a measuring stick. "Not today." He recorded a number on the board with the chalk and pencil marks. "I will do my work while you are in school, between orders for other customers."

The boy eased over to the peg board and danced his fingers over a smooth last. "*Herr* Tafel?"

"What is your question?" Aware Joseph had afternoon chores, he glanced at the clock and confirmed he needed to send the boy home soon.

"Did you go to school?"

Kurt exhaled tension. "Six years—fall and winter terms."

"I don't like school." He moved to the table and touched the heel of *Herr* Hebing's repaired boot.

"Is the work hard?" He remembered his struggles to get columns of numbers to make sense until his oldest brother showed him how they used numbers in shoemaking.

Joseph shook his head. "I know my letters. Mr. Hopewell shows me new things with numbers. But…the older boys laugh at me. My classmates ignore me. Mama tells me to make a friend." He faced Kurt and displayed both hands. "How?"

Studying the confusion on the boy's face, Kurt sat on a stool and rubbed his chin. When he was a schoolboy, he made friends easily. "Do you share?"

"Yesterday, I let Caleb take a bite of my apple. Then he snatched the whole thing and ran to the other side of the schoolyard."

"A problem—sounds like Caleb does not

understand sharing."

"What do I do?" He sat on the floor and looked into Kurt's face.

Kurt remained silent for a long moment. "Do you join the games outside?"

"Too much jumping and running…I finish last."

"Hmm." He compared Joseph's problem making a school friend to his task of introducing himself to the residents of his new home. "Give me until your next visit to find a proper suggestion." Phrases from the family letter returned. Three of his brothers included words about wives or sweethearts. While he enjoyed learning the news and wished his family well, the information rubbed his heart like rough bark. He silently recited the names of the *Frauen* at the most recent dance and failed to find any who lightened his heart. Closing and releasing his hands, he fought the memory from last night's dream—when he held Polly in a waltz.

Chapter Seven

After Sunday morning worship service, Polly lingered in the church narthex. In the sanctuary, Pastor Harter expounded on a Bible story to the children, including Joseph. Outside the open double doors, a light rain continued. The scents of damp wool and fresh mud caused her to wrinkle her nose. From the corner of her eye, she confirmed the entry lacked a simple mat to capture dirt from shoes. She turned and glanced toward the new, large Bible lying on the altar. Hiding a sigh, she calculated the cost of a rug, a great assistance to the cleaning lady, at pennies compared to the dollars the men of the congregation spent for a fine, leather-bound Bible with gilt edges A moment later, she joined a group of women gathered at the end of the room, including Eliza Cook, the hardware owner's wife.

"No, a thin paste makes a better gravy. You continue to stir while it bubbles around the vegetables to avoid the lumps." Eliza counseled a younger woman.

"You will do well to follow Mrs. Cook's kitchen advice," Polly inserted. "Did you taste her seasoned green peas at the most recent church dinner?"

Eliza blushed. "You flatter me. Our garden blessed us with a second pea crop this year."

Gathering a little confidence from the cheerful expressions of the other women, Polly moistened her lips. "I want to let everyone know the winter silks and wide lace arrived. We have some gorgeous colors. We also have a new supply of light fabric, ideal for chemisettes."

Mrs. Franklin shook her head. "My girls and I dress plain—and modest. Our household has no need for lace or a little chemise."

"Has the wide ribbon suitable for bonnets arrived? I've trimmed the frayed ends so many times it is difficult to tie a proper bow." Mrs. Cook fingered the end of deep-red ribbons on her black headgear.

Polly reviewed the new items in the recent shipment. "New ribbon arrived and some is wide enough for the purpose. Please, stop in and view the colors."

"Bonnets." Mrs. Franklin sighed.

"What about your girls, Mrs. Franklin, have they winter dresses?"

"You are a good saleswoman, Mrs. Black. I will inspect Rebecca's frock...she has grown much since spring." Mrs. Franklin tapped her umbrella tip on the floor. "I suppose a plain style in a pretty color will not cause a distraction."

Polly darted her gaze toward a group of three older girls sitting and whispering in the back pew and identified Rebecca, the oldest Franklin child, by her thick, dark curls. She kept her smile small at the kind words.

"Excuse me, ladies."

Polly blinked slowly before she pivoted toward the familiar, unwelcome voice. "Good day, Mr. Rush."

"May I have a word, Mrs. Black?" He nodded to each of the other women and pointed to an unoccupied portion of the room.

Manners and kindness. She recalled *Fraulein* Mueller's concise description of how to deal with difficult customers. Adjusting the umbrella hooked over her arm, she smiled a farewell to the group before following the lumber dealer. *How many times have we spoken? Twice?* She recalled the odd ending to the conversation on his wagon and hid a frown. "What do you hesitate to say in front of others?"

George Rush held his hat firm against his chest. "I want to apologize. The other day…in the wagon…I was too bold."

Glancing toward the ceiling, she remained silent for a long moment. "I won't mention a word to others."

"The core of the matter remains. I can't raise my daughter alone. I miss her terribly during the week." He glanced into the sanctuary, where Hannah, only the top of her head visible above the pew's back, sat beside another girl.

She surveyed the children and felt an invisible string tug her toward Joseph. "I understand. Have you pondered on the matter of a housekeeper?"

He looked toward the floor and then at her face. "My opinion on hired help remains firm. What I want to do…might we start over…you and I?"

She drew a breath and stilled. Studying her hands, she clasped them tighter. "I gave you a plain answer. I am content with a quiet life and do not seek a husband."

"Bah—a healthy woman your age gains true happiness only with a husband and children—several to pass on the family name." He lowered the hand holding his hat to his side and began to raise and point with his free hand.

She focused on taking the next breath and backed

half a step until her shoulder brushed the wall. *He has no right to lecture me on the advantages of marriage.*

"This evening," he lowered his voice, "after the others leave for the farm, I shall call at your home. Expect me at seven o'clock."

She glanced toward the plain ceiling but did not discover an obvious reason a widower could not call on a widow, even one of her description. In the next breath, she pushed aside an image of Kurt sitting at her table eating beans and asking questions. Choosing to ignore Mr. Rush's earlier stated goal, she lifted her right hand a few inches above her skirt. "You have permission to call. I will serve tea and cake. We can get acquainted proper."

"Capital. Until later." He ignored her hand, stepped back, and shifted his attention to the children exiting the sanctuary.

"Mama," Joseph hoarse-whispered from a distance of four feet.

Advancing to him, she touched his shoulder and drew him close. "Did you pay attention to the Bible story?"

"Uh-huh."

"Real words, son." She stayed aware of Mr. Rush placing a hand on his daughter's shoulder and escorting her toward the door.

"Yes, Mama. Pastor told us about the boy David when he killed a giant soldier. Who were you talking with? Can we go home? I'm hungry." He spoke rapidly and softly.

Polly adjusted her shawl, stifled a laugh, and ignored his first question. "You're always hungry. I think you are getting ready to grow again. Today, we eat and spend an hour or two with *Frau* Keil."

"Frau Keil has the best smelling apartment." He rubbed a circle on his stomach.

A few steps from the church property, Joseph extended one hand beyond the umbrella's edge and caught raindrops. "Was Papa tall? Will I grow up to look like him?"

"He was tall enough. You inherited his handsome hair." A vivid memory of her first meeting with Bernard returned. Exiting Madam Robineau's front door on a late summer afternoon, she had not paid close attention to a man climbing the stairs. After a near collision on the step, Bernard doffed his cap and had introduced himself in English with a charming *Deutsch* accent.

"I want to grow tall, like *Herr* Tafel—and strong. Once he let me touch his muscles." Joseph chattered about the new neighbor while he strolled beside her toward the bakery.

One...pause...two...pause. She counted even, calming breaths. If she blinked too slow, an image of large, gentle hands setting a darning egg beside her flatware returned. "I think you like *Herr* Tafel. Be careful you do not become a pest. He needs to tend his work."

"He gives me chores—sweeping. Yesterday, he gave me a peppermint and called it my wages."

"Clever." She chuckled. Pausing before stepping from street to sidewalk, she shook her head. *Regardless of his charm,* Herr *Tafel must remain a friend—like Hans Hoffmann or* Herr *Hebing.* She resumed walking the final yards to *Frau* Keil's apartment steps.

"The rain stopped." Joseph reached above his head

and tapped the umbrella's underside.

"Yes." She lowered and collapsed the umbrella before she surveyed growing patches of clear sky between ragged clouds. She savored a puff of rain-washed air before familiar wood smoke rode the next breath. "Wipe your feet on *Frau* Keil's mat."

"Yes, Mama." He scampered up the wooden stairs.

Remember, the immigrant is your friend. Startled at the sudden return of one of her mother's favorite sayings, Polly paused on the lowest step. She gazed at the quiet street and remembered her father bragging about his grandfather, a soldier at Yorktown. Leo's sour expression when she first mentioned calling at the Keil's bakery formed as clear as if her brother stood before her. Shaking aside memories of insults to immigrants spoken by her father and brother, she took a step. A shiver danced across her shoulders at the image of Leo displaying admiration for Mr. Rush. *The lumber dealer wants to marry. He appears to dote on his daughter and ignore other children, including Joseph.* She mouthed the thoughts toward the sky. *If I choose to marry, then the man must accept my son and treat him with kindness.*

Joseph faced her from the top of the stairs. "Hurry, Mama. I smell chicken."

Jerked to the task at hand, she climbed the steps and wondered if *Herr* Tafel enjoyed a fine, Sunday dinner.

****

Kurt joined the uneven line of exiting parishioners and dropped a single coin into the offering box. With a nod of greeting to a familiar man, he continued out of the building and down the front steps. Aware the rain had stopped, he curved his lips into a smile. Today, a longer sermon might have been a good thing. He hummed the melody of the dismissal hymn and noted the expanding patches of clear sky between the clouds.

"Are you going to Althoff's today?"

Turning toward the familiar voice, he smiled at Hans Hoffmann. "*Ja.* They offer a fine dinner plate on Sunday. I find the meal a pleasant change from the tavern's stew or my humble cooking. Will they have dancing today? The new pavilion lacked shingles and doors the last I walked past."

After a glance toward heaven, Hans frowned. "One time, when it rained during the night, I learned they cover the dancing area with large canvases. When the sky cleared, they rolled the coverings away, and the music began."

Kurt suppressed his building laugh into a wide smile. *Music, to me, is one of life's joys. I do not believe Hans agrees.* He recalled the stable hand's wrinkled brow and whispered counting while dancing with Louisa. "To me, an intelligent brewer and beer garden owner is another reason to like Elm Ridge. Excuse me. We talk again at Althoff's, no?"

A few minutes later, in a group including Jacob Thayer, a master carpenter, Kurt inquired about progress on the dance hall.

"Not long," Jacob replied. "Another week and the plasterer can begin. This late in the season, it is not wise to say how long to dry."

Kurt and the others in the group muttered about the influence of weather on a great many things—from harvesting the remaining corn, butchering hogs, and laying in a wood supply.

"Papa." A dark-haired beauty dashed up to Jacob.

Kurt glanced from daughter to father and back again. He estimated her age at sixteen and recognized her as one of his favored dance partners. But he hesitated for a brief moment before recalling her name…Bertha.

"Christian and Amelia plan to walk to the beer garden. I want to join them." She stared at her father from clear, blue eyes.

Jacob tipped his head and laughed toward the sky. "Do you go to keep them honest? Or do you plan mischief?"

"Really, Papa. You know I am kind to Christian." A momentary frown crossed her face.

"And your sister—does your sweetness extend to her?" Jacob's eyes twinkled as he teased.

Bertha emitted a noisy sigh. "Amelia is bossy. She never lets me forget she is older."

"May I escort you?" Kurt uttered the invitation before the words passed through his brain. "My company will make the number even." As silence settled over the trio, he waited. "With your father's permission."

"Go. I wish you well, *Herr* Tafel." Jacob lifted his hands.

Moments later, Kurt and Bertha joined a young couple waiting at the corner. After hasty introductions, he offered his arm to Bertha and fell into step behind Christian Giesel, a stonemason and Amelia's intended.

"Thank you for offering to accompany us." Bertha glanced toward him.

Kurt alternated his gaze from the couple a few steps ahead to the delicate hand on his forearm. "A man would be a fool not to offer. Few men call me such—at least not within hearing."

Giggling, she adjusted her arm.

"Aside from dancing on Sunday, how does the fair Bertha Thayer spend her time?"

"Regardless of Papa's comments, I am a dutiful daughter. Most days, I assist *Mutter* with the household chores. At times, I do housework for hire. Papa likes to keep me close and insists the jobs be short-term and in the village."

He held the question of how long since she left the schoolroom behind his teeth. "Which do you prefer—home or wages?"

Touching the knot of her dark-green shawl, she hesitated only a moment. "Wages—for then, I have money to buy books. Two weeks ago, I finished work for the Schneck family. *Frau* Schneck bore her second child in August."

"What sort of books are your favorite?" He glanced toward her thumb rubbing on his sleeve. Noting a sparkle in her eye, he suspected she sought adventure. "Dare I guess you favor stories set in exotic places?"

"I enjoy a variety. The list for my recent wages includes Immanuel Kant's finest work—plus two lighter books. Papa places an order with a bookseller in St. Louis every autumn. I look forward to the arrival and do not mind when he holds back a title or two for St. Nicholas gifts."

Kurt added the knowledge to his already good opinion of *Herr* Thayer.

Jingle-jingle. Clop-clop.

Kurt guided them to the grassy verge and halted as a buggy passed on the muddy street. Each glance toward Bertha prompted thoughts of his brothers. *Two are married. Another will speak vows before Christmas. Only young Helmut and I remain without partners.* He slid his gaze toward Bertha. He observed a lively and attractive young woman. Two years ago, he'd locked his heart and limited his emotional displays around young women to smiles during a dance or idle conversation. He could not imagine a *Fraulein* of Bertha's tender age dismantling the obstacles and affecting his heart.

****

"Are you certain you want to share your vegetables? You have been generous to Joseph and me." Polly paused at the bottom of the bakery apartment steps. She lifted her attention to the sky and noted scattered clouds in the east. However, in the west, where most of the storms formed, a thick, lumpy blanket shielded the afternoon sun.

Frau Keil opened her mouth to speak at the same instant a steamboat whistled from the river.

Joseph, balancing an empty basket on his head, set his hands on his hips and stepped forward.

The container slid off his brow and into his flailing arms.

"I think I need practice." He steadied the basket on his head with one hand.

Pressing her lips, Polly halted her question. She needed to accept the idea that children brought home strange notions. She suspected Joseph mimicked a drawing in a book.

"You worked diligently in our garden this summer. Louisa and I could not have stayed ahead of the weeds." Charlotte opened the garden gate. "It is fair you share the bounty. No?"

"I appreciate the produce. The next time we go for a picnic, I will pay for the horse and gig." She paused beside a raised bed containing a row of late cabbage and withered potato vines.

Charlotte cut a large cabbage and gestured for Joseph to bring the basket. "The weather is turning. I believe our drives to the clearing above the river are ended for the season. In winter, my habit is to share Sunday dinner with friends and spend the afternoon enjoying cards and table games."

"You are always welcome in my humble home." She counted guests since the fire on one hand with fingers remaining. *Mr. Rush this evening—I pray for kindness and manners.*

"I will remember." *Frau* Keil exchanged her knife for the digging fork. "One hill of potatoes, I think. I'll add a few carrots and onions to give you all except the meat for a fine stew."

Polly squatted and helped Joseph find and rub the mud from several round potatoes.

"This summer..." Charlotte lifted a corner of her apron to her face. "Louisa...you...and your son...gave me great comfort. Bernard...his death was so sudden. I was lost...adrift...in my mind."

"Go, wash at pump." Polly stacked potatoes in Joseph's open hands. Sealing her lips, she contained her thoughts on the baker's death. An entire set of dreams were crushed under the wagon wheels on a May afternoon. However, thanks to Charlotte, the ache in her heart lessened a little every week. "Louisa is a good worker...talented baker."

"Yes, she is." Charlotte tugged two round onions

from the next garden bed. "The day she arrived and inquired about employment, I sensed she was a good person. Bernard grew to trust her. I wish…oh, never mind…wishes cannot change facts. I am in good health, and the business provides what I need. I have many blessings."

"Do you think Hans and Louisa will marry?" Polly did not see the stable hand often, but at each encounter, he appeared to have matured years instead of weeks.

"In time…he saves money from his wages." She bent and loosened half a dozen carrots from a forkful of disturbed dirt. "Have you thought of your future?"

"Are these clean enough?" Joseph displayed the rinsed potatoes. Settling the tubers in the basket, Polly gestured toward the carrots. "Go wash those, and we will join you at the pump in a few minutes."

"Yes, Mama." He limped toward the garden gate.

"You ask of my future—I suppose you want to know if I seek marriage. I enjoy my work with Mrs. Clark. I find life pleasant enough." She lifted the basket. "I keep hoping Joseph will make a true friend at school. But so far, he only talks of teasing or shunning."

"Give the boy more time. School has only met for two weeks." Charlotte brushed one hand across her apron.

Polly skimmed a finger over a thick onion. "What do you know of George Rush?"

"Rush," Charlotte muttered. "Do you mean the partner in the lumber company?"

"The same." She studied the older woman's face and found hesitation.

"The business has a good reputation. Neither of the

families trade here—they prefer the American merchants." Charlotte stored the fork in a corner of the fence and faced the gate. "I think they supplied the lumber for your new building."

"Yes. Mrs. Clark was very firm in purchasing the materials from Americans but hiring *Deutsch* carpenters. Her brother-in-law assisted in engaging *Herr* Thayer. Do you know him?"

"*Ja,* he runs a large crew. Nice family. No gossip or rumors follow in his wake."

She hesitated and organized her next words. "Mr. Rush—do rumors trail him?" Interpreting Charlotte's tilted head and pursed lips as questions, Polly drew a new breath. "His wife died recently...in childbirth. I-I-I think he means to court me."

"I am sorry to hear of his wife. I talked to her once or twice at Cook's Hardware. Well, Eliza and I talked—Mrs. Rush spent much time glancing toward her shoes. I suspected her shy—at least, when *Deutsch* words are sprinkled in the conversation."

Nodding, Polly signaled agreement with the description. "At church, I saw her as standing in her husband's shadow. I seek more information to understand his manner."

"Other children?" Charlotte paused one step past the gate.

"A daughter, Hannah, younger than Joseph—she is living with relatives on a farm some distance from town. He speaks fondly of her."

"Be careful, Polly. Don't let him hurry you into a decision you will regret."

Latching the garden gate behind her, Polly watched Joseph lay the carrots in a row on the cistern cover. He appeared to be more independent and confident than mere weeks ago.

Moments later, with the carrots added to the basket, Joseph lifted the container and staggered a few steps forward. "I get strong—like *Herr* Tafel."

"In time, son...in due time." She glanced toward Charlotte. "Neighbor. Cobbler. Before Elm Ridge, he lived in Pennsylvania. Joseph enjoys going to his shop."

The bakery owner chuckled. "We have met. He purchases a rye loaf each Wednesday morning while the bread is still warm from the oven."

"Joseph, I will carry the basket now. Go fetch the umbrella and then bid *Frau* Keil a proper farewell."

Without a word, he set the heavy basket on the ground and dashed up the stairs. At his return a moment later, he paused three feet in front of Charlotte. He bowed deep from the waist. "*Auf Wiedersehen* until our paths cross again."

The ease with which her son sprinkled the proper *Deutsch* phrases into conversation caused Polly's heart to swell with pride. She offered her own parting words and realized some of her truest friends in Elm Ridge spoke *Deutsch* with an occasional English word, the exact opposite of her speech.

Two hours later, while a light rain pattered against the window, Polly added two pinches of tea leaves to her brown, round teapot. She regarded the visitor to her home and reminded herself to be kind.

George Rush leaned back in one of the plain chairs at the table. "Eight miles separate Hannah and me—too far."

Fifteen minutes and we've exhausted the topics of weather and today's sermon. She sent her gaze to the area under the steps and confirmed Joseph and Swifty played a game involving a piece of string. Standing near the corner cupboard, she lifted the lidded sugar container. "I believe the water is almost at the boil. Do you take milk in your tea?"

"No...thank you." George tapped one work-coarsened finger on the table's edge.

Almost convinced his slightly downturned mouth was his normal expression rather than a silent comment on her mismatched dishes, Polly returned to the table. She set the sugar beside the half of a pound cake resting on the circular board and inventoried the items between the two place settings...knife, butter, strawberry jam. A moment later, she stood at the stove and poured water from kettle to teapot.

George swiveled his head and straightened. "Neat. Tidy. I approve."

Did you invite yourself to inspect my home? Swallowing the rude comment before the words spilled, she carried the brewing tea to the table. "The building is a simple space, but more than adequate for Joseph and me."

"My mill sawed and sold the lumber." He looked at her directly and lowered his voice. "We purchase an entire raft of white pine floated from Minnesota Territory each spring. Franklin and I store the logs in our yard a full year before sawing. Makes for a nice, straight board with minimum warping. Fewer complaints from the carpenters."

She swirled the teapot and failed to find any sort of privileged business information in his conversation. Pretending more than the casual interest she felt, she listened to the clock in the shop strike the hour.

"We sell windows, too. Have a dandy of a man doing the fine work. Glass comes all the way from Cincinnati. Steamboat service these days sure is an improvement from my first years in Elm Ridge."

"I understand you were one of the first businesses in town."

He nodded, lifted the knife, and cut a thick slice of cake. "I built the first waterwheel on Rumble Creek twelve years ago. Gordon started work on his grain mill mere weeks later. We've been in competition of some sort or another ever since. Like to think he wishes me no ill, however, I don't agree with a lot of his ideas."

"Mr. Gordon, the mayor?" Politics seldom entered into conversations around her, but the name and a faint idea of reputation poked from a corner of her mind.

"The same." He laid the knife with the handle almost touching his plate. "I landed with little more than a keg of hardware, a few tools, and a ton of determination. Boats stopped at the levee whenever they chose, sometimes a full week between. Franklin and his young family arrived a few months later with more supplies. He's the mechanic—I negotiate most of the sales. Didn't have a lick of competition until three…four…years ago when a fellow built a small mill on Skunk Creek south of town." He shrugged. "One man outfit—cuts local wood—what doesn't go to the steamboats."

"The boats do use a great deal of fuel. Our packet from St. Louis stopped once, sometimes twice, each day to replenish the supply." She poured fragrant, amber liquid into his delicate cup before filling her own.

George added two rounded spoonsful of sugar to

his tea. "My wife, whoever I settle on, will have a grand house. Have you seen it?"

Shaking her head, she stirred one scant spoonful of sweetness into her drink."Mama." Joseph stood near her elbow. "May I have cake?"

"No, remember what I said after our supper."

With a sigh, the boy returned to a collection of acorns under the steps.

Polly shifted her attention to George. "I understand you built on Seventh Street—a full two stories."

"Correct." He slathered a thick layer of jam on his cake. "Eight large rooms—four downstairs—four generous bedrooms upstairs. Proper staircase"—he glanced toward the open, steep steps to her loft—"with oak bannisters. Three chimneys—fine kitchen stove plus two smaller coal burners for heating. One of the largest homes in Elm Ridge. Certainly, the grandest frame house." He paused with his cup halfway to his mouth. "Gordon has a large home—brick."

"Frame sounds appropriate for a man in the lumber business." She cut herself a thin slice of cake and dipped her knife into the butter. She thought of the time and effort to keep the many rooms of a large house clean and tidy.

"Never considered building with stone or brick. A man in my position needs to live true. Took some talking, but I got my way before the builders dug the foundation."

She savored the first bite of cake and swallowed. The fresh butter, purchased yesterday, complemented the fine texture and subtle sweetness of the cake. "Tell me more."

"I insisted on setting the front wall a full fifty feet

back from the street. I don't want the street dust and noise to be a bother. Already, in the less than two years since the house was finished, traffic has increased." He swallowed his final bite of cake and licked dots of bright jam from his fingers. "Pity I only need two rooms at present—except for the scant hours on Sunday when Hannah and the others visit. Visit"—he spat the word—"my daughter needs to live in her father's house."

Polly sealed her lips to keep her secret promise to avoid mention of a housekeeper. "I can see the village is expanding. Do you think the church will thrive?"

"Every day I pray for the health and growth of the congregation. Did you know I was on the committee to invite the first preacher?" Reaching for his tea, he met her gaze.

"I believe Mrs. Franklin mentioned the fact in passing." *She also says you want to replace Mr. Gordon as mayor.*

He nodded. "Nice woman, Mrs. Franklin—tends her own business and children. I believe she sets a good example—her and the girls dressing plain. I shake my head and wonder at the state of the world each time another woman at church abandons simple dress for lace and whatnots. Flowers and feathers on bonnets make for a distraction during worship."

To hide the flash of anger at his attack on her livelihood, she glanced out the window. Full dark had replaced the gray, early dusk present at her guest's arrival. Standing, she gestured toward Joseph as he and the kitten played a crude game of marbles with acorns. In the light from the single, lard oil lamp in the sewing area, she cleared her throat. "Dark comes early, especially on a dreary, rainy day. Joseph, time for you to wash and go to bed. I'll come listen to prayers in a few minutes—after Mr. Rush says his farewell."

The boy groaned loud enough to fill the entire room. "I want to stay here and play with Swifty."

"School tomorrow." She pointed toward the washstand. "Wash. Bed. No argument."

"Swifty?" George muttered. "Did the lad name a kitten?"

Polly brought a linen towel to the table and wrapped the remaining cake. "Certainly. We are hoping the kitten will grow into a good mouser and become a trusted employee. She deserves a name."

Swifty, as if prompted to demonstrate, dashed under the drape to the shop.

"Foolishness." George frowned with both lips and eyebrows.

"Mr. Rush, did you have a dog when you were a boy?" Memories of Ticker, an old hound, howling in the middle of the night to scare the fox away from the chickens, returned with her next breath. She sighed. Fondness for the dog was one of the few things she and Leo agreed on as children. Since the arrival of the kitten, she found herself thinking of the family dog more often.

"No time for pets. From the time I was able to carry a brick in each hand, I worked. God created animals to serve man—horses for work, chickens for eggs, swine for meat. Dogs are all noise—bark at every passerby doing honest business." He set his cup onto the saucer with a loud *clink*. "Sorry to hear you have a mouse problem. Guess a cat might have a use—but I'd never waste my breath to name one."

"You missed a great joy by not having a pet." She paused in front of Joseph and waited while he blotted the towel against his face. She placed one finger under his chin and tipped his face.

"Good?" He looked up with wide eyes.

"Well enough. Now off to bed. I'll be up soon."

"Good night, Mr. Rush." Joseph bowed to the guest before he turned and limped up the steps.

"I hope you brought a lantern, Mr. Rush. I believe the rain has stopped, but clouds are hiding the moon." She gathered the dirty dishes and set them beside the washstand's basin.

He tapped one finger against the table's edge. "Don't underestimate me, Mrs. Black. Or should I say Miss? In the spirit of Christian kindness, I am willing to overlook a mistake in your youth." He pushed back his chair and stood. "You best mind your tongue—and manners. Ordering me from your home—not proper."

Surprised at his threat to her already fragile reputation, she blinked. "I mean no insult, Mr. Rush. However, morning brings work. I find a day unfolds in a better manner when I have a good rest." She won the struggle to keep her face serious.

Pursing his lips, he lifted his hat from the peg.

Please—make your final comment and go. You spoke three words or less to my son the entire time you've been under our roof. She straightened her shoulders and faced him.

In the blink of an eye, he stepped close, set one hand behind her head, and lowered his lips to her mouth.

Oh...what? Frozen in place, she accepted his kiss with closed lips.

He pressed his lips firmer.

Recovering a few of her senses, Polly lifted her hands and placed them securely against his chest. With steady pressure, she increased the distance between them. Instead of basking in the glow of a welcome kiss, she felt as if he attempted to claim ownership. "Enough."

"For now, Mrs. Black. We shall converse again." He settled his hat, opened the door, and departed through the back porch.

She closed her eyes for a moment and pictured Leo's flour mill property adjoining the sawmill yard. She worried her bottom lip and wondered what tales her brother told. "Please Lord," she whispered, "don't allow loose words of Joseph's parentage to destroy the reputation I have started to weave. I could not bear to have Joseph, or *Frau* Keil, suffer because of my past."

Meow. Swifty strolled into the room and circled her feet.

"Yes, my little friend, we need to protect Joseph." *The most certain way to guard my son is to marry.* "Not George Rush"—she poured water to wash the few dishes. "I will marry a decent man able to accept my son as his own. My husband must be a man with Christian love in his heart—and able to understand the need to name a pet."

Chapter Eight

Smoothing the gingham remaining on the bolt, Polly glanced out the workroom window. Monday dusk settled over the street view. She blinked and returned her gaze for another look.

Across the street, a sign, bright-blue and rich-brown against clean white, hung from the cobbler's shop.

"Abigail, I believe *Herr* Tafel has a placard."

"A man finished hanging it less than an hour ago. From here, the sign appears a handsome piece of workmanship." Abigail lifted the cash box from the shelf under the counter and set it beside the ledger.

"It is a pity the fire damaged our thread and needle emblem beyond repair." Polly plucked one pin from the green pincushion and secured the end of the uncut cloth. Shivering, she remembered the morning after the fire. Soon after sunrise, Polly, Abigail, and Abigail's sister had met at the fire site and collected metal and pottery items which were still usable. They found the sign in half a dozen pieces in various degrees of singed wood. The bracket had been discovered bent, broken, and entangled with the wire dress frame. She sighed and carried the fabric to the display shelf.

Abigail muttered numbers and moved a pencil down the ledger lines. "One more month of good business and I will inquire at the sign maker. Step-by-step, we return to profit. I dare say, without a sign, we held an advantage over the cobbler."

"In what way?" Polly remembered her first weeks in Elm Ridge and finding her way from one shop to another by the signs mounted on the buildings or names painted in the windows.

"The families who were our customers before the fire know our location. Only newcomers are not aware this building is a dress shop." Abigail met Polly's gaze for an instant before returning to her bookkeeping.

"I did not think of the situation from that perspective. A new sign before the spring steamboats bring a surge of new residents will work well." She shifted her attention to the dress form in the far corner of the workroom. A fine-weave wool in a rose color brightened the space. "You have made good progress on Mrs. Winston's new gown."

Abigail returned the ledger to the low shelf. "She refused lace or trims. However, she did consent to a more stylish cut to the bodice. I don't understand why the men of our church consider a little contrasting binding or a few decorative pleats to be a distraction. I find an attractive dress gives me confidence."

"You might have answered your own question." *Confidence—too often mine is only on the surface.* Mrs. Clark retrieved her bonnet from the peg. "Soon, the mornings will require more than today's light shawl. Have you started sewing yourself a proper cloak for winter?"

"One more week and I'll pay you for both the wool and black silk to line the hood." She patted the bolt of light gray she'd selected as soon as she pulled it out of the shipping barrel. "Speaking of winter—when does packet service become unreliable?"

"Last year, the boat arrived daily until the end of December. I sent in a large order last week to allow plenty of time. You have no need to worry about letters to your friends in St. Louis for several weeks."

Polly glanced to the shelves. "I look forward to more fabric on our shelves. Perhaps, it will be advisable to pray for a mild winter."

"You'll be at direct odds with Old Mr. Winston." Mrs. Clark knotted her shawl. "When I stepped into his store today, he was predicting a long, hard winter and retelling a tale of driving cattle on the ice across to Missouri."

"Recently?" While aware Elm Ridge was north of St. Louis, she found it difficult to feature the entire river frozen long and hard enough to support a herd of cattle. In the city, river traffic to and from the south stopped only for a few days during a typical winter.

"No, I think the incident was eight or nine years ago. I remember a bitter winter the year before my husband died. However, Mr. Winston's stories get more elaborate each year they're removed from an event."

A rush of cool air, simultaneous with the shop bell's tinkle, acted as punctuation.

"May we—" Polly froze mid-turn toward the door.

"*Guten Abend,* ladies." Kurt removed his cap and adjusted a thick, gray bundle under his arm.

"Have you come for more linen thread, *Herr* Tafel?" Abigail tucked a smile into her question.

"Not today." He tipped his head toward the drape to the living quarters. "Greetings, Joseph." Returning his attention to Mrs. Clark, he paused. "Today, I come to deliver an order to Mrs. Black—special request."

Abigail retrieved her basket from the floor behind the counter. "Need I stay?"

"No," Polly inserted. "Go home to your favorite chair and a warm supper. Joseph will chaperon." Instinct told her the only person apt to begin a rumor against her reputation was George Rush—and gossip was double-edged for a politician.

"Very well, I leave the place in your capable hands. I shall see you in the morning." Abigail departed with a rustle of skirts and tinkle of the bell.

After locking the door and pulling the curtain on the small window, Polly pointed toward Kurt's package. "Step into the workroom and show us what you have."

"I puzzled over your request for moccasins and stockings for some hours." He unrolled the bundle and revealed the wool stockings with the addition of a low slipper.

"May I touch?" Joseph paused a hand above the junction of wool and leather.

Polly nodded and lifted one garment. "Nice, even stitches—where did you find matching yarn?"

"When I learned *Fraulein* Mueller knit the socks, I asked her for a little. Do you think they will do?" He shifted his gaze from Polly to Joseph. "You need to walk around large or deep puddles. Can you remember?"

Joseph held his eyes wide and rounded. "I remember."

"Sit down, son. Put on your socks-with-shoes and tell us what you think?" Polly forced her gaze to avoid Kurt.

The boy grabbed both modified stockings and sat

on the floor. He pulled on first one and then the other. "Warm."

"Good." She eased around the table for a better view. "Cold feet do not help you pay attention in church or school."

"Can you wiggle all your toes?" Kurt asked.

Joseph nodded, then scrambled to his feet.

Squatting beside him, Polly pressed her thumb along the rounded toe. A pound of worry evaporated from her chest with each test. "Good...you allowed room for growth. How much do I owe you?"

"Materials and a little time...I believe we settled on half the price of shoes at Clemons' Dry Goods." Kurt eased back until his hip touched the sales counter.

"Are you sure?" *This appears to be quality leather. You are giving me a bargain.* She stayed quiet as Swifty crept into the room.

"Yes, if you lack funds, I will accept a portion and put the rest on an account. I enjoyed the challenge of the project." He kept his gaze directed toward the dress form in the corner.

"I put money aside for shoes." She did not desire charity. Long ago, when she learned she was to be a mother, she set her mind to pay her own way in either coin or labor. "I believe your kindness deserves a reward. Would you honor us and share our supper?"

****

Kurt hid his surprise and alternated his gaze between Polly and Joseph. "Are you certain you want to add me to your table? I do not want to intrude."

"You will not be trouble." Her words emerged in a rush.

"Please, *Herr* Tafel. I will share." Joseph lifted his

93

gaze from his new shoes to Kurt's face.

"I will stay. I ask for something in return." He held his gaze on Joseph and struggled to keep his lips in a serious line.

"What do I need to do, sir?" Joseph stiffened.

Sir? The boy frightens easier than I imagined. Or is it good American manners? "I want you to tell me all about the kitten examining your shoes."

"Swifty." He squatted.

The kitten retreated at a speed consistent with her name.

Joseph extended one hand and circled his thumb against three fingers. "Come, Swifty...*Herr* Tafel is a friend."

Standing still, Kurt marveled as the kitten stalked toward the boy.

"New shoes—for school—and church." Joseph addressed the kitten and stroked her head. "I smell new leather and clean wool. What does your nose find?"

Breathing deep, Kurt detected simmering onions from the next room. Without moving his head, he stayed aware of Polly gathering sewing tools from the table and placing them in a tin. "I think a kitten fits well into your household. Has she learned home?"

"She comes to the pump with me in the morning. Today I coaxed her inside without trouble—I did not need to sit still with bread dipped in milk." Joseph grabbed the edge of the worktable and stood without moving his feet.

"Very good."

"Do your kittens come into the shop?" Joseph spoke so quick the words blurred in the air. "I saw the gray leap all the way from the top of your woodpile to the ground once. She is brave. Does she have a name?"

"Slow down, young man." Kurt risked a glance toward Polly and noticed she pulled the curtain across the large window. "You and I will talk about kittens while your mother does the last-minute supper preparations."

Polly held the drape to the living quarters aside. "Business day is done—time to feed a schoolboy and our...neighbor. Joseph, your next task is setting the table...three places."

What flew through her mind during the long pause? He followed her into the living quarters.

A short time later, Kurt stood at the washstand and dried his hands. Directing his attention to Joseph, he watched the boy place a wide butter knife, three-tined fork, and round spoon near each water glass. "My kittens come in and out of my apartment and shop at their own pleasure. I have been calling them Smoke and Coal. They scurry away if a customer arrives or the clock chimes. My wood pile is not so tall. Soon I will buy a larger supply for winter. Then we will test the kittens' skill for climbing and jumping." He intersected Polly's gaze. "I notice more farmers with carts of stove wood on the streets."

"Mrs. Clark and I were speaking of the river closing before you arrived. Like you, this will be my first winter in Elm Ridge." She set a jam jar and butter plate on the table.

"Do you expect it to be very different from St. Louis?"

"River traffic halts." She unwrapped a partial loaf of wheat bread. "I understand the number of weeks without packet service varies with the weather."

Kurt draped the towel over a rod at the end of the washstand. "When the river closes, I shall miss the mail service."

"Does your family write often?" She glanced toward a tin box on a high shelf.

"*Mein Mutter* and second brother send most of the letters. *Vater* often adds a line or two at the end." Blinking, he banished the image of his father scratching a few sentences at the bottom of the page. His father managed to put both a bit of news and advice in a few words. He imagined his family's reaction to the moccasin socks and hid his smile.

She nodded while carrying a bowl of stew to the table. "I hope you like vegetables simmered with very little meat. I have not been to the butcher since Friday."

"I'm not a fussy eater." He absorbed peace from the quiet domestic scene. *She moves with an easy grace from one task to another. Mrs. Black will be a credit to any man.* He sealed his lips and focused on the table set with mismatched dishes. "Please, sit." She set the final filled bowl at her own place.

What if she asks me to pray? I know only Deutsch *prayers.*

"Joseph, please say the blessing." She touched her son's wrist.

"Heavenly Father…"

Kurt paid close attention and translated many words into *Deutsch,* his language of religion. Twice the boy hesitated and then continued with a complicated word. Moistening his lips, he joined in a hearty "amen."

"Very good, Joseph." She touched his elbow.

The boy lifted his spoon and dipped it into the stew. "I'm hungry. I didn't want to repeat any parts."

Kurt shifted his gaze and beamed at Polly. In his family, the table prayer passed from one person to another around the table each day. When seven gathered at the Tafel table, his day was Wednesday. Now, with only three at the table, he knew the pattern was different. He lowered his gaze to his food at the realization three sat around the Tafel table tonight—the same number as here. He brought a spoonful of peas and cut turnip near his nose. "Mmm, simmered with peppercorns and…?"

"A sprig of rosemary." She lifted a sliced carrot near her lips. "Tell me, *Herr* Tafel, who made your fine, new sign?"

Tension, gathered while he thought of his family, slipped from his shoulders. "*Herr* Knapp. Is he among your *Deutsch* friends?" He waited for her to shake her head. "To find a good, *Deutsch* workman, the best places to inquire are the tavern and beer garden."

"If a person refrains from drink and dance?"

He cut a slice of bread and offered it. Knowing certain Americans frowned on such entertainments, he sorted words and discarded mentioning blacksmith or barber shops. "Then the task is more difficult. Where do ladies gather and exchange news?"

"At the grocer," she replied. "After church service, we often dawdle and speak of recent events."

"Your opportunity is limited." He offered the next slice of bread to Joseph and touched the knife blade to the remaining portion of loaf. "Is Mrs. Clark considering a sign? Can you handle the language if I send *Herr* Knapp?"

"Abi—Mrs. Clark continues to collect funds for a new sign. Like many things—the fire destroyed the needle and thread emblem. As to the language—we manage. You are kind to show concern." She lowered her gaze from his face to her stew.

He nodded. Cash was dear. The funds he brought from Pennsylvania dwindled faster than expected. The expenses of renting a shop, purchasing supplies, and socializing to spread the word consumed coin daily. "When women arrive with shoes for repair, shall I suggest a new frock?"

"You speak an enchanting idea." A smile danced in her eyes.

"One problem…no lady customers…yet."

She leaned back and tilted her head.

Serious thinking? Nein, *her eyes sparkle with humor.*

"Would you have me check the shoes our customers wear?"

Grinning, he collected the remaining piece of potato on his spoon. "You have an excellent idea. We can be like the butcher and baker sending customers to the other shop—dress and shoes."

She laughed.

In silence, he compared the beauty of her laughter to melodious church bells. He allowed his gaze to linger on her twinkling, hazel eyes.

Joseph looked from one to the other and scrunched his brow.

"No problem, son." Polly turned her attention to spreading a thin layer of strawberry jam on her bread. "*Herr* Tafel, would you be so kind as to continue the tale of your travels? I believe you mentioned the town of Riverport, in Ohio, during our most recent walk to church."

"My pleasure." Kurt organized his thoughts. He soon launched into a description of one of the colorful characters who boarded the steamboat at the Ohio town. Aware of Joseph at the table, he selected his stories with care and omitted certain details of men's behavior after too much whiskey. Soon, a second portion of stew vanished.

Polly carried the remains of a pound cake to the table and prepared tea.

After the conclusion of a story which included a man falling into the river at a levee, Joseph cleared his throat. "*Herr* Tafel, is it dangerous to travel?"

"Do not misunderstand my tales." Kurt opened his hands and shook his head. "The great number of people I met on my journey were kind and honest. The few others…they provide the colorful stories."

"Mama and I stayed in the room during much of the trip from St. Louis." Joseph frowned.

Kurt glanced from the boy toward Polly and noted protectiveness in her eyes. "She kept you safe."

The clock chimed the hour.

Pushing his chair away from the table, Kurt stood. "I have taken enough of your precious time."

Joseph slipped from his chair. "Thank you again, *Herr* Tafel, for the warm shoes."

"Oh—one minute—I will fetch the money." Polly rose and hurried around the table.

"If you are short—"

She waved one hand to banish his comment. "I set aside from regular needs." She stopped at the corner cupboard, rose on her toes, and retrieved a small, red crock.

Minutes later, Kurt paused at the end of his shop.

He tipped his head and studied the stars in a clear sky. "What are you telling me, God? Why do you put an American woman into my life? You give me love of music, but she does not dance. Will she object when I light my evening pipe? Certainly, in this place, you can guide me to a suitable immigrant *Fraulein.*"

A door slammed in the distance.

He glanced toward the darkened dress shop and sighed. *Tonight, no matter what thoughts I mutter into my pillow, I suspect I will dream again of a sweet woman with light-brown curls framing her face.*

Chapter Nine

Sunday morning, Polly shivered and pulled her shawl close. She glanced at the closed shops and listened for street traffic. "Soon," she muttered softer than a whisper, "I must purchase the cloth and begin sewing my cloak." She blew out a breath and stepped into the miniature cloud.

"Look, more frost." Joseph pointed toward a wood pile in a shady spot. "The wood grew white hair."

"Not exactly." She reached for his bare hand. "Come, we need to walk steady. You know Pastor Harter tends to call out the late arrivals."

"Will the pump freeze, Mama?"

"Not today." She glanced at her son and gave silent thanks for his new, wool coat and warm slipper-shoes.

"Did I tell you Thomas wants to be my friend?" He glanced toward her face.

A dozen times. She nodded and checked for riders or wagons before stepping into the street.

"I think *Herr* Tafel sewed magic into my shoes. None of the boys talked to me in the schoolyard until I wore them." He stated the same basic observation for the third time this morning. "I want Thomas for a friend. Did I tell you our hands match—same size? Except...he has a scar on his left hand...or maybe his right...a burn from a long time ago."

"I am pleased you have a friend. Perhaps the magic

in the shoes will help you make another. A person may have more than one."

Thud-thud.

Determined to continue forward, Polly pretended she didn't hear a running person approaching.

"Wait. Can you spare a minute?"

Joseph stopped and turned his head.

She recognized the voice, hesitated, and glanced over her left shoulder. "Good morning, *Herr* Tafel. I thought perhaps you were ahead of us today."

"*Nein.*" He drew even with her and touched his cap. "Brushing my coat…and…other tasks delayed me. Swirling his right hand, he encouraged her to resume walking. "We travel these last two blocks together. I do not wish to make you late for worship. Is all well at the dress shop?"

"We are well. Business is steady." She stepped with a lighter tread than moments ago. Sneaking glances as they proceeded side-by-side, she enjoyed the view of his tall, generous frame, clean-shaven jaw, and pale eyebrows. Each day, since he shared their table Monday evening, she fought the urge to cross the street and visit the cobbler's shop.

But Joseph, on his best behavior, returned from his daily calls on their neighbor promptly.

"*Herr* Tafel, did you notice my new coat? Mama says I can wear it for a long time—all winter—and beyond." Joseph extended his arms and wriggled fingers out of sleeves which covered half of his hands.

"Your mother sewed you a fine coat."

Polly took a hurried step. "Come, we still have an entire block to walk."

"*Herr* Tafel, how long is beyond?"

"You ask a serious question. Are you a philosopher?" Kurt hesitated.

"I don't think so." Joseph shook his head and wrinkled his brow.

Rubbing his chin, Kurt resumed long strides. "Beyond is a clever thing. It is always hiding around the corner or behind a door. Beyond stays out of sight…skillful and sly."

Polly looked to the sky to conceal her smile from her companions. *He managed to make an interesting story out of an impossible question. I wonder…?* She suppressed a sigh and banished the absurd idea. *Leo is correct about one thing—if I seek a husband, he should be an American.* "Does your business improve?"

"*Ja,* one man tells another and soon a person with poor shoes seeks my skill."

"*Gute,* good." She briefly pressed her lips. Without bidding, she remembered he was born in Pennsylvania and her birthplace was Virginia—two places which touched on a map. Aware they arrived at the church, she eased to a halt. "Thank you for accompanying us, *Herr* Tafel."

"*Frau*…Mrs. Black." He maneuvered to face her and removed his cap. "This afternoon, after church services, I am visiting with a carpenter and his family. Would you and Joseph be inclined to join us?"

Polly backed a step and held one hand against her chest. "What? 'Tis rude to walk into a family's home with two extra mouths for the hostess to feed."

"When I spoke to the man on Friday, he claimed a friend would be welcome." He held his flat, leather cap close to his body.

"No. But we thank you." She risked a glance and

squeezed Joseph's hand in a signal to remain quiet. "We have our own plans for the afternoon."

He glanced toward the sky before intersecting her gaze. "Perhaps another time."

She nodded.

"Now I must hurry. I want to be in my seat before the bell rings." He glanced toward the steeple three blocks distant. In the next instant, he reached out and grasped Joseph's small hand. "Farewell, my friend. Enjoy your day."

"And you, sir." Joseph bent in a small bow.

She experienced the odd sensation of observing both man and boy in a stage play.

"My dear Mrs. Black." Kurt lifted her right hand toward his lips. "I look forward to many future conversations." He dotted a kiss on her pale glove.

Staring at her hand much longer than polite, she half-expected the linen glove to burst into flame. "Yes…of course…I…we must go and find a pew."

****

Three hours later, Kurt patted his stomach and surveyed the empty bowls and platter. Settling his gaze on his hostess, he set his butter knife across his plate. "A wonderful meal, *Frau* Thayer."

"*Ja, Mutter.*" Johannes, the only Thayer son, echoed the compliment and pushed back his chair.

"*Danke, danke.*" *Frau* Thayer, an agile woman standing one inch over five feet, reached for the pickle dish. "Johannes and Hilde, stay and help. The rest of you—out, out—enough time at table."

With a glance to his host, Kurt stood. "You are very kind to invite the newcomer to your home."

"No trouble." As the group exited the dining room,

Jacob Thayer surveyed his family, plus his eldest daughter's betrothed. "As you can see—one more mouth to feed is hardly worth the notice."

"*Herr* Tafel, will you go for a stroll with us?" Bertha, the second daughter, dashed from the opposite end of the parlor to stand in front of him. "Amelia, Christian, and I plan to walk beyond the cemetery and view the grandest houses in town. Have you seen them?"

He smiled at the dark-haired, blue-eyed young woman with a lively spirit. According to a comment early in the meal, she celebrated her seventeenth birthday three days ago. He glanced toward his host to gauge if his daughter was often this bold. "Will your father trust me as a chaperon?"

Laughing, Jacob waved a hand toward the front door. "Go—another set of eyes will help to keep Christian and Amelia honest before December's wedding." A moment later, the carpenter lowered his voice and spoke directly to the young, blond stonemason who would soon be part of his family. "Take care, Christian. The owners of certain of the grand homes complain if a passerby takes so much as a hickory nut from the ground."

"I stay aware." Christian released Amelia's hand.

A few minutes later, the quartet stepped into late October sunshine and strolled away from the river. Kurt drew a deep breath of the cooler air, adjusted his flat, leather cap, and extended his arm toward Bertha. With a nod toward Christian, he indicated the other couple should take the lead. He contemplated the tone of both Jacob's and Christian's early friendly comments, and comfort, warm as a winter coat, settled around him.

Yes, it is good to make new friends, both older and younger than myself. Although Christian has as many years as my brother, Helmut.

"Are you ready for winter?" Bertha leaned close.

He savored a whiff of peppermint and recalled a covered, glass dish on the Thayers' sideboard. "I'm well stocked with materials for my trade. Or did you refer to food and fuel?"

"All of it." She gestured wide with her free hand. "Little remains in our garden—all is in crocks or protected in the root cellar. Papa tells us the woodcutter, *Herr* Widder, will make a large delivery before the end of this week. Papa wrote to the bookseller. In a week or two, even after books are set aside for St. Nicholas Day, I will have something new to read in the evenings."

Kurt made careful note of the wood seller's name. He trusted a carpenter's evaluation of wood and wanted to buy from a dealer who sold dry, not green, logs. "Reading must give you great pleasure."

"I enjoy books more than needlework or knitting. Do you read in the evenings?"

"Books and I are not great friends." He held back the information that he found reading long pages in *Deutsch* difficult—and impossible in English. "I do miss a newspaper. Do you suppose a printer will be among the spring immigrants?"

"I would be delighted. I scored well when we wrote school essays. After living in Elm Ridge for ten years, I know everyone of importance—and many not so important. Do you think a newspaper would pay me to write articles on the news of the town?" She switched from a sedate step to a schoolgirl's skip. "Do women write for newspapers in Pennsylvania?"

He struggled to keep his smile small and voice level. He found her exuberance contagious. "I think only a foolish man would deny you an opportunity. I tell you, the few newspaper men I've known were sharp businessmen—not thickheaded."

"Don't pay heed to my daydreams." She shook her head until every flower on her bonnet quivered. "I change my mind often. *Mutter* counsels patience until I find my proper place in the world. *Vater* despairs I will marry a man unable to support me."

Kurt blinked. *Does she mistake kindness for more? She is an excellent dance partner and daughter of a man I hope to count among my friends.*

"The grand mansions of Elm Ridge await our inspection." Christian spoke loud and directed attention to a large, two-story, brick home set on a lot three times larger than most. "Mr. Gordon, owner of the large flour mill, lives here. He is one of the early settlers—also the mayor. Have you met him?"

"*Nein.* I have only heard his name in passing." Kurt stopped at the edge of the street and studied the red brick structure. The white trim contrasting to the brick compared well to his memories of houses in Philadelphia. "An impressive home. How many people are in the Gordon family? A man would need servants, or many children, to keep the house and grounds in good condition."

"This home has a very practical floor plan." Christian appeared to ignore the immediate question. "Symmetrical, central staircase, good window placement for ventilation—three stoves and two chimneys."

Listening to the younger man, Kurt compared the smaller, frame dwelling and outbuildings on his parents' property. *With much work, I aim to own a decent house. But anything equal to this mansion is beyond my dreams.*

Bertha released Kurt's arm and stepped toward a young orchard. "The family is Mr. Gordon, his wife, and a married son with two young daughters. A second son is away at school. I know of a cook and a gardener. In addition, I think they hire day labor, depending on the season." She gestured her sister to join her on the brown, trampled grass. "Look, Amelia, I believe the Gordons have planted more trees since we last walked here. What do you suppose they are?"

Mindful of *Herr* Thayer's warning, Kurt hid his surprise as Christian followed the sisters toward the orchard. Shrugging, he joined them.

"What do you think?" Bertha stood near a tree which stood a few inches taller than she and handed him a brown leaf.

Studying the leaf's shape, Kurt ruled out several fruits. "My guess is pear. Are the others apple?"

"At least two are cherry. Mrs. Gordon brings the most delicious cherry tarts to the Fourth of July celebration." Bertha licked her lips.

Kurt turned and counted trees planted in straight rows. *Fourteen—much work to keep them pruned and bearing well.* He flexed his hands at the memory of trimming the four apple, one pear, and one plum tree on his parents' property. "I see plenty work for more than one gardener." He looked to his left and estimated the size of a plot within a fence. "Is that the kitchen garden?"

"*Ja*, not of much interest this late in the season. During the spring and summer, you often see the elder Mrs. Gordon tending the vegetables and flowers." Bertha touched his elbow. "Come, we have more places to show you."

Kurt lingered in the street at the front of the house and studied the building. Admiring the brick porch pillars and steps, he noted blue-and-green glass in the fanlight. "Mr. Gordon's business must be prosperous. Am I correct the mill is located along Rumble Creek?"

"*Ja*, a quarter mile upstream from the sawmill," Christian confirmed.

For the better part of the next hour, the two couples viewed the homes along Seventh Street. Interspersed between the large, newer homes were a few older cabins. As they stood in front of a frame home with a long, wide front porch, Kurt faced Christian. "You are very knowledgeable and have a reply for all my architecture questions. Do you plan to design homes in the future?"

"My primary interest is the chimneys." The stonemason pointed toward the nearest brick structure and the thin smoke rising straight. "I do much work on the foundations, but the stacks—combining the form and function—is my real joy."

"He is modest." Amelia touched Christian's elbow. "Our new house, three blocks south of the church, is his design. We will have four rooms downstairs. As the children arrive, we will divide the upper level."

Christian reddened. "The additional bedrooms wait for money and time, my dear. But I promise two stoves—kitchen and parlor—installed before our wedding."

At the couple's gentle teasing, Kurt concealed a building chuckle.

Clearing his throat, Christian gestured toward the house. "If you study the roofline on many of the older buildings, you will find history. On this one, it is plain the log portion was first, with the chimney at one end— very inefficient. Next, a frame portion, with the higher roof, likely a sleeping loft, was built. If you walk a little farther, you will see…"

"A more recent addition in the back—much like my shop," Kurt contributed.

Christian faced Kurt. "The building at Apple and Third Streets?"

"*Ja,* you know the place?"

The stonemason nodded. "Three years ago, when I first arrived in Elm Ridge, *Herr* Thayer hired me to build the foundation piers for the two rooms in the back. I never inquired when the other portions were built."

"You explain a great deal—especially why the floors in each portion are different. When I climbed to the roof to inspect the chimneys, I could not make good sense of the different rooflines."

Bertha set a hand on Kurt's forearm. "Come, we are almost at the final and largest of the homes."

"One I am glad I do not live in," Christian added in a hoarse whisper.

Curious at the comment, yet wishing not to speak foolish, Kurt held his tongue. A moment later, they cleared a line of brush, and he sighted a large, frame structure painted dark-blue with white trim. The house stood two full stories, plus an attic with small dormers. He counted three chimneys in the *L* shaped roofline.

Studying the windows, he could not envision a logical floor plan. "Who lives here?"

"Rush." Bertha mixed a sigh into the single word. "He and Mr. Franklin own the sawmill and lumber company. Well, the only one of any size. Papa says the lumber is sound and cut true. However, in the next sentence, Papa calls Mr. Rush a hard, stubborn man who refuses to admit he knows even a few simple *Deutsch* words."

"Does he have a large family?" Kurt ambled to the edge of the street and studied the second-story windows. No matter the angle he chose, he failed to visualize a floor plan.

"He has a young daughter—not yet in school. His wife died recently in childbirth. I should find Christian charity in my heart for the man, but it is difficult." Bertha stood at Kurt's elbow.

"Best you return to the street." Amelia gestured toward Kurt's boots on the grass. "Mr. Rush will call you a trespasser."

"*Ja,* true," Christian agreed. "This is the most troublesome house I have worked on in Elm Ridge."

Kurt stepped back to the pounded dirt and raised his brows. "Due to the height?"

"Partially," Christian glanced around. "*Herr* Thayer drew a plan. I strung my line and began to dig for the foundation. Then, Mr. Rush visits the site and makes changes. Three times he argued with a master builder about the location of the building. In the end, *Herr* Thayer placed the house too far from the street. Each spring, the runoff in the back comes almost to the small porch. But Mr. George Rush insisted."

Rush—George Rush. Kurt concentrated for a

moment and placed the name to a man he'd encountered at the blacksmith shop. While not physically imposing, the man's voice carried command. *Mr. Rush and the slave overseer on the Louisville dock spoke with a similar stern tone of voice.* "His partner, Mr. Franklin, does he live in a large, grand home?"

"Large, but not grand," Amelia replied. "He builds an addition every few years to make room for his many children." She counted on her fingers. "Eight, no, nine—I think another girl was born in March."

Christian laughed. "Listen to you. Are you the *Fraulein* who chatters the names of a dozen?"

"As many as God wills." She turned and stood toe-to-toe with her sweetheart.

"Good answer." Christian touched her nose with one finger.

Bertha strolled to the other side of the street. "I believe we should return home. *Herr* Tafel, do you enjoy playing cards?"

"My skills are far less than the men I met on the riverboats. But I enjoy an honest game." Kurt joined her and offered his arm.

"Perhaps we should partner you with Hilde. She shows promise."

As he listened to the others chatter about Sunday afternoon games, Kurt realized he was unfamiliar with more than half of the names mentioned. Twice during the return to the Thayer home, he reminded himself he lived in Illinois—not Pennsylvania. He failed to recall Joseph mentioning a game other than marbles in the schoolyard. *What sort of entertainment does Mrs. Black enjoy?*

Chapter Ten

Late Thursday morning, Kurt stood, stretched, and glanced toward the pair of recently resoled shoes on his worktable. Stepping to the shelves of supplies and tools, he selected a rag and a small bottle of neat's-foot oil. Moments later, he held a repaired brogan in one hand and conditioned the leather with the oiled cloth. He submerged his senses in the familiar oiled leather smells and the steady, soft sound of the shelf clock. *I repair factory shoes—moderate quality leather—hasty workmanship–uneven stitching.* He ignored street noises and rubbed the shoes to an appearance equal to, or better, than new.

Jingle-jingle. The bell on his shop door interrupted the near silence.

"*Hier,*" he called before rising from his low stool. "*Guten...*" He moistened his lips and switched to English. "Good day, do you bring shoes to repair?"

"Are you Mr. Tafel? Or do you prefer *Herr*?" The tall stranger twisted his lips at the *Deutsch* word.

Kurt set the brogan and rag on the table and strode toward the waist-high counter separating the entry and sales portion from the main workroom. "I will answer to Mr. Tafel. Your name, please."

"Rush—George Rush. I came to issue a warning." He stood with his feet planted shoulder width and held both hands behind his back.

The words *American, hard*, and *stubborn* from Sunday afternoon at the carpenter's home returned. Kurt assessed the muscular man wearing sturdy boots, plain trousers, and black coat. Dark-brown hair peeked from the rim of a common, low-crowned hat. He confirmed his own sighting at the blacksmith. "Your name...I hear it tied to a sawmill. Correct?

"Largest and best lumber dealer for miles around." George added a slight nod to his words.

"When I am in need of boards or window frames I will remember. However, my need for lumber is in the future. We speak first of today. Do you bring a caution for the coming winter weather?"

"Stay away from her." He glared at Kurt and held his mouth in a frown.

Kurt blinked. *He reminds me of the schoolmaster when the class became restless.* "Pardon me, I do not understand the detail. What is the woman's name?"

"Don't pretend ignorance—I seen you escort Mrs.—" He spat into a bucket containing a thin layer of sawdust. "Polly Black goes around town letting people believe she's a proper widow. Bah—no vows said for that union. My information is on good authority—not rumor."

"The seamstress?" *Good manners allow her to choose time to tell of her son's father—I have no need.*

"Mother to a mongrel." George wiped the back of one hand across his mouth.

Kurt rubbed his chin and considered the insult. The words he would choose to describe Joseph included innocent, bright, and inquisitive. "Who is she to you?"

"By year's end, she'll be my wife. Public vows and church blessing. All proper."

"You plan to marry her?" Mr. Rush's words, insults to the child in one breath followed by a claim to the mother in the next, spun in Kurt's brain. He tipped his head toward the rafters and closed his eyes, but he did not find an image of Polly, with her demonstrative love for her son, wed to the man in front of him.

"You better believe me. Two months—or less—and I give her a respectable name. Mrs. George Rush will have status in Elm Ridge." He brought one arm out straight and slapped the counter. "A man needs to take charge—put his life back to rights after a tragedy."

Meeting the other man's gaze, Kurt failed to picture the mild-mannered seamstress with the harsh-speaking man. "Mrs. Black...has she agreed?"

"She will." He tapped one work-coarsened finger against the smooth wood.

Kurt rubbed his chin. *He tells a tale to match the wildest stories told on the riverboats.* "You mean to court her?"

"In a sense."

Kurt circled his forefinger beside his ear and recalled the sons of widows with stepfathers in their Pennsylvania village. The boys' relationships with the men ranged from affection...to toleration...to fear. *Joseph—and Polly—deserve kindness and tenderness. I doubt Mr. Rush knows the meaning of the words.* "If the lady refuses?"

George leaned forward and wagged one finger under Kurt's nose. "I've got power in this town—growing power. I missed election to the village council by a mere three votes last spring. Once I have me a new wife, perhaps a son of my own, I'll snatch the mayor's office out of Gordon's hand. He's weak. Does he take steps to discourage immigrant filth like you and yours? No, he puts an advertisement in a St. Louis *Deutsch* newspaper. Not right to have people with queer language and customs elbow their way into honest American business." He paused only long enough to draw a deep breath. "You been in America how long? A year?"

Straightening and increasing the distance between their faces, Kurt positioned one hand in front of his mouth to stifle the urge to laugh. "Rush—is your name Scottish?" He waited for a slight nod. "Our family made shoes for a good many Scotsmen back in Pennsylvania. Fair number of them spoke with an accent so thick the tavern master could not separate their *aye* from their *ale*."

"Pennsylvania?" George blinked several times. "How many years you spend in the East?"

"All my life." Kurt allowed a small smile. "My father also born in Pennsylvania. Grandfather, he arrived on a ship the same year George Washington took the office of president. Which of your ancestors crossed the ocean? Father? Grandfather?"

"But…but…you speak *Deutsch*. You frequent the tavern…and dance at the beer garden."

"I learn *Deutsch* at home. I also hear and practice enough English in my father's shop to do business with all."

George widened his eyes, opened his mouth, and closed his lips before sound escaped.

Stepping around the counter, Kurt eased his way past his customer until he touched the doorknob. *Mr. Rush is not the first narrow-minded American I meet.* He recalled conversations overheard on his travels—

communities along both the Ohio and Mississippi Rivers were banning liquor, dancing, and cards on Sunday. *How will a working man find enjoyment on his one day away from the job?* "Have you delivered your message? Or do you have more to say?"

"Keep your hands off my woman." George pivoted, strode across the threshold, and slammed the door.

Kurt stood for a long moment and listened to the faint, familiar sounds of footsteps on the sidewalk, the jingle of harnesses, and the slap of reins urging a team into motion. Beneath a calm shell, his stomach churned as if recently escaped from a drunkard itching for a fistfight. "I think he forgets the woman has a say in the matter," he whispered in the quiet shop. "Mrs. Black…Polly…deserves a man who will love her…and accept Joseph as his own." He shuffled into his workspace, sank to a stool, and cradled his head in his hands. "She has no brother or father to speak in her defense," he mumbled toward the floor. "Is it proper for the newcomer to interfere?"

****

Late in the afternoon, Polly snipped a thread and released a sigh. Mrs. Winston's new, winter, church dress lay finished across her lap. She stabbed the needle into the plump, green pincushion. "Finished." She stood and shook out the largest wrinkles from the gown.

"Was that the final hem?" Mrs. Clark paused in her task of pinning a pleat in a chintz gown on the dress form.

"Only the pressing remains. I will put the iron on to heat." Taking care to avoid adding creases, she draped the garment across the worktable.

The shop bell announced a potential customer.

Polly hurried toward the counter. "Good day, ladies."

The older of the two women cleared her throat. "*Sprechen sie Duetsch?*"

"*Ein wenig.*" Polly volunteered a little knowledge. With pauses to think every few words, Polly introduced herself and gestured toward Abigail. "*Frau* Clark owns the shop."

"*Frau* Thayer. My daughter, Amelia."

The younger woman, a few years past girlhood, studied the stocked shelves from wide, blue eyes. "I need…new frock…special."

Polly increased her smile one size at the broken, accented English. "*Sonntag?* Do you require a Sunday dress?"

"*Ja*—wedding and winter." Amelia touched a spool of deep-blue trim. "I like much." Her cheeks bloomed in a charming hue.

"Wonderful." Polly studied the younger woman's slender figure and pictured which bodice seams to cut large to allow for future alterations. With a careful look at blonde hair peeking from a beige bonnet and the woman's fair complexion, she stepped from behind the counter and patted several bolts of cloth. "Wool…tight weave…light and warm. Color?"

Amelia stood at Polly's shoulder and stroked a fine, rich blue. "Beautiful…how much?"

After consulting the price list, Polly figured some numbers on a slate. In a mixture of *Deutsch,* English, and hand gestures, she explained the fabric's price. She paused to find *Deutsch* words not used since leaving St. Louis. "Cost of fabric and labor—no lace."

Frau Thayer shook her head.

Amelia shifted her attention to a different weave in a lighter blue. "Less money? I want three rows ribbon trim on skirt."

"*Ja,* we figure the cost with new fabric." Polly consulted the price list and repeated her calculations. This time, she included the cost of the trims and buttons in addition to fabric and labor. She tapped her chalk against the final number and displayed the slate to Abigail.

Fair, Mrs. Clark mouthed.

Polly displayed the slate to the Thayer women. "Fabric, three rows trim on skirt"—she displayed three fingers and gestured—"ribbon on bodice"—she drew a line with one finger before touching the button dish—"flat buttons and labor. *Gute?*"

Amelia exchanged silent words with her mother before she spoke. "*Ja, mein Vater* complain, but not much."

"Now, we decide style." Polly retrieved a stack of sketches from a shelf below the counter. Motioning Amelia to join her at the worktable, she pointed to the placket concealing her dress buttons and then behind her neck. "Front...or back?"

"*Vorder,* front." Amelia fingered the top, flat button on her dress. "No servant—dress myself."

During the next half hour, with many gestures and several bursts of laughter, Polly guided Amelia in the design of a unique, practical winter Sunday dress. Polly displayed the various drawings.

Frau Thayer added the occasional word or head shake.

"How long to make?" Amelia fingered the dark

ribbon selected for the skirt.

Polly pressed tight her lips and sought silent advice from Abigail. *Aside from the chintz on the form and the two children's dresses, do we have major orders?*

Abigail responded with only a raise of her eyebrows.

With the realization Abigail was assigning the special dress to Polly, she drew a deep breath. "When is the wedding?"

"December…second Tuesday." Amelia sighed. "Christian, *mein Schatz,* promises the house will be ready."

"*Gute*—dress will be finished one week before wedding. *Frau* Clark will measure today. Can you return for a fitting…" she consulted the calendar tacked to the workroom wall "eleven or twelve November?"

Amelia removed her shawl and bonnet and handed them to her mother. "*Ja,* afternoon—like today?"

"Will you bring the heirloom collar and cuffs you mentioned?" Polly unhooked the loop holding the drape between workroom and sales area. In a moment, the space became secure for a customer to remove her dress.

Amelia nodded before she released the final button on her calico gown and slid the garment to the floor. "*Herr* Tafel speaks well of you, *Frau* Black."

"The cobbler?" *Stop being foolish. How many* Herr *Tafels are in Elm Ridge?* She leaned toward the table's center and retrieved one of the rejected ribbons.

Frau Thayer waved her daughter toward Mrs. Clark and her measuring tape. An instant later, she leaned close to Polly and spoke in slow, careful *Deutsch.* "At Sunday dinner, he described your shop as well-stocked with two talented seamstresses. We discuss, *Herr* Thayer and I, and decide Amelia purchase new dress here. *Frau* Osten is a fine woman, but her sight is failing since a spring illness."

Glancing toward the curtained shop window, Polly let the *Deutsch* speech settle in her brain. *Shoes and dresses.* Herr *Tafel, you give me a test.* "I am flattered. I…we…will take extra care."

"*Herr* Tafel is an excellent dance partner." Amelia rotated left at Mrs. Clark's hand signal. "My sister, Bertha, tries every Sunday afternoon to claim more than her share of waltzes with him."

Polly lifted one hand and pressed it against her chest. The growing church she attended taught dancing, drinking, gambling, and smoking were sins. Pastor Harter mentioned the waltz as the most intimate and evil of the dances. She willed an image of Kurt twirling a young, attractive woman on the dance floor to fade. "*Herr* Tafel is a kind neighbor."

Swifty zipped into the room toward a sliver of sunlight on the floor.

"Oh—" Amelia raised one hand toward her mouth. "A cat—a surprise."

"A kitten. She runs fast, and we hope she will soon learn to catch the mouse." Polly halted the next words on her tongue. She had no need to tell customers who gave the kitten to the shop. "All good?"

Amelia nodded.

The back door slammed.

"One minute." Polly pushed the narrow curtain to the living quarters aside and searched for her son. Approaching him, she held one upright finger on her lips. "Customer."

Joseph nodded. "My friend...Thomas...he helped me with my spelling words."

"Good...and were you a friend to him?" She squatted to make their eyes near the same level.

"I helped with his sums." The boy extended his left hand and coaxed the cat toward him. "I like having a friend."

"Do you want to celebrate?" She eased to her full height. "I think one sugar cookie is hiding in the jar."

He smiled. "Yes, please, a sugar cookie will fit exactly into my stomach."

Handing him the cookie, she resisted ruffling his hair. "I need to return to work. Eat your cookie and do your chores. Tonight, we have biscuits with our supper."

"I like biscuits with jam—do we have red jam?"

"Let the color be a surprise." She slipped into the workroom.

Amelia fastened her final button.

"How old?" *Frau* Thayer pointed toward the curtain.

"My son is five—first term in school." She steadied her lips into a small smile. "All good with the dress? You will remember the fitting?"

"*Ja,* I remember." Amelia settled her bonnet.

Several minutes later, after the Thayer ladies departed with much mixture of *Deutsch* and English words, Polly fingered Mrs. Winston's dress and sighed.

"What is the matter?" Abigail pinned the slip with Amelia's measurements to the bolt of cloth. "We had one of our best orders today. Your language skill made it possible. I would have been lost after *guten Tag.*"

Instead of the practical wool dress on the table,

Polly envisioned Kurt dancing with a young woman. "Nothing is wrong. I must put an iron to heat."

"Perhaps the next time you visit your bakery friends"—Abigail glanced toward the clock—"you can ask to learn more sewing terms. If the *Deutsch* seamstress's sight is failing, we might gain customers—always a good thing."

"I'm glad we have an order from *Frau und Fraulein* Thayer. I will take care and make her a beautiful gown—and hope she tells others about the shop." Herr *Tafel is a neighbor and a friend. He is kind to Joseph and polite to me.* She recalled his warmth in the brief moments he lifted her hand and brushed his lips on her glove. Never, not with Bernard, nor any of the men who courted her in St. Louis, did a simple gesture on a public street stay so vivid and central in her dreams.

Chapter Eleven

Friday morning, Polly hurried along Plum Street toward Winston's Grocery. She paused for a moment outside the building with small, high windows and a wide, green door. Drawing a deep breath of cool air carrying a trace of wood smoke, she repeated her determination to purchase only necessities and pay on her account today. Restocking her cabinet after the move to the new apartment had grown her balance owed to over five dollars. With a final pat to the pocket holding her coin purse, she stepped inside.

The air in the store held the competing scents of fresh-roasted coffee beans and dirt clinging to the root vegetables.

Polly took note of one man standing at the counter facing the grocer. She nodded and passed Mrs. Hill at the bean barrel before she continued to the onion crate. After selecting a plump onion, she stepped toward the display of red apples and dark squash. While inspecting produce, she heard portions of the conversation between the grocer and the other man.

"Entire account—plus ten dollars."

"Yes, sir. What explanation shall I give?" Mr. Winston spoke softer than the customer.

"Call the payment a gift."

She sealed her lips and selected another apple. Turning toward the carrots, she lifted her gaze and confirmed the speaker was Mr. Rush. Aware the fine hair on her neck tickled, she forced her hand to search for a firm carrot. *Many reasons for him to be in the store—perhaps he is starting an account for a housekeeper.* She concentrated on taking even breaths.

An instant later, Mr. Rush, looking neither right nor left, hurried out the door.

Polly tightened her hold on her basket, glanced toward Mrs. Hill busy inspecting thick turnips, and approached the counter. "Good day, Mr. Winston."

"The same to you, Mrs. Black." The white-haired grocer glanced at the closed ledger beside the scale.

"Today, I want to purchase two pounds of flour and a small bag of peppercorns." She handed him two drawstring bags and a short, square tin. "I also want a scoop of tea."

"Certainly. Can I interest you in any other spices today? Last week, we received some fragrant cinnamon." The grocer opened the flour barrel and placed two large scoops into the larger sack.

"No, thank you." She sidestepped to the end of the counter and placed four eggs into her basket. While he weighed the flour and scooped tea, she arranged the cloth in her basket to reveal all of her selections.

Mr. Winston set the flour, peppercorns, and tea on the counter, inventoried her basket, and mumbled numbers. He lifted his pen and hesitated. "Anything else?"

"I'll pay on my account—today's total—plus three dollars." She held her coin purse in one hand.

The grocer looked beyond her toward the door for a long moment and shifted his weight from one foot to the other. "Your account's paid. A credit remains after today's purchase. The gentleman said it was a gift."

"Mr. Rush?" She swallowed quickly to prevent a contradiction of the term *gentleman* from escaping.

"He didn't mean for you to know." Mr. Winston flushed.

"Rather difficult not to hear from the apple barrel." She tipped her face and studied her shoe tips while heat climbed her neck. His declaration of desiring a wife, not a housekeeper, rushed into her brain. In the next instant, she recalled her plain refusal and stiff behavior when he left her home after tea. *I do not want to owe him. However, it would be wrong to blame the grocer. Only a foolish merchant refuses good coin.* Drawing a deep breath, she counted to five, lifted her head, and prayed her exterior remained calm. "In that case, please add six of the peppermints. My son loves them almost as much as Mrs. Clark."

During the return to the shop and the few minutes to put the groceries on her shelves, Polly again reviewed Mr. Rush's actions. *He invited himself into my home—ate half the sugar in the bowl—and made no mention of leaving.* She dropped the candies into an empty jam jar and placed a flat, ceramic tile across the opening.

The sound of the shop bell, muffled by the curtain, pulled her to the present.

Polly stepped into the shop and discovered Mrs. Clark latching the cash box.

"Mrs. Winston was pleased with her dress. I expect to see her wear it to worship the day after tomorrow." Abigail glanced toward the clock. "Are you done with errands so soon?"

"I finished at the grocer. Is this a good time for me

to go to the butcher and baker? Do you need anything special?" Polly eyed the bright bell over the door.

"Nothing for me," Abigail stated. "My sister is shopping for our household today."

"Very good—I shall try to be back within an hour." She returned to the apartment, snatched her basket, and exited through the back porch. Twenty minutes later, Polly entered the bakery and smiled. Cinnamon and apple, two of her favorite scents, filled the shop's air. She nodded to a departing customer and approached the counter. "*Guten Tag, Frau* Keil. Does Louisa have apple pie in the oven?"

Charlotte smiled. "We are happy to see you. What may we put in your basket today?"

Wiping her hands on her apron, Louisa appeared in the workroom entrance. She spoke in English with her hands imitating folding and pinching movements. "Not pie...small...folded...you call...turnover?"

"Yes, you used the correct name." Polly stepped close and gave her young friend a quick hug. "Is all well?"

"*Ja,* busy—preparing for winter after each day of baking."

"What did you purchase at butcher today?" Charlotte brought their attention to the paper-wrapped lump in Polly's basket.

I will reply in Deutsch—*or try.* "Beef...neck bone...I make soup with noodles."

"Wheat or rye bread to finish?" *Frau* Keil showed pleasure in her curved lips.

Polly considered for a moment. "Rye...a small change from regular order. Do you have ginger cookies? I would like six. One more question...not about baking."

"I return to baking...listen while I work." Louisa excused herself and hurried to check the oven.

Polly stepped to the counter, but she aimed her words across the pass-through shelves. "Tell me, do you know the Thayer family?"

"Thayer is a common name in our community." Charlotte squatted and removed cookies from the glass case.

Polly gathered a few more *Deutsch* words into a sentence. "Yesterday, *Frau* Thayer and her daughter, Amelia, visited the dress shop."

"Hands always in motion? Less than your height...daughter an inch taller?" Charlotte added a seventh cookie to the order.

Polly nodded.

"I believe you met Jacob's wife." The bakery owner slowed her speech. "He is a carpenter...built your new shop...and many other buildings. A nice family of three girls and one boy. The oldest girls hire for housework when a wife is sick or gives birth."

Aware it was not her news to spread, Polly withheld knowledge of Amelia's impending wedding. "Good. Mother and daughter gave a fine impression." She hesitated a moment, praying her awkward *Deutsch* would not be mistaken for nosing into another's business. "I wondered if you had a hand in sending them to the shop."

"*Nein,* my customers have not inquired after a seamstress. If the time is right, I will mention your name."

"*Danke.* One more question—not related." She opened her coin purse. "Did your husband have reason to do business with Mr. Rush? Is he honest?"

Charlotte pursed her lips for an instant. "Rush and Franklin Lumber has a good reputation. They do little business with *Deutsch*—aside from the carpenters."

"He...I..." She sealed her lips and placed two coins on the counter. After closing the purse and slipping it into her pocket, she met Charlotte's gaze. "He has hinted he knows the name of Joseph's father— and our lack of a marriage certificate. I apologize for not paying close attention to my brother and his friends during the months we were both in Elm Ridge. I have concern Mr. Rush will tarnish your reputation."

Charlotte set her hand on Polly's arm and leaned close. "I know the truth. I feel certain Bernard would have married you if your brother had not threatened his life. For a full year, he checked at the levee and among his English-speaking friends. He sent at least two letters and waited for your arrival."

"You have told me." Polly glanced toward the street and prayed no customer arrived for another few minutes.

"News of your arrival with a young boy confused Bernard. He fretted over the situation. I do not know his exact plans, but I think he would have found a way to acknowledge Joseph." Charlotte straightened.

Polly paused. In all the serious conversations with Charlotte this summer, long hours working through grief, she had never taken the time to consider the effect of her sudden appearance. *I should have written instead of moving when I learned he was in Elm Ridge.* "Bernard had a good heart. I wanted to warn you in case Mr. Rush starts a rumor."

"I thank you."

Tinkle-tinkle. The shop bell interrupted the conversation.

Polly lifted her basket and turned from the counter. Forcing a smile, she nodded at the arriving customer.

"Take care, my friend."

With Charlotte's words fresh in her mind, Polly left the bakery. *Rumors catch and spread faster than a grass fire in a town the size of Elm Ridge. I will take Joseph to Bernard's grave—soon—to prepare him for schoolboy lies.*

****

"*Ein Minute.*" Kurt lifted his gaze before his shop bell ceased jingling. "*Herr* Widder, a pleasure to see you again. You arrive on a fine afternoon."

"I have your cart of wood. Where do you want to unload?" A sturdy man of medium height, wearing a shabby, brown coat, held a red, cloth cap with both hands.

Kurt wiped his knife on a rag and slipped it inside the leather sheath. Turning toward the wood dealer, he smiled, pleased the man arrived less than a week after he spoke with him at the tavern. "I shall put my new sign in the window. I finished a placard directing customers to find me in the yard." A few minutes later, Kurt paced along the board base for his winter wood supply in cool, afternoon air. "We stack tight. I have a canvas to protect from the worst of rain and snow."

"Good plan." The broad-shouldered man climbed to the top of the load of stove-length logs. He looked from the current meager racked wood to his feet and back. "I unload, not stack. I need to return to the farm in good light. Is this your first winter in Illinois?"

"*Ja*—do you have advice." Kurt moved to the

cart's rear.

Herr Widder removed his coat and draped it on one of the cart's front posts. "Keep watch of your supply. Frozen mud and snow on the roads make delivery uncertain in deep winter."

"I plan to." He was familiar with weeks during January and February when only sleighs or sledges could navigate the roads. However, in Elm Ridge, the river was the primary route of supply, not the land routes toward Springfield or Peoria. Kurt reviewed highlights from the multitude of advice the tavern customers offered newer residents. While many farms would be isolated, he lived within the village. He felt confident about walking from one business to another—except during an actual storm. He lifted a small piece of wood and tossed it into the yard. "We begin." A short time later, Kurt rolled an especially thick log toward the growing untidy heap.

"*Herr* Tafel. *Herr* Tafel. I want to help." A high-pitched voice grew near.

Turning his head toward the street, Kurt grinned. "We do hard work, Joseph."

"I'm getting stronger." The boy paused, raised one arm, and fisted his hand.

Herr Widder laughed and tossed a small piece out of the cart. "What have we here—a red-haired cyclone?"

"Go ask your mother. Be quick." Kurt took advantage of the interruption to wrestle a large piece to the rack.

Climbing from the cart, *Herr* Widder wiped his forehead with a stained handkerchief. "One load of wood warms me three or four times."

Kurt chuckled at the old joke. "I can offer water—now or at the end."

"I'll accept a drink for the horse—now is good." *Herr* Widder pointed toward the pump.

"Fair, the offer for you still stands." Kurt set a tin pail into position and grasped the pump handle.

A few moments later, *Herr* Widder held a small water bucket for his mare.

Joseph reappeared. "How can I help?"

"First, I will introduce you to the woodcutter, *Herr* Widder." He waited for the boy to nod. "This eager schoolboy is my neighbor, Joseph Black. Do you want him in the cart or on the ground?"

"Go in the cart—a boy's hands are good for the small stuff." *Herr* Widder carried the empty pail to the pump.

In a pair of blinks, Joseph climbed into the cart and tossed slender, dry branches over the wheel.

"Out the back, Joseph." Kurt pointed toward the jumbled wood on the brown grass.

"Yes, sir, *Herr* Tafel." The boy reached for more wood. He jumped back against the opposite railed side. "One of the sticks—it's moving."

"Get down—now." Kurt ran to the cart's front, grabbed the axe secured in a bracket, and vaulted into the cart. *Not Joseph. Not another child.* He swung the axe at the dark, moving shape.

Thunk. Whack.

The memory of Greta's screams blotted out the sound of metal against snake and wood. *I will not fail again. People are foolish to trust me with a child's life.*

"Halten." A firm hand on Kurt's arm accompanied the command.

Kurt exhaled and blinked. Drawing a deep breath, he waited while his present surroundings clarified.

"The deed is done. Time to stop." *Herr* Widder, standing on the wheel hub, spoke directly into Kurt's ear.

"Dead?" Kurt panted. His heart beat wildly while strength vanished from his limbs. He sagged against the cart's side.

"Chopped him in three, four, half a dozen pieces. I never seen snake blood fly so fast or high."

Looking toward his boots, Kurt spied the reptile's front portion twitch. "Rattler?"

"*Nein,* harmless black." *Herr* Widder extended one hand toward the axe.

"Joseph, are you hurt?" Kurt steadied his gaze on the boy trembling beside the unloaded wood.

"I-I…not see many snakes. I surprised." The boy's lower lip quivered.

Kurt assessed the damage inside the cart. Kicking aside a few wood scraps, he jumped to the ground. "I am sorry, *Herr* Widder. Add any damage to your cart to the cost of the firewood."

The woodcutter took the axe from Kurt's relaxed grip. He stepped into the cart, used the tool to rake out the corpse and stray bits of wood. "I might need to replace one floorboard." He shook his head. "Last time I see such fury…my daughter…after her mother die…dig fierce in our garden. For a time, she appeared to be digging a well. Yes, my Christine has much energy when angry."

Kurt stood still and listened to his heartbeat slow toward normal. Studying the woodcutter, he decided the less he said, the better.

"Herr Tafel." Joseph tugged on Kurt's sleeve. "Do we bury snakes?"

He glanced toward the shed where a pitiful collection of general tools was stored. "Later—I will bury in my garden plot before dark. Best you go home now."

"I didn't help much." The boy looked at his magic slipper-shoes.

"We start again tomorrow." He touched Joseph's shoulder. "Go. I think you have chores at home."

Herr Widder stored the axe on the cart's front board and stared after Joseph's back. *"Gute Junge*—a boy to make his father proud."

Kurt sighed. "His father is dead." *I think.* "We finish the unloading—not much remains." He shoved aside a bit of snake and lifted a short log. Using the physical task as an excuse to remain silent, he decided the time had come to ask Polly, or a reliable source, a direct question about Joseph's father.

Chapter Twelve

The foundry's one o'clock whistle called the workers for the Saturday afternoon hours. Kurt tightened the press another quarter turn on the three layers of soaked leather. With a stained rag, he wiped the water drops from the floor. He straightened and glanced out the window. Fair sky confirmed he was correct to plan on only a piece of bread for lunch and then continue to stack his wood supply.

Jingle-jingle-creak. Light footsteps followed the sound of the shop bell and stiff hinge.

He pivoted, blinked, and stepped toward the sales area. *"Guten Abend, Damen."*

"Guten Abend, Herr Tafel." Bertha Thayer smiled and laid her fingers against her shawl's knot.

Hilde, age ten, clutched a cloth-wrapped bundle against her chest and stared at the shop's wall of tools and lasts.

"How may I assist two lovely young ladies today?"

Dipping her head, Bertha gazed toward the floor.

"My shoes." Hilde loosened her hold on the tan package. "The dancing shoes have worn soles. Can you mend?"

He advanced another step around the counter and extended his hands. "Allow me."

She nodded until the white feathers on her bonnet waved.

A moment later, he set the bundle on the counter and pulled the cloth away. He hoisted one shoe and examined the sole. "Yes, I see the problem. I can repair." He examined the second shoe and encountered a place where the sole was worn paper-thin. "Good workmanship, a skilled cobbler made these shoes— many dances ago. I will fix to give you many more."

"*Gute.*" Hilde sighed.

"*Ja, gute.*" Bertha found her tongue. "How long? Cost?"

Kurt calculated the amount of time and materials to put both new soles and heels on the pair. He currently worked on an order for a teamster. The dancing shoes, for a paying customer, meant another short delay for Joseph's surprise. "One week."

Hilde clapped her hands. "They will be ready for the first Sunday dance in the new hall."

"And the price?" Bertha rested three fingers on the counter's edge.

Kurt quoted the same price he expected from any customer for similar work. Aiming his gaze at the young ladies' feet, he contained a chuckle. "Hilde, have you checked the fit? I suggest we take an extra minute and be certain your sister's shoes give room to wiggle toes."

"But...but..." Bertha blushed.

"I notice shoes, *Fraulein* Thayer. The pair with worn soles is the same you wore at the dance two weeks ago—and again Sunday—when I visited your home." He studied a wrinkle form and disappear on her brow during one breath. "You are kind to give shoes to a younger sister."

"*Mutter* purchased new shoes and gave me her old.

136

I pass mine to Hilde."

He blinked in surprise. Among his family, shoes, coats, and other items were passed in birth order until useless. He glanced to the ceiling at a memory of Helmut, the youngest brother, inspecting a coat worn so thin the garment was no warmer than a shirt. "Shoes from *Frau* Thayer—not *Fraulein* Amelia?"

"*Nein.* Amelia's feet are larger than *Mutter's.* Only *Vater,* and soon Johannes, require larger shoes or boots." Bertha curved her lips and held his gaze.

Kurt proceeded into the workroom and returned with a low stool. "For you, Hilde, please sit and allow me to check the fit."

A few moments later, Hilde sat on the stool and held her skirts close and modest. Pressing a thumb around the edge of the round toe, he smiled. "I suggest a little soft wool in each toe until your feet grow. Fit perfect by spring?"

"*Herr* Tafel." Hilde loosened one shoe and reached for her scuffed half-boot. "Please, will you dance the schottische with me when Althoffs open the new hall?"

He curved his lips into a generous smile at the youngster's hurried words. "Will your *Vater* allow?"

"*Ja.*" Her bonnet feathers jiggled when she nodded. "Papa gave permission to dance with family friends. I grow tired of dancing only with Papa or Johannes."

"I will be honored. But I will speak to your papa before we dance."

Hilde grinned. The instant her second low boot was secure, she sprang off the stool. "*Danke, danke, Herr* Tafel. I will do my very best to avoid treading on your toes."

"Do not worry, *Herr* Tafel. Hilde keeps good

rhythm—she is accomplished with all the circle dances." Bertha fingered the edge of her pale shawl. "When the hall opens, I do hope you will waltz with me. You are my favorite dance partner."

He considered the young lady for a long moment. *She is attractive...lively...intelligent. Too tender of years to consider a man of my age—and I her. My heart stays steady in her presence. Unlike...* "My intention, at every afternoon of dancing, is to sample many partners. I will include you."

He nodded to the departing girls before he recorded the order in his ledger. He set the dancing shoes on a shelf and sighed. Bertha Thayer was a pleasant dancing partner, nothing more, but he puzzled how to make it clear without insult. He placed a sign directing any customers to the yard in his window and locked the door. "I go and stack wood. I need to rid myself of the habit of comparing every waltz partner to a charming neighbor who does not dance." He continued to mutter as he hurried through his apartment, out the side door, and toward the remaining jumbled wood on the yard.

He recalled a conversation with Mr. Cook at the hardware store and recited activities forbidden to members of the American Christian Church. "They do not dance. Nor do they drink...or gamble. Would Polly frown and complain when I smoke an evening pipe?" he asked the stove wood. "I cannot help myself—my heart becomes excited in her company. When I dream of guiding her in a waltz I wake both exhausted and happy."

****

Near the end of Sunday worship service, Polly lowered her gaze at seeing Pastor Harter stare at her for the third time during this morning's service.

"Receive the departing blessing." The man raised both arms.

She clasped her hands, closed her eyes, and waited for him to finish. "Amen." She joined her voice to the other worshipers.

"Mama," Joseph whispered. "Why did you bring picnic things to church? Is this a day for a big dinner after service?"

She turned toward her son and placed one finger across her lips. The rule against conversation in the sanctuary was unlike the more casual worship in the St. Louis church she formerly attended. She sidestepped into the aisle and ushered Joseph to walk in front of her to the narthex. After greeting the pastor, Polly sighed when Joseph darted into the early November sunshine. In the next moment, she retrieved her basket and joined two other ladies in conversation a few paces beyond the open door.

"Mrs. Black."

At the sound of the authoritative male voice, she shifted her gaze and felt ice form in her previously comfortable stomach. "Good morning, Mr. Rush."

"Are you well?"

"Yes, Mr. Rush. My son and I are in good health."

"I want to show you my house." He held his hat still against his chest.

Polly swallowed. "Today?"

"No—Sunday is my time with Hannah." He glanced toward the small girl beside him. "I will collect you Tuesday afternoon—four o'clock."

"You suggest a very poor time. Joseph returns from school soon after four. And Mrs. Clark will be unable to chaperone."

"What?" He leaned toward her.

Backing one step as he invaded her personal space, she nodded. "I must guard my reputation, as well as yours." She darted her gaze to the scattered pairs and trios of people remaining on the church grounds. "For Hannah's sake."

The child formed her mouth into a perfect circle.

"I don't understand." He shook his head.

"I suggest"—Polly moistened her lips—"please hold a conversation with a married lady, perhaps Mrs. Franklin, before you issue another invitation to an unmarried woman. Excuse me." She pivoted and searched the dwindling number of parishioners for Joseph. A moment later, she spied him talking to his friends and using wide gestures. She approached and paused two paces from the youngsters. "Joseph, time for us to go."

"Yes, Mama." He clapped one boy on the shoulder and whispered a few words before hurrying to her side.

When they stepped on the sidewalk, Polly led them away from the familiar route home.

"Where are we going? Is *Frau* Keil going to drive the horse? This is not the way to the bakery—or the stable." The questions tumbled out of Joseph's mouth in a hurry.

"We are going to a special place—new to you. What did you talk about with the other boys?" She offered her hand, but he did not touch her fingers.

"Thomas and Robert are my friends. I told them about the snake."

Enough about the snake. Each time you tell the story—and I've lost count—the creature gets longer and thicker. I am grateful Herr *Tafel kept the conversation on other topics during today's walk to church.* "Did you talk about anything else?"

"Thomas showed us his new marble—from the store—green and black. Robert has a red marble."

Polly blinked. "I'm surprised the parents allowed the boys to bring toys to church."

"Pockets." Joseph patted one on his coat.

She sent a stern glance toward her son. After raising her gaze toward heaven for a moment, she sighed. Today was not the time to dwell on the challenges of forbidden objects secreted in a boy's pockets. She had a much more important topic to discuss.

"How far are we hiking? What did you put in the basket for lunch?" He limped beside her.

"We are almost there. Look across the street and tell me what you see."

Joseph tipped his head first to one side and then the other. "I see a wooden fence and two stone pillars. The space between the posts is narrow and rough, not like a proper street."

"Very good. Now, we will cross the street and test if you can read the words carved into the columns."

Standing in front of the left marker, Joseph shook his head. "I know the letters, but I do not know the words. The other one has a word and a number—a year—I think."

"This first one"—she pointed—"reads *Elm Ridge Cemetery.* The other says *Established 1829.*"

"Eighteen twenty-nine," he whispered. "Was that a long time ago?"

"Long enough. I was a small girl, not old enough to

attend school. When the first person was buried here, the village of Elm Ridge was new and small—only a few buildings."

"Did the knights in my storybook live then?"

"No." She considered. "The stories you enjoy were already many generations old."

He widened his eyes. "Are the stories older than the man with a cane at church?"

"Yes, many years older. I think"—she guided him along the central wagon track—"this place became a burial ground when Mr. Winston, the grocer, had dark hair."

He tipped his head back and stared.

Pressing her lips, she contained a laugh. Stepping from the rutted road, she guided them into the *Deutsch* portion of the cemetery. "I brought you here today because I think you are old enough to learn your father's name."

"Was he Joseph—like me?" He pointed toward his chest. "Or Thomas—like my friend?"

Polly smiled at the excitement in his rapid questions. Her instinct to protect him argued again with reality. She suspected rumor and gossip would soon be loose in the town to attack both mother and child. "No, his name was not Joseph—or Thomas." She halted in front of a new stone beside lumpy ground. "Help me spread the picnic blanket. Before I tell you his name, I want a promise."

He tugged one corner of the blanket into place. "Do I need to keep a secret?"

"Not exactly." She paused to arrange jumbled words. "Let me explain." She sat beside the basket and patted the space on her other side. "Your father was a good man—honest. Some people in Elm Ridge do not agree. Therefore, I do not want you to talk about your father to others unless they mention his name first. Do you understand?"

"A half-secret?" He tilted his head and squinted.

She nodded and suppressed a smile at his simple description. *My son gives me courage to tell him the basic story.* "The people who did not like your father might call him names—bad names young boys should not repeat. Some of the same people might also insult me—and you. I do not want you to use those words."

"Samuel, at school, calls me a carrot." He removed his cap and lifted a lock of hair.

"I expect you to deny being a vegetable." She offered him a chuckle and a jam sandwich. *I keep him away from the levee and tavern for I do not want him to learn cursing.* "Do you understand the sort of words I do not want you repeating?"

"I think so. Will you tell me Papa's name?" He bit his sandwich and chewed.

"Bernard Keil." She sipped water from a jar and waited.

"Ber…" Joseph repeated the name three times. "Wait"—he lowered his sandwich and stared from widened eyes—"like *Frau* Keil?"

"Yes." She pointed toward the stone. "His name is engraved on the marker. *Herr* Keil was a good man—a baker. Soon after you and I arrived in Elm Ridge, he died in an accident. He is buried here." She gestured toward the lumpy ground beside the blanket.

Joseph stared at the marker for a long moment. Shifting his attention to the uneven ground, he leaned toward her. "Are we sitting on him?"

Shaking her head, she struggled to remain serious. "His body is in the ground, but his soul is in heaven."

"In the sky—like a cloud?" He tipped his head. "Good afternoon, Papa."

She opened her lips, and a rumble of laughter rose from deep within her chest. "No need to talk loud. Souls in heaven have good hearing."

He took another bite and gazed toward the grave marker.

Polly studied her son to the sound of migrating geese overhead.

Joseph chewed slowly and looked steadily in the direction of the stone.

I believe he is sorting all the new information. A cloud drifted in front of the sun and she shivered.

"Mama, why didn't Papa live with us?" He turned his face toward her.

"Do you remember how Uncle Leo talked about the *Deutsch* people?"

Joseph nodded. "He used some of the words you asked me not to repeat."

"Correct. Your papa and I arranged to be married. Then Uncle Leo returned to St. Louis and did not permit the wedding." *From the best accounts I managed to find, Leo waved a pistol in front of Bernard's face.* Memories of those first days filled her mind, and she pulled her shawl tight. *My brother locked me in my room—treated me like a prisoner. If not for Madam Robineau entering for short visits, I would have gone mad. I did not see the kind* Deutsch *seamstresses for two weeks.* "I did not learn where Bernard moved for a very long time."

"I don't think Uncle Leo likes me." He frowned

and examined his jam-decorated fingertips.

Polly remained silent and recalled the evening after Joseph's birth. Tired from the ordeal, she had spoken little. But she heard the full minute of cursing from Leo's lips after he saw the baby's crippled foot. Within the week, Leo boarded a steamboat for Fort Benton.

Joseph licked jam from each finger. He stood and limped to the tombstone. "Are all the letters Papa's name?" He traced each groove with his right forefinger.

She joined him in front of the marker. "These two words, in the biggest letters, are his name. The numbers are the years he was born and died. The words below are a *Deutsch* saying—telling us he rests with God in heaven."

"Oh." He recited each letter of the name.

A cold wind gust stirred the leaves and penetrated her shawl. "Time to go home." She focused on a pair of yellowed leaves skittering across the picnic blanket.

He tipped his face toward her. "Can we visit Papa again?"

"Do you want to?" She stooped and set the empty water jar into the basket.

Joseph nodded. "I want to hear stories about Papa. I want to learn what he liked."

"He liked yellow flowers." She folded the blanket. "In the spring, we can bring a handful of blossoms. Do you like the idea?"

"I like yellow flowers, too." He patted the stone's smooth top.

She swallowed to banish the memory of the pleasant smell in the boardinghouse parlor when he smoked his evening pipe. Lifting the basket, she extended her hand.

Joseph swiped his hands on his trousers and marched independently beside her. "Look." He pointed. "More people are visiting in the cem...cemetery."

"I see them." Polly studied the group of five young people a few rows away. *The young lady with the green shawl looks familiar. Perhaps when we get a few steps closer I will recall her name.*

"Good day," Joseph called.

"Hush. Let others tend to their own business." She paused to select a different route to the entrance. Aware the group was speaking *Deutsch,* she fixed her lips into a small smile.

"Ein Minute"—the tallest girl turned and hurried toward Polly—"you are seamstress, no?"

Thayer. Fraulein *Amelia Thayer.* The very instant she recognized the voice, she focused on the white stone with the same surname. *"Guten Abend."*

An instant later, Amelia presented the muscular young man now at her side. "Mrs. Black, I introduce you to Christian Giesel, my intended. Christian, Mrs. Black is sewing my wedding dress."

Polly searched her memory for *Herr* Thayer's occupation before she addressed the future groom. In the next instant, she felt Joseph's small, warm hand clasp her fingers. She skimmed through a short, mental list before speaking in hesitant *Deutsch.* "How pleasant to meet you. Are you a carpenter?"

"Nein. I train as bricklayer with my uncle in St. Louis." He replied with a mixture of languages. "Three years ago, I arrive in Elm Ridge. I do much work for *Herr* Thayer—brick and stone foundations and tall chimneys."

"He is modest." Amelia glanced at Christian with

obvious affection.

Polly gestured toward the group remaining near the grave marker. "Are the others your brother and sisters?"

"*Ja.*" Amelia beckoned the others to come forward. "Today my brother, Johannes, suggested a visit to Uncle Hermann's grave. I introduce you now to the living relatives."

Smiling at the careful phrasing, Polly stepped forward.

Amelia pointed toward each of her siblings in turn. "Bertha, Hilde, and Johannes, please greet Mrs. Black, a seamstress at the dress shop, and her son."

"A dress shop"—Hilde clapped—"I want to visit a proper dress shop. Where?"

Polly smiled at the blue-eyed, rosy-cheeked girl and estimated her age at near ten. "We do business at Third Street and Apple—beside Mr. Fox, the cooper."

"Across the street from *Herr* Tafel?" Bertha fingered her bonnet ribbons.

"Exactly." Polly blinked at the dark-haired, more delicate featured member of the family and remembered Amelia's comment during the dress shop visit. *My sister, Bertha, attempts to claim more than a proper share of waltzes with* Herr *Tafel.*

"*Herr* Tafel is repairing shoes so I can dance." Hilde skipped to Amelia's side.

Amelia set one hand on her youngest sister's shoulder. "Silly girl. You can dance without those shoes."

"Not well. These boots are getting small and pinching my feet." Hilde directed attention to dark, rounded toes peeking from under her gingham skirt.

"I am certain *Herr* Tafel will do a fine job

repairing your shoes." Polly halted, uncertain if she was voicing too many English words.

Hilde pointed toward Joseph's feet. "What kind of shoes?"

"Magic," he replied. "*Herr* Tafel turned stockings into shoes. They are warm, but he cautioned me to stay out of puddles."

Amelia set her lips into a straight line and sent a warning glance toward her youngest sister.

"Have you ribbons at your store?" Bertha broke the silence. "When we fetch the shoes, Hilde and I might shop for hair ribbons—to celebrate the new dance hall."

"*Ja,* we sell ribbon in many widths and colors. I look forward to your visit. Now, we go and let you enjoy the rest of your cemetery visit." Polly backed a few steps before turning toward the central wagon track.

The moment they passed the cemetery marker post, Joseph released her hand. "Mama, does the young girl, Hilde, go to school?"

"I think so." She checked for riders or wagons on the street.

"Where? She does not learn from Mr. Hopewell."

Polly sighed. Elm Ridge, like many villages, contained schools divided by language, religion, or both. "I think she attends the *Deutsch* school on Hickory Street. If we see her again, you may ask."

"I will remember. Mama, I think it is good for *Herr* Tafel to repair shoes so a girl can dance. Do you know how to dance?" He hurried to cross the street with her.

In the next blink, Polly remembered an evening when she was in her second year of school. "My papa taught me to dance—when I was a few years older than you*."* An instant later, she frowned as other memories of her father rushed in. She found it impossible to remember his smile or laugh without also recalling his negative habits: cheating in business, drinking whiskey, playing dice.

"Mama?"

She shook her head and focused on the present.

"Did my papa, Bernard, dance?" He paused with his hands on hips and head tipped.

Good question. He never talked of going to any of the many Deutsch *dances or beer gardens in St. Louis. He sang...or tried.* She smiled at the memory of Bernard humming a tune when he entered the boardinghouse after a day's work. "Your papa and I did not dance together." Herr *Tafel dances. He is an honest, good man, I think.* She recalled his casual mention of eating supper at the tavern—a place where men drank beer and smoked tobacco. During the remainder of the walk home, she pondered the quality of a person's character compared to habits her church permitted.

Chapter Thirteen

Kurt pegged a sole into place and listened to the foundry whistle fade at one o'clock on Tuesday. In the mills and businesses of Elm Ridge, men returned to work from their lunch break. Several of the shopkeepers locked the door and prepared for their own meal and errands. After one more peg was tapped into position, Kurt ran a thumb along the sole's edge.

Harnesses jingled and wheels creaked as a team pulled a barrel-filled wagon down Apple Street.

A few minutes later, the shop locked, Kurt strode toward a large building on the north side of the town square. A quick *guten Tag* or nod of the head to those he met on the sidewalk did not slow his progress. He ignored the first two doors of the wide building. Today, his business was at neither Clemons' Dry Goods nor the unmarked door. He paused outside his destination and studied the red-and-white striped post. Moistening his lips, he reminded himself to speak only English inside this business. He opened the door and stepped into the barber shop.

"Welcome." Andrew Hill glanced toward Kurt, nodded, and returned to his work on an elderly man with a generous stomach. "Be with you soon's I finish trimming Ol' Tom."

"No hurry." Kurt removed his cap and assessed the barber and his business. The man, short and stocky, was clean-shaven and sported short, dark-brown hair. The shop appeared tidy with two plain chairs for waiting customers. A row of shoulder-height pegs waited for his coat and hat.

"Don't recall seeing you in afore," Mr. Hill spoke while using a straight razor to trim the customer's thin, white hair.

"Not been in." Kurt hung his coat and cap. "I set my tools down in Elm Ridge recent—six-and-twenty of September to be exact."

"What sort of tools?" The customer curled large hands over the ends of the chair arms.

"Shoemaker—cobbler—rented the building at Third and Apple. Land agent told me the wheelwright left a month before."

"Don't believe but half the words from a land agent's mouth." Ol' Tom twisted his lips from smile to frown and back.

The barber grunted agreement.

"Which part is false? Need I fear the wheelwright's return?" Kurt failed to recall any hint of the previous occupant at the other businesses where he introduced himself.

Mr. Hill shook his head. "Doubt Silas McMaster will rise from his grave to bother you."

"Will you tell me the story?" He kept his mouth in only a hint of a smile, lest the barber realize how much Kurt enjoyed a loose-lipped man cutting hair.

"First off." Mr. Hill paused after a long stroke. "McMaster died in the spring—one of them lung fevers got him just as the trees started to leaf."

Ol' Tom coughed twice into his lap. "The late Mr. McMaster died with debts to most every merchant in

Ellen Parker

town—and a few up the river. Tools, stock, most everything was claimed to cover a portion of the debt. I expect you found the place bare."

Kurt nodded and remembered the thick dirt layer, more than expected for being one month vacant. "Stoves and the building's shell pretty much describes the place I found."

"McMaster business hardly settled when a building burned at that corner." The barber nudged his customer to bow his head. "It was a near thing for the cooper. Mr. Fox came close to losing his entire business."

"I noticed scorch marks, but he didn't tell me much about the fire." Kurt sealed his lips against revealing the source and extent of his knowledge of the July blaze. "Fire can be a hazardous thing."

"Necessary—need to keep under control." Ol' Tom mumbled into his chest.

Mr. Hill took a final swipe with the razor. "Careful now, new fella will think you talking about a team...or a wife." He shot a glance toward Kurt. "You got a name?"

"Tafel...Kurt Tafel...late of eastern Pennsylvania." Drawing a breath, he decided to tell the basics before one of the men commented on his accent. "My family lives an easy day's drive from Philadelphia."

"We don't get many from those parts." Andrew exchanged razor for towel. "We see plenty of men from Ohio and Kentucky. In spring and summer, we have whole boatloads of *Deutsch* immigrants. Nope, can't recall another Pennsylvania man. Now, I'm not an authority. There are a few folks in these parts who don't volunteer information. I see no reason to pry. If a man wants the past to be past." He shrugged. "I be too fond of my fingers and straight nose to stick them into another man's business. Know what I mean?"

Kurt nodded. He recalled a good many men on the riverboats who he realized did not appreciate questions. Brushing debris from the customer's neck, the barber stepped back. "Done with ye, Ol' Tom."

"Thank ye, kindly." Tom pushed to his feet and stepped away from the swivel chair.

Kurt moistened his lips and mixed a measure of courage with his next breath. "Either of you know a man named Rush?"

Tom froze with a coin in his hand. "Do you mean George Rush...partner in the sawmill?"

"Yes, sounds like the same. His name surfaced in conversation the other day. Just enough was said to make me curious."

Tossing the coin to the barber, Tom turned and retrieved a gray, cloth cap from a peg. "He lost his wife five, maybe six, weeks ago—'bout the same time you unpacked your tools. Sad business. I heard the stillborn was a son."

Kurt recalled deep frown lines on his recent caller's face. *More than weeks to make such deep creases. His grief did not resemble* Vater's *after Greta died.*

"He has a daughter." Mr. Hill honed the razor on a wide, leather strop. "Less than a week ago, he talked of her the entire time I trimmed his hair. I understand she lives with relatives on a farm nine, maybe ten, miles out the north road. He complained about seeing her only on Sundays."

"A sensible man would hire a housekeeper." Tom paused with one hand on the doorknob. "Rush built a large, monster house out on Seventh Street. He should be able to find a few dollars a week to hire an able-bodied woman."

Kurt settled into the barber chair. "Does he really have the largest house in town?"

"Close—he's ambitious. Tried twice to get on the town council. Man never knows about an election." Tom opened the door and met Kurt's gaze. "According to my wife, Mrs. Rush never smiled."

Kurt heard the door close before he organized a response.

"How do ye want this—same part in the center?" Andrew pulled a comb through Kurt's thick, blond hair.

"*Ja*—yes—and straight across the back, if you please." Aware of heat climbing his neck, Kurt closed his eyes. The tavern keeper had warned him Mr. Hill spoke only English.

The barber chuckled. "You lasted longer than most. Last week, I had a *Deutsch* customer who lapsed after three words. Now." He packed serious into his tone. "In my own opinion, George Rush is determined—protective. Some people call him hard. I did see him whip his horses a time or two. Never heard one way or t'other how he treated his wife."

Pondering the multiple steps between whipping a stubborn horse and slapping a grown woman, Kurt almost missed the barber's next comment.

"Now his business partner, Franklin, you'll never meet a man more kind and fair than Samuel."

"Are you saying Rush's not square?" Kurt blinked, thankful his back was to the barber.

"Honest in business…according to both American and *Deutsch* carpenters. Generous at his church from all accounts. Let me think a minute on where he spends his Sunday morning."

Listening close, Kurt caught the mumbled names of three churches.

"American Christian...brick building a mite south on Sixth Street." Mr. Hill nudged Kurt's head.

Kurt tipped his head as directed. "I know the place...a tidy, modest building. Each Sunday, I walk past on my way to worship."

The barber stroked the razor. "You ever wander by his house?"

"Once." He glanced at his loosely clasped hands. "I failed to make sense of the window arrangement—didn't fit with any floor plan in my experience."

Andrew sidestepped and lifted hair with his comb. "I hear bits and pieces, from all sides, as men sit in my chair. The stories floating in the air two summers ago were enough to burn a fella's ears. Rush wanted the front door fifty feet from the street—he refused the builder's advice. Now, he's left with a nubbin of a back porch and water lapping at the step during spring melt."

"Sounds foolish to ignore a builder's advice." Kurt frowned at the amount of hair drifting toward the floor. *Will I look like a shorn sheep when he finishes?*

"I agree. You plan to do business with Rush?"

Aware of a razor near his ear, Kurt resisted shaking his head. "I use more leather than lumber in my business. I don't expect to need boards or posts until I build a proper garden fence in the spring. By the way, how long have you lived in Elm Ridge?"

"Four years last July...my family and I come from Kentucky." Andrew launched into a monologue about the businesses which had come and gone during his time in the town. He spoke mainly of the American community but included a few notable events centered around the *Deutsch* immigrants.

A short time later, Kurt stood and handed the barber his payment. He nodded at his mirrored image, while shorter, his hair remained in a familiar style. "Thank you. I understand more about my new home now."

"Pass the word—I don't speak *Deutsch*. But hair is hair, and coin is coin."

During the return trip to his shop, Kurt mused on the character of George Rush. *Whipped his horses. Wife never smiled. Sets his mind on something and doesn't stop until he wins.* He recalled Polly's delightful smile when Joseph received the sock-moccasins. *Please, be careful, Polly—your smile is too precious to lose.*

****

Polly changed position to take better advantage of the Tuesday afternoon light. While the day was not bright, the two windows in the workroom allowed sewing without lighting a lamp. Turning from the dress form draped with basted bodice pieces, she lifted the first blue sleeve of the wedding dress and addressed Mrs. Clark. "How deep did you cut the sleeve-to-bodice seam?"

"Twice the usual." Abigail continued to adjust the gathers on a child's dress. "*Fraulein* Thayer is a young woman...and practical. I think it is good to leave an allowance for future alteration."

"I agree." Polly allowed a smile to lift her lips and thought of the recently ordered shop sign. *I purchased the wool for my cloak. Tonight, after the supper chores, I will cut the pieces. If I work into the nights, I will finish by Sunday.*

The jingle of harnessed horses in the street interrupted her musing.

She ignored the urge to glance out the window and pinched a tiny, precise pleat. In the next instant, she slipped a pin into position. Her mother, and later, the *Deutsch* seamstresses at the St. Louis boardinghouse, stressed the importance of even stitches and meticulous pleats. She believed a well-made, simple garment hung well and flattered.

Abigail stood, leaned, and collected ribbon to decorate the child's frock.

When the first sleeve was pinned into place, Polly stepped back to inspect her work. She treated the wedding dress as the most important garment trusted to her skills. If *Frau* and *Fraulein* Thayer were pleased with the work, Polly expected them to speak well of the dress shop to others in the *Deutsch* community. She remembered the varying quality of the bakery customers' clothing. From girlhood, she believed a dress should fit properly and not require a tied apron to define the waist.

The shop bell announced a potential customer. Confident Abigail would greet the patron, Polly reached for the threaded needle.

"Good afternoon, Mr. Rush. How may I help you? Have you come to purchase a ribbon for Hannah?"

"I wish to speak with Mrs. Black," he growled.

Polly closed her mouth so tight her back teeth ached. With a glance out the window, she confirmed the daylight remained steady. If he intended to interrupt a work day to view his house, she would give him a sharp word. Jamming the needle into the green, velvet pincushion, she drew a breath containing reason and manners. "One moment, please."

"There you are…pretty as one of them illustrations in a periodical." He removed his hat from well-trimmed hair."

She smoothed her apron and approached to within inches beyond arm's length. "What have you come to say?"

"I want to speak in private." He set his hat on the counter where it nudged a dish of buttons toward the edge.

She swallowed to create a delay while she sorted the mix of curiosity and caution swimming inside her body. "Mrs. Clark and I do not keep dress shop secrets. We believe the practice is bad for business." She sneaked a peak at her employer and stifled a display of relief at Abigail's nod.

"Well, since you use those terms." He placed one hand flat on his chest.

Change the clothing, and he would be one of the illustrations—a knight begging a favor—from Joseph's storybook.

"I ask you to join me for supper at the hotel. They serve a fine veal chop on Tuesdays. I shall call for you at a quarter hour before seven."

"I've not agreed." She hid her clenched fists amid her skirt's generous folds. Regardless of how he intended, she heard more demand than invitation.

"Fair enough. What's your decision?" He shifted his stance and lowered his arm.

A glance toward the ceiling did not give her the proper words. "Today is impossible. Tonight's supper already bubbles on the stove."

He extended his lower lip and stared.

Meeting his gaze, she searched for a better excuse. In a glance toward the divider curtain, she prayed he would not comment on the scents of pork, onions, and apples seeping from the Dutch oven. She did not want him to invite himself to dine. "You did not include Joseph in your invitation."

He studied the floor and mumbled.

Tick...tock...tick.

"Mrs. Clark"—he faced the shop owner—"would you be so kind as to watch the boy? I'll pay for your time."

Polly pressed tight her lips and fastened her gaze on Abigail.

"'Tis impossible...plans tonight." Abigail stared at Mr. Rush.

Polly swallowed and focused her attention on George. "I decline the invitation. You must understand my responsibility to my son."

"Find another person," he snapped.

With a glance toward the clock, she struggled for composure. His stance reminded her of her brother, Leo, shouting orders. "You have left me with less than three hours. The work is waiting. My son returns from school soon. I do not have the time to walk across town, beg a favor from friends who likely have their own plans, and return. The sewing will fall behind schedule."

Mrs. Clark cleared her throat. "The shop is busy. We have two large orders and several smaller ones which require our attention."

Bless you, Abigail.

He alternated his gaze between the women before

settling on Polly. "Tomorrow—same time—I expect you to have your household in order."

Surprised, she felt her lungs refuse to breathe for a moment. She opened her mouth, but no sound emerged.

"No excuses." He grabbed his hat from the counter.

Abigail lurched for the teetering button dish.

Pivoting, he marched toward the door, exited, and slammed the barrier hard enough to shake the glass inset.

Rude...demanding...powerful. She swallowed as the final descriptor flashed in her mind. "I can scarce believe it. Does he think I'm a child to be ordered about?"

"His wife's less than six weeks in her grave," Abigail whispered.

Polly shifted her gaze to the larger workroom window and sighed.

Mr. Rush yelled at the team and slapped the reins.

Staring through the glass, Polly dared not breathe until the horses plodded around the corner at Second Street. "Mr. Rush exhibits an odd notion of courtship. If she sought a man so soon, a woman's reputation would be forever ruined."

"True. What do you plan to do?" Abigail stepped toward the child's gown on the worktable.

"I felt cornered into accepting the dinner invitation." She returned to the dress form and reached for a threaded needle. "The hotel is a public place. I think he will be cautious of his speech around others." *A man like him—with political ambition—will not want to appear foolish in front of other men.* "The moon is near full. I will have light if the situation requires me to walk home alone. Will you stay at the shop with

160

Joseph?"

"Certainly. He's an easy lad to supervise."

Polly exhaled relief. "I appreciate your kindness. Mr. Rush will ask questions over our supper…difficult ones…I fear. I must prepare some answers."

"Don't trust him, Polly." Abigail lifted her gaze from the dress-in-progress to Polly's face.

"Advice I'm already following. What I do not understand…why does he resist hiring a housekeeper?" She placed the first basting stitch.

"Men"—Abigail spoke at a near whisper—"some are focused more on an heir than the family in front of them."

Heir? Does he focus on a son and heir and fail to consider the wife and mother as a whole person? Does he ignore the fact a woman holds opinions and desires of her own? Polly recalled George's behavior when she served him tea. *He used half the sugar in the house. I needed to remind him to leave. His kiss—* She shivered and frowned. *He smelled of damp sawdust and cheap soap.* She smiled and stole a glance at the building across the street. Herr *Tafel wears the fragrances of tobacco and leather—more pleasant to my nose.*

****

At twenty minutes before seven the next evening, Polly stood in front of the square, washstand mirror and inserted a pin into her hair.

"Mama, why are you leaving the house to eat supper?" Joseph placed the final spoon onto the table.

She slid an additional hairpin into place and sighed. Not counting the days she sent him to school, she seldom left her son in another's care. "Mr. Rush invited me to dine at the hotel."

"Don't you like fried potatoes with bacon?" He exaggerated a sniff of the bacon-and-onion scented air. "Smells delicious."

She turned to face her son. "I like them very much. However, Mr. Rush wishes to talk with me, and our conversation over supper will not be interesting to you."

He sat at the table and traced a tiny circle on the bread knife's handle. "Does Mr. Rush ever smile? He looks angry at church."

She considered her response and could not find an instance when he smiled in her presence. "I want you to mind your manners for Mrs. Clark—no fuss at bedtime."

"Yes, Mama."

"We'll be fine." Abigail spooned hot food from the frying pan onto a plate. "A new issue of *Godey's Lady's Book* arrived. I intend to enjoy every page."

"Sounds delightful. I do hope they have an interesting dress pattern in this edition." She lifted her bonnet from a peg.

Rap-rap-rap.

"One minute." She gave a quick, silent command to silence Joseph before she hurried through the enclosed porch. Opening the door, she gestured Mr. Rush inside. "You are prompt. I will only be a moment to don my bonnet and shawl."

"Punctually is a virtue." George stepped into the main room, removed his hat, and nodded toward Abigail and Joseph.

A short time later, after exchanging comments on the clear sky and rising moon, Polly and George arrived at the hotel dining room.

"Two for supper." He displayed two fingers to the first employee they encountered.

"Yes, sir, Mr. Rush. We have a table laid for you." The young, mustached man gestured them to follow into the large, busy dining room.

Polly muttered "thanks" to the waiter when he pulled out her chair. Settling on the cane seat, she glanced to the place setting and then the young man. "Please, sir, what is your menu this evening?"

"Spareribs with all the usual, ma'am." He offered a hint of a bow and departed.

George wrinkled his brow.

She clasped her hands under the table and met his gaze. "Do you dine here often, Mr. Rush?"

"Often enough to know Wednesday is spareribs." He released his top coat button. "You?"

She delayed a response by giving some attention to the high, brightly-painted ceiling. When she leveled her gaze, she hid a smile. "The first evening Joseph and I were in Elm Ridge, we dined here."

"They do a good business." He nodded once when the waiter deposited glasses of water. "I count only three empty tables at present."

She skimmed her gaze over the other diners, two matrons and at least a dozen men. "Mrs. Fox says court is in session. I expect the proceedings bring a fair number of people to town."

"True—the judge, and some of the lawyers, come from as far as Springfield." He rubbed a clean-shaven cheek. "I expect you want to know more about my house."

"From all accounts, your house is new and large." She leaned back as the waiter set plates of steaming spareribs, mashed potatoes, sliced carrots, and a warm roll at each place.

Without checking the flavor, George inserted the tip of his butter knife into the salt cellar and sprinkled the seasoning over his food. "Indeed—the final shingle was placed two years ago last month. Jane"—he scooped buttered potatoes onto his spoon—"I believe you met my late wife—fine, dutiful woman—good mother."

She nodded and separated a bite of meat from the bone.

"Jane insisted on the best possible kitchen stove. I purchased one from the local foundry, which is larger than the one at your apartment. Then again, it heats a bigger room. I ordered our parlor furniture from a firm in Louisville. My dining table, also a special order, seats ten adults with plenty of elbow room. Three bedrooms are furnished—mine, Hannah's, and one for guests. A person really needs to see the rooms to appreciate them." He lifted a rib with both hands and paused it six inches above the plate. "How late do you work on Saturday? I could give you a tour before dark."

Polly swallowed surprise with her meat. "We stay open until six—past sunset at this time of year."

He finished the rib in several rapid bites and blotted his lips with a napkin. "Perhaps a different day of the week. You must leave the shop for errands while Mrs. Clark continues the business."

"We have an arrangement." Scooping potatoes with her spoon, she suppressed a sudden shiver. "You seem in a great hurry to escort me to your home, Mr. Rush. Why?"

He paused his fork so quick the carrots quivered.

"Well, I expect you want to see the place—get your mind settled and all before the wedding."

She set her knife across her plate and straightened. Hiding her hands below the tabletop, she pressed on a suddenly sour stomach. "I have not agreed to marry you, Mr. Rush."

"You came to supper." He thumped his water glass on the table and stared.

His manners are no better in a public place than in the dress shop. She drew a deep breath and counted to four in silence. "Mr. Rush, eating supper with you at the hotel is an entirely different matter than marriage."

"Don't make a scene." He leaned toward the table's center.

Let the other guests hear. Unexpected courage arrived with her next breath and strengthened her voice. "A woman needs to enter marriage of her own free will, sir—not at the end of an ultimatum."

"Hush." The command emerged sharp.

"Your situation, Mr. Rush, calls for a housekeeper. I suggest you seek a willing person among the residents of the village or surrounding farms." She clenched her napkin with both hands. Aware her voice grew louder with each word, she pressed her lips and fixed her gaze on a wall sconce over his shoulder.

"I expected you to be willing—considering you have a boy." He took a sip of water.

"Joseph—my son is Joseph." She mixed relief into words at normal volume. "I do not want to marry you, Mr. Rush. Should I ever seek a husband, my concern would be his character—not the size of his house. I believe Joseph will develop into a fine, young man—regardless of lack of a male in the household."

165

"Mongrel…cripple…worthless," George muttered between bites of buttered roll.

Aware of a quiver building in her fingers, she pushed back her chair and stood. "I'm leaving, Mr. Rush. Please, do not call or issue further invitations."

"What?" Mouth open, he gazed at her.

Adjusting her shawl, she pivoted and strode toward the door. *Feet, don't fail me.*

Chapter Fourteen

Friday, half an hour after the shop closed, Polly set a pan of biscuits into the oven. She hummed "O for a Thousand Tongues to Sing" and reviewed the day. She smiled at the progress on *Fraulein* Thayer's dress. In silence, she calculated the amount of work remaining before the young woman came for her fitting. After cleaning every speck of flour from the board, she wiped her hands on her apron and gave an anxious glance toward the back door. *Why is Joseph taking such a long time to fetch the final pail of water?*

The lamp on the sewing table glowed with a soft, steady light.

"One event today puzzles me," she whispered to the empty room. "Past two o'clock, Mr. Rush halted his team in front of the shop and sat for at least a quarter hour. Is he spying on me? Does he take note of our customers?" With a shake of her head to banish thoughts of the unpleasant man, she reached deep into her sewing basket and extracted a slim book, purchased today at Clemons' Dry Goods. "*The Adventures of King Arthur and his Knights,*" she read. A similar volume, full of Joseph's favorite stories, was destroyed in the fire. "I suspect he will beg me to read every tale before Monday morning."

"Mama, guess who found me at the pump," Joseph called out while still on the back porch.

Swifty, the cat, scooted ahead of her boy the instant the door opened two inches. Then, with the elegance of her kind, the young cat settled on her favorite perch, the third step to the loft and claimed a perfect observation spot for most of the room.

Polly faced the door and stilled. Forcing a swallow, she struggled to keep her smile small. "Welcome, *Herr* Tafel. Are you having a good week of business?"

"Good evening, Mrs. Black. Please tell me when Joseph's chores are done. I brought a surprise." He removed his flat, leather cap and held it in his right hand.

Sliding her left hand holding the book behind her back, she sidled closer to the sewing basket. In the next instant, she slipped the book under several items in the roomy container. "Let me check one thing." She stepped for a better view of the tin pail of wood beside the stove. "Chores are done—the water was the final item."

"Please, *Herr* Tafel, may I see what you carry in your sack?" Joseph stood straight with arms at his sides, the perfect pose of a student reciting in class.

"First, you must close your eyes." Kurt swung a small, coarse-cloth bag from behind his back into plain sight. "No peeking."

Joseph placed one hand over each eye and nodded.

Watching Kurt's hands more than his face, Polly almost missed his wink. Curious, she leaned forward. She remained silent when he placed a child-sized brogan onto a chair. An instant later, she gasped as he placed a second shoe, not an exact copy of the first, beside it.

He nodded in her direction and mouthed a single

word.

She hid her mouth behind one hand.

"Open your eyes," Kurt urged.

Joseph looked at Kurt's hands for an instant before he spotted the shoes on the chair. "What? Wow. Look, Mama—shoes like *Herr* Hoffman wears on Sunday." He extended one hand and touched the firm leather. "Are they my size? Thank you. Thank you."

Allowing her smile to grow, Polly lowered her hand. The only time she recalled equal excitement in Joseph's voice was the year the *Deutsch* seamstresses in St. Louis decorated a cedar Christmas tree in the boardinghouse parlor.

Joseph lurched forward and wrapped his arms around Kurt's waist. "*Danke.*"

"Sit...try them on." Kurt gestured toward the second chair.

"One moment"—she shifted her attention to the sewing basket and slipped her hand below the book. *I wondered why* Fraulein *Mueller insisted on giving me a second pair of stockings for Joseph.* "I feel the victim of a conspiracy."

"Con...conspire...I don't know the word." Joseph pursed his lips and contracted his eyebrows."

"A surprise—planned by two or more people," Kurt offered.

Polly handed her son the new stockings, almost identical to the pair used to make the magic shoes. "You must give proper thanks to *Fraulein* Mueller the next time you see her."

"I remember." He nodded and removed one magic shoe.

A whiff of biscuit caught Polly's attention. She

hurried to the oven, grabbed a towel, and opened the cast-iron door. Sliding out the pan, she viewed the small, golden breads. "*Herr* Tafel, you must stay for supper."

"Please…please…I will share." Joseph tugged on one new stocking and tipped his face toward Kurt.

"I will consider your kind offer." He beckoned Polly closer. "Now pay attention, young man. This shoe"—he lifted the larger of the two—"see how thick the sole is? Compare the size to your smallest finger."

Joseph matched his finger to the sole and nodded.

"This shoe always goes on your left foot. Can you point to your left foot?"

"Left is my big foot." The boy made a final adjustment on the second new stocking.

Polly squatted beside his chair. "Good."

In the next moment, Joseph slipped the shoe over the sock and grasped the laces.

"Can you tie a bow?" Kurt paused his lips in a tiny smile.

"I will try." The boy crossed the laces, made a loop, tucked an end, and crossed the laces twice again. "Is that a bow?"

Polly pressed her lips to stifle her laugh.

"My goodness." Kurt leaned forward to inspect the result. "You have made an interesting knot."

Shaking her head, Polly compared the mess of laces to the tangle when she dropped the thread box. "I think we will have lessons in the proper way to tie shoes—later. Here, let me straighten the snarl and tie it correct. Watch and learn."

Several moments later, Kurt held the second brogan. "Are you ready for shoe number two?"

"Yes, sir."

"See how thick the sole is? See the difference when you put your little finger on the edge? This shoe always goes on your right foot."

"Big sole, small foot." Joseph squinted. "Why?"

Polly glanced toward the ceiling and stifled a laugh.

"Do you remember the day I measured your feet?" He waited for a nod. "When you stood on the wood strips, I measured how thick to make the sole."

Polly tied the second laces. "Okay, now stand."

"The shoes feel...different." He scrunched his brow and looked at his shoes.

I never bought you such fine shoes before. "Walk to the door and back."

Clump. Thump. Clump. Thump. Each shoe made a different sound against the wide floorboards.

"What do you think?" Kurt motioned the boy to halt in front of him.

"They are beautiful, brown shoes...I never...I stand...level."

Kurt squatted and pressed a thumb hard into the toe of first the left shoe and then the right. Turning his face toward Polly, he nodded. "I made them long. A little soft wool in the toe will make them comfortable until he grows."

"An excellent idea." She glanced toward the stove before meeting his gaze. "Now, you must stay for supper—no argument. I will pay for the shoes, but I do not have the money on hand today. Tonight, please share a humble meal of beef stew and biscuits.

"*Danke* for supper. No hurry with the money." He stood. "I will consider a warm meal more than a first payment."

"Look—I can move faster." Joseph clumped and thumped from the back door to the shop drape and back.

"You have made my son very happy." She observed the sparkle in Joseph's eyes. Joy fluttered like a butterfly at the base of her throat. She blinked back unexpected tears. In the next instant, she remembered another time Joseph's entire face beamed with happiness. *Poor* Herr *Hoffmann—after the fire, my son hugged him with all the strength in his five-year-old body—unaware the burns on Hans's back still healed.*

"Look, Swifty...new shoes." He paused, squatted, and pointed, doing his best to direct the cat's attention to the footwear.

Polly hurried to the cupboard and collected another place setting. A contented sigh escaped her lips. "Tell me, *Herr* Tafel, where did you get the idea to make one sole thicker than the other?"

"*Mein Grossvater*—he always fashioned a double sole on *Grossmutter's* left shoe to lessen her limp." He sidestepped to the washstand. "Do you want me to help—or only to wash?"

"Wash, sit, eat, and tell us more of your travels." She transferred biscuits onto a white plate.

"My pleasure." He poured a ladleful of clean water into the basin.

A short time later, Polly surveyed her son and their guest. Quick smiles flashed on both man and boy between bites of carrots, turnips, and peas simmered with meaty beef ribs. She lifted a buttered biscuit and viewed the scene with a deep sense of satisfaction before resuming the conversation thread. "Two weeks in St. Louis…did you enjoy your time in the city?"

"Very much." Kurt captured broth and a small piece of onion with his spoon. "I carried letters to a few businessmen. They were all very helpful in suggesting suppliers."

"Is there much construction on the riverfront?" She made a quick comparison of the area before and after the Great Fire of 1849. This year, on the spring morning she and Joseph boarded the packet for Elm Ridge, scaffolding surrounded many new, brick buildings.

"The air in the entire city throbs with construction sounds. And the brick kilns glow through the night. Did I tell you I saw a juggler?"

Polly listened, supplied a comment when he paused, and watched Joseph's meal disappear.

"Enough of my stories." Kurt set his empty dish near the table's center. "Has your shop been busy?"

"We are having an excellent week. The orders give me sewing for every evening. I seldom find time to work on my household sewing and mending." She brushed biscuit crumbs from her fingers and wished guilt of labor on the Lord's Day, the only way to complete her cloak in a timely manner, shed as easy.

Joseph turned and pointed toward the shop. "What does Swifty have in her mouth?"

"Is it a mouse? We noticed signs in the shop two days ago." She became aware of her arm muscles locking into place. No matter how many times she witnessed a cat catch prey, she felt a sliver of pity for the meal.

Swifty demonstrated her affection for Joseph by dropping the creature beside his chair.

"It…it moved…not dead." Joseph gulped before he

whispered.

"I see." Polly forced her attention on the rodent taking a tiny step.

Swifty placed one paw on the smaller animal.

Polly swallowed. "*Herr* Tafel, how does one teach a cat to kill, not maim, their prey?"

"I don't know. I suppose the first step is not to frighten the kitten." In slow, silent movements, he stood and eased between Joseph's chair and the stove.

Released, the dazed mouse crept forward.

Swifty pounced. The kitten bit into the mouse's neck and shook her head.

Holding three fingers against her lips, Polly forced herself to remain silent.

The rodent's tail swung in time to Swifty's head and then hung limp.

"I think Mr. Mouse is dead now. Good job, Swifty." Joseph clapped.

The deed is done. Polly glanced toward Kurt and encountered a warm look from his clear, blue eyes. Fearful the heat on her neck would become a blush and bring too much attention, she returned her focus to Joseph's new, special brogans.

****

"Yes, good job." Kurt shifted his left foot.

The kitten zipped across the room carrying her supper.

"Thank you." Polly released a large breath.

Joseph stood and took one step toward Swifty.

Startled and possessive, the pet gripped her trophy and darted toward the shop.

"I want to watch." He glanced toward his mother.

"*Nein.*" Kurt touched the boy's shoulder.

"Let Swifty eat in peace." Polly gathered the cloth cover for the jam jar. "You saw enough to learn she is a good worker."

Kurt watched an additional, silent message pass from mother to son. "I will try to watch my pair of kittens closer. So far, I've not seen signs of mice in my building. However, the weather is getting cooler, and the pests might seek warmth from my stove." He gathered dirty dishes. "Allow me to help. *Mutter* taught her sons household basics."

"Joseph, you are in luck tonight." She replaced the usual wash basin with a deep, tin container. "Thank *Herr* Tafel for wiping the dishes and emptying the slops."

"*Danke.*" Joseph stood straight as a wooden soldier for a moment, then he made a deep bow. "The lowliest servant of the castle thanks you from the soles of his new, wonderful shoes."

Kurt struggled to confine his building laugh to a genuine smile. "Go in peace, young man."

"Stay out of the shop." Polly tossed the directive toward Joseph's back.

A short time later, Kurt dried the final bowl. He studied Polly's hands as she held the Dutch oven. At first glance, her fingers appeared ordinary, but he had witnessed evidence of strength and skill in the slender digits.

"Done," she announced. Hanging the wiped cast-iron pot near the stove, she faced him. "All that remains is to discard the dishwater."

He snapped his towel open and draped the cloth over a chair back. "You are a talented woman, Mrs. Black. You make instructions sound pleasant to my ears."

She lowered her gaze.

"I do not wish to embarrass you. I state the truth. You sew…cook…teach your son good manners." He hesitated with his hands on the deep basin. "One day, you will make a man very happy. I pray for you to settle with a good man…who will give joy to your heart."

"You flatter me." She glanced toward the sleeping loft where Joseph had retreated.

"I speak the truth." He carried the dirty water through the porch and into the early night. Studying the almost full moon and a scattering a bright stars, he thought of George Rush standing in the cobbler's shop. *The American is a hard man…ambitious…determined. His wife seldom smiled.* A shiver from more than cool air raced across his shoulders.

A few moments later, the slop bucket emptied and stored, he surveyed Polly's apartment. He observed Joseph playing under the stairs and Polly selecting a garment from her sewing basket. Suddenly, he felt like a guest who overstayed his welcome. He cleared his throat. "I will go now. Thank you for the delicious supper and conversation."

"Draw one of the chairs closer and sit. I can mend and visit at the same time." She knotted a thread. "I want to ask you a question."

"Very well." Uncertain of the exact regional rules necessary to protect her reputation, he positioned a chair near the back door. Crossing one leg over the other, he lightly gripped his knee. "Does your question concern shoes?"

She smiled and selected a pale button from a dish

beside the glowing lard oil lamp. "Not tonight—your recent words stirred my curiosity. Do you think women marry to be happy?"

He rubbed his chin with two fingers and reminded himself to speak English. "I believe women...and men...marry for a great many reasons. I know of marriages arranged by family. Others are made for money...prestige...children...safety." He ticked off the words on his fingers and shifted in his chair. "From my humble point of observation, I think life goes better for both if they share affection for each other—a little joy and laughter makes work go better."

"You sound like a philosopher." She poked the needle another time to secure the button to a child-sized shirt. "Life can be difficult...plans can be disrupted." She lifted her gaze. "A person does well to remember life on earth is temporary—the lasting reward is in heaven."

"Is laughter forbidden?" He waited for her slight head shake. "I see pleasure in many things...sunrise, the scent of ripe apples, the racing notes of a polka...these happy things are good to share—no? A friend at your side increases the joy. Do you understand?"

She clipped a thread and fixed her gaze on him. "Are we friends?"

He uncrossed and recrossed his legs. Wriggling his fingers, which itched to touch her hand, he gave thanks his chair sat beyond reach. "I value you, Mrs. Black. Your voice is pleasant. Your smile is beautiful. I desire to be counted among your friends. Do you have room in your circle?"

"You give me undue honor, *Herr* Tafel. I shall

consider it my good fortune to be included in your company of friends."

"I am glad we have it settled." Tipping his face toward the floor for a moment, he won a struggle to limit his grin. He stood and turned toward the peg holding his coat and cap.

"Don't leave." Joseph straightened. "May I show you my game?"

Polly lifted the short scissors. "Stay. Spend the evening. Your company is a welcome change from routine."

"Are you certain?" He reviewed his recent activities and discovered too many evenings of sitting on his steps, smoking his pipe while thinking of Pennsylvania.

Joseph tossed an acorn from one hand to the other. "Please."

After a glance to Polly for silent permission, he squatted beside the boy. "Explain the game."

"The boys at school use marbles…from the store. If I take the cap off, an acorn rolls almost the same…sometimes." Joseph flicked one of several nuts on the floor and sent it sliding a few inches.

"Tell me, at school, do the boys draw a circle in the dirt?"

Joseph nodded. "I practice with an invisible circle. Mama does not allow chalk marks on the floor."

"I understand. Will you let me try?" Kurt opened his palm and waited for the boy to place a nut on his hand. Setting the practice marble on the floor, he touched his middle finger to his thumb, flicked the finger, and sent the acorn toward the pretend circle's center.

"Wow. You shoot an acorn better than Thomas managed with his new green-and-black marble."

Kurt blinked to banish memories of schoolyard games. "A person needs to practice. You shoot one, and I will watch."

Joseph set a nut into position, circled thumb and index finger, and jerked his finger against the acorn.

The toy rolled a few inches.

"You do it better." The boy collected scattered acorns from previous plays.

"Let me show you a trick." Kurt set three acorns in front of the boy and one near his own hand. "Can you copy the way I hold my right hand? Make the circle with thumb and longest finger. See?" A quarter hour later, he stood. "You are doing better. Remember the new way to hold your hand...and practice."

"Mama, did you play marbles at school?" Joseph turned toward her.

"No, son. When I was a schoolgirl, we played different games." She adjusted the close-woven, gray wool on her lap.

"Time for you to practice." Kurt worked the kinks out of his joints and pointed to the dozing cat. "Your pet will supervise while I chat with your mother." He stepped to the shelf which held a small collection of books. *All English.* "What are you sewing?"

"A winter cloak." She moistened the tip of black thread and poked it through a needle's eye.

"For yourself...or another?" Blinking, he broke the stare at nimble fingers connected to an agile mind. He awaited her response with more eagerness than any question he asked a dance partner. Polly poised the threaded needle near the cloth. "The shop is doing good business, and often, I work on garments for others in the evening. Tonight, I save for my own mending and sewing."

"If you did not work as a seamstress, how would you spend your evening?" He touched a small, metal, lidded box on the highest shelf. *Scorched…saved from the fire…this must be very precious.*

"Sometimes I read stories. My favorites are found in *Godey's Lady's Book.* Joseph prefers tales with kings, knights, and castles."

"Fables?" He sat, crossed his legs, and focused on her fingers. "We read from the Grimm Brothers stories in our household. *Mutter* teased us about wearing out the print. By the time my youngest brother, Helmut, finished school, most of the pages wore smudges from dirty fingers. I suppose my nephews read it now—or listen while my brother reads."

"All boys in your family?" She adjusted the garment across her lap.

"*Ja*—five brothers in the household. Our sis—" Swallowing a sudden, sour taste in his mouth, he hesitated before his next words. "Our sister died young—three years old."

Polly shifted her gaze to her stitches and gathered a deep, quiet breath. "You mentioned nephews…how many…how old?"

Speaking of the three nephews and one infant niece in the next Tafel generation, Kurt relaxed. "The oldest, tall for his age, started school fall term—like Joseph. On an evening with only family in the house, I expect they sing. I have fond memories of music in the parlor."

"Do you sing often?"

"At church…or when alone in the shop. I never

joined a singing society like my eldest brother—he has the best voice in the family. Do you know this one?" He began humming "*Muss i den*, Must, I then." When he reached the chorus, he repeated it an extra time. He stood and extended his hand. "Set aside your work and dance with me. You hinted you danced when you were a girl."

"True"—she curled her lower lip over her teeth—"many changes in my life since I danced. Now, I am a mother…with responsibilities…and I attend church."

"A little fun sprinkled with work is a good thing. God will forgive." He sang the second verse.

"You tempt me the same as the serpent coaxed Eve in Eden." She slipped her needle into the cloth and set the garment on top of her basket. "The tune is familiar. I expect my feet have forgotten the steps. I will trample you."

"Prove it." Aware his heart sped faster than the liveliest dance tune, he wriggled his fingers in an eager invitation. "Come…smile…laugh…have a little fun. We are private…save for a boy and a cat."

"You sing in *Deutsch*—tell me the story in the song." She smoothed her skirts.

"Later. Now I change the tune to one our American neighbors enjoyed." He collected his thoughts and began singing a reel with nonsense words. She tipped her head to one side and smiled. "I remember the same tune with different words."

Touching her hands only when required by the figure of the dance, he guided her for three verses—when he exhausted his ability to create suitable words. He ended with a flourish of a turn and a deep bow.

"Oh, my." She held one hand against her chest and

smiled with her entire face. "I forgot how many daily cares disappear during a dance."

"Music is good medicine." He lifted her right hand. "*Herr* Doctor Tafel recommends music and dance for your health." In the next instant, he dipped his head and brushed his lips across the back of her bare hand. He longed to linger on her soft…tender…tempting skin. He dabbed a second kiss before he lifted his head. Warmth raced from his fingers toward his heart. Blinking, he released her hand and regretted the loss. "Enjoy?"

She stood perfectly still and changed her mouth from a circle to a smile. Kurt pressed his lips and detected a flavor from her skin. *Lavender? Scented soap? Would her mouth taste of the raspberry jam she spread on biscuit?* He swallowed and came to his senses. Turning, he removed his coat and cap from the peg.

"*Herr* Tafel." Joseph approached to within one large step. "Thank you again for the shoes…and the marble lesson."

"You are welcome. Enjoy the brogans, young man. I expect your mother will seldom allow you to wear them inside the house."

"I will take care of the shoes, *Herr* Tafel. I will practice with the acorns and win the game when Thomas allows me to use a real marble."

"Good." He switched his attention to Polly. "I bid you farewell, Mrs. Black. I shall remember this evening in your company with great fondness." A few moments later, Kurt lingered in the street. In the dim moonlight, he spied a man hurrying along Apple Street. He shrugged. Tonight was the wrong time to accuse another of prowling the village streets at a late hour. He studied the sky until he found Orion's Belt. "She's a wonderful, smart, vibrant woman. Lord," he whispered into the night. "Please, do not allow anyone to damage her smile."

Chapter Fifteen

Polly glanced at Swifty sitting sentry on the third step to the sleeping loft and reached for the butter dish's cover. "Finish your last bite of lunch, Joseph. The clock has already struck two. I want to complete all the Saturday shopping before early dusk."

"Must I go? I promise to be good." He popped the last portion of bread crust into his mouth.

She regarded her son. Since he started attending school, he seldom accompanied her to the shops. However, the timing of customers yesterday prevented her from doing errands on Friday. "You must not pester Mrs. Clark."

"I will read my book. The knights in the stories did not go shopping with their mothers."

He is too young. He needs to have more independence. The familiar debate circled in her mind.

The shop clock chimed the half hour.

"I will have a word with Mrs. Clark."

Fifteen minutes later, reciting her shopping list under her breath, Polly stepped inside Winston's grocery. She carried her basket directly to the potato barrel and selected enough to last until Tuesday. At the keg of dried peas, she opened her small, cloth bag and measured three generous scoops. "Good day, Mrs. Clemons." She greeted the lady as they both inspected onions.

The dry goods merchant's wife responded with a definite frown and a slight nod before she switched her attention to the squash.

Polly glanced down. She saw no stains on her dress and all her buttons were fastened. Nothing obvious should have prompted the other woman's atypical behavior. A few moments later, she stood at the counter and added two eggs to her basket.

"Put them back." Mr. Winston added a point of his finger toward the eggs and practically growled the words.

"I will pay...today...in full." She forced her gaze to remain on the grocer's face. Today, she had the coins to cover the two bits due on her account and purchase several days' supplies.

"Pay your debt and leave my store." He pointed to her level-full basket.

She blinked at the usually cordial man. "Why?"

"My business doesn't sell to the likes of you." He grabbed two potatoes from her basket and set them on a shelf behind the counter.

Likes of me. She worried her lower lip and stiffened her knees against a building tremble. *I suppose one man told another until my exit from the hotel supper is common knowledge.* "Tell me, what has changed since my previous visit? I do hope you are not inclined to believe gossip."

"A merchant has the right to do business with who he pleases." He snatched the bag of peas. "I choose not to sell to you."

"The cloth sack is mine." Aware her cheeks were heating, she focused on the spice jars visible over his shoulder.

Shrugging, he loosened the drawstring over a crockery bowl. With a firmer-than-necessary shake, he ensured not even one dried pea remained.

She set a coin for her account balance onto the counter. "I believe you give too much weight to words from the wrong people." She opened her mouth and closed it without additional words. The question—did he choose to do business with the ladies in the rooms over the American tavern—the two who practiced the world's oldest profession?—dried in her throat.

"Go"—he swished his hands above the counter.

She drew a deep breath for courage and grasped her basket's handle. "Good day, Mr. Winston." She spun on her toes, kept her back straight, and marched toward the door.

The second American grocer, Mr. Davis, demanded her exit from his store the moment she touched an onion.

Clenching her basket's handle to steady her fingers, she stepped across the threshold of the third grocery. She smelled mold in the still air. Glancing at darkened apples and shriveled potatoes, she suspected pigs might refuse the produce. In the next moment, she departed and cursed Mr. Rush under her breath. *I know a good butcher and baker—where will I find the other things?* She straightened her spine, snapped her fingers, and set off for a shop on Fifth Street. *I pray I can find the proper* Deutsch *words to buy what I need.*

****

Monday evening, Kurt set his fork on the delicate plate and glanced around the bakery apartment. "Excellent meal, *Frau* Keil and *Fraulein* Mueller. The sweet cherry *Kuchen*"—he rimmed his lips—"better than my *Mutter* bakes."

"*Danke*—you are too kind." Louisa lowered her gaze.

"I speak the truth. If I am ever in need of more than a loaf of hearty rye bread or a sweet cinnamon bun, I shall buy a fruit *Kuchen.* "

Charlotte collected the dessert dishes. "You best wait until you have a guest or two. If you, and the young boy who frequents your shop, ate an entire *Kuchen*...you would have the stomachache, and he would have an angry mother.

"Perhaps I should seek a tin cupboard among the merchants." He curved his lips and hoped she understood his good-natured tease.

Frau Keil laughed.

He pushed his chair from the table and stood. "I will assist in the cleaning after such a fine meal. You were so kind to share your table when I requested a simple conversation." *Perhaps not so simple a topic. Frau Keil speaks little of her late husband. I do not trust the snatches of conversation in the tavern.*

"Are you certain you want to dry dishes?" Louisa wrapped the remaining *Kuchen* in a linen cloth.

"Accept your good fortune, Louisa." Charlotte set a shallow, wooden tub on the worktable. "I recall you saying you wished to write a reply to your friend Bertha, the carpenter's wife, in St. Louis."

Louisa nodded and walked toward the peg holding her shawl. "*Ja.* I will write a letter, make the bread sponges, and retire for the night. Unlike Hans and me, you do not require a chaperon."

Changing a laugh into a cough, Kurt choked. The widow Keil, an admirable woman, aroused no feeling within him beyond friendship. "Now that you mention his name—where is your *Schatz*?"

"Hans, and *Herr* Bergmann, left after lunch to inspect some horses. I believe the farm is some distance on the Peoria Road. They will return tomorrow, during the afternoon." She slipped out the door.

Listening to Louisa's footsteps fade on the outside steps, Kurt sighed. From his humble perspective, he thought Hans and Louisa well-suited and wished them happiness.

"From the way your cheeks colored when I suggested we speak on the church lawn, I suspect you desire to speak of Polly Black and her son." Charlotte poured hot water over bits of shaved soap in the tub.

"I am uneasy with gossip and rumors. I hear whispers that *Herr* Keil fathered Mrs. Black's child. Do you know the truth?" He sealed his lips and glanced toward the floor. After his poor phrasing, he would not fault the lady if she requested he leave.

Tick...tock...tick.

Charlotte rubbed a soapy rag over a saucer. "*Ja, Herr* Keil is Joseph's father."

"I sense more to the story." He dried the first clean dish.

"Bernard Keil arrived in Elm Ridge during September of forty-five. He promptly opened the bakery. At the time, I was a widow working as a laundress." She emptied the dregs from the teapot. "Each time Bernard brought aprons, towels, and other items to the laundry, we exchanged a few pleasant words. He did not make any unwelcome advances. He minded his own affairs. I noticed he attended church regular."

One by one, Kurt discarded assumptions formed from the scattered comments.

She rubbed a stubborn spot off a spoon. "In the spring, when the wildflowers bloomed, he invited me for a Sunday drive. He rented the gig and horse from Bergmann. We drove out the South Road to a lovely spot with a view of the river."

Setting the lid beside the dried teapot, Kurt conquered the desire to have her hurry the story.

"That day, *Herr* Keil stared at the swollen river and told me of Polly Black. I am not certain of the exact times—but some months after his first wife died, he moved to a different St. Louis boardinghouse. Polly lived in the same residence. A trio of *Deutsch* seamstresses were teaching Polly the fine points of their trade. Many evenings in the parlor, she and the other ladies sewed while he read the *Deutsch* newspaper aloud. I also believe much pipe-smoking and general conversation in both English and *Deutsch* took place."

Nodding at the account of a proper courtship, Kurt wiped the final piece of flatware.

"The arrangements for marriage were in place— each tells—told—a story with the same details. However, Polly's brother, Leo, returned from a lengthy trip to the West. He forbade the marriage—to the point of threatening Bernard's life if he did not leave the city. Polly claims Leo locked her in her room for weeks and burned any correspondence. Bernard did not know of the boy."

Kurt figured the months and nodded. "*Herr* Keil sent her a letter?"

"I am aware he paid Mr. Cook to write in English. I believe in early summer—but I am uncertain of the

Ellen Parker

exact time—or if he had written earlier in *Deutsch.*"

Kurt frowned and arranged the sparse facts. "He received no word?"

"Correct—no letter. Bernard made inquiries at the levee, and among the American merchants, during the entire summer. I believed him when he said he had done the same in his early months in Elm Ridge." She wrung the rag after the last dish was clean. "One year and two weeks after *Herr* Keil arrived, we married. Over the four years and eight months of our marriage, he taught me much of the bakery business."

"Mrs. Black arrived this May?" *I will continue to do her the honor of a widow's title.*

"*Ja,* but troubles arrived earlier, in March."

"Did your husband receive a letter?" He set the final dish on the table.

Charlotte poured the dishwater into the slops bucket. "*Nein,* worse than any letter—Leo Black—the same man who aimed a gun at Bernard in St. Louis, arrived with money in his pockets."

Kurt stilled and failed to find mention of Polly's brother in any of the conversations with the seamstress or in the American shops he visited.

"Mr. Black acquired the smaller of the two grain mills. The bakery purchased from this mill—good product from the previous owner. Mr. Black raised the price. Soon, the quality suffered...lumpy...damp...sour before we reached the bottom of the barrel." She set dishes into the cupboard and gestured Kurt to sit. "I did not hear all the arguments between my husband and the miller. Fierce—the few I did witness. Twice, Mr. Black tramped into the bakery and shouted when customers were present. English—always English with him—

190

never did I hear even a simple word of *Deutsch* cross his lips. At the end—days before Bernard died—he raged and threatened the bakery's reputation if we purchased from Gordon's mill."

"Blackmail." Kurt spat. "He used his knowledge of Joseph as a threat."

"Polly walked into the shop a day or two later. Bernard puzzled over how to deal with the situation. I want to believe he would have found a way to acknowledge the boy."

Kurt arranged a crude timeline, but he found large gaps. "What happened to Leo? I hear no word of him when I speak to Americans."

"A few weeks after Bernard's death, a cyclone destroyed the mill and a nearby home. Mr. Black was injured. Polly, and others, persuaded him to sell the ruined building to the foreman, a local man of decent character, and leave town. Leo knew little of milling— many *Deutsch* farmers stopped taking grain to him. I suppose Mr. Gordon benefited the most."

Rubbing his chin, Kurt studied the bakery owner. "Yet, you chose Polly as your friend. She told me of the fire and your kindness."

"I will never have children of my own." She sighed. "Polly is a capable woman—intelligent and caring. I am selfish and want to treat Joseph as a nephew." She settled on the settee and regarded him with narrowed eyes. "You ask more questions than is common for a neighbor."

"I-I am fond of the boy." He paused and searched for neutral words. "The mother...she has a sweet smile."

Charlotte glanced toward the ceiling. "Follow your

heart, *Herr* Tafel. Louisa tells me you dance with many at the beer garden. Who lightens your heart when you waltz?"

"You ask a difficult question." *Polly warmed my fingers with excitement when we danced the reel.* "Many people settle for a mate they can tolerate."

"Too much drink and bad habits grow from such a marriage…soon, one or both are miserable. I am twice widowed…unsure if I am in the best position to give advice." She crossed her ankles. "Follow your heart."

The clock chimed the hour.

Kurt stood. "I will take my leave. Thank you for the delicious meal and enlightening conversation. You have given me much to ponder." A short time later, Kurt paused on the sidewalk beside the dress shop. He studied the pale light spilling from the window. *She works into the night…sewing a respectable life for her and Joseph…one stitch at a time.*

Chapter Sixteen

Tuesday afternoon, Polly set three widths of black ribbon on the worktable. "Black cotton is an excellent choice for the new mud ring. With narrow, black stripes in the primary fabric, the alteration blends into the original. I suggest a four-inch width. The current style is to hide the seam with a wide ribbon, then finish with a ring or two of trim above the new fabric. See…here is a drawing."

"I don't know." Mrs. Fox fingered the tightly woven cotton on the bolt.

The back door slammed.

Polly shifted her attention to sounds from the living quarters. On most schooldays, she could visualize Joseph's movements from the sounds of his stocking feet or his high voice coaxing the cat out of her napping spot.

Clump-thump.

She stared at the drape and frowned. *He knows the rules—leave his shoes on the back porch.* Sealing her lips before she voiced a scold, she faced her customer. "Excuse me, I must have a word with my son."

"No trouble." Mrs. Fox smoothed the skirt spread across the worktable.

The moment the curtain swished behind her, Polly stilled. The cross words climbing her throat slid below her stomach. "What is the matter?"

Joseph stood at the table with his face hidden in his arms. "The boys…" he mumbled.

"What did the boys do?" She listened to more complaints about the children in the schoolyard than about the lessons. Although, in recent weeks, her son spoke well of two or three friends.

He lifted his head. "I'm sorry, Mama."

She stepped forward, set two fingers under his chin, examined his face, and failed to see any signs of fisticuffs. "Tell me what happened."

"The boys…Thomas…my friends…" He wiped at escaping tears and swallowed. "They called you names. Bad names…words you told me not to use. And words I did not know. What is a har…harlot?"

Polly's heart turned heavy as stone. "We will discuss names after the shop closes. What did you reply?"

"I called them liars." He blinked with moist eyelashes. "I no longer have friends. I liked games with the other boys."

She struggled to hold back angry words meant for the adults who cursed in front of children. *I sinned— and confessed to God. Others have no right to insult my innocent child.* She eased to the wash basin and dampened a cloth. A moment later, she wiped his face. "Better?"

"A little." He planted one elbow on the table and rested his head against his open hand.

"Put your shoes and coat where they belong. You may look at the King Arthur book while I finish with a customer. After you do your chores, we will talk about your ill-mannered schoolmates."

"Yes, Mama. Thank you, Mama." He wrapped his

arms around her waist and snuggled against her apron.

She pulled off his cap and ruffled his hair. "I must return to the shop."

"Where's Swifty?" He eased back.

"First, see to your shoes and coat." She drew a deep breath and glanced toward the ceiling. Trouble, from adults, after she embarrassed Mr. Rush at the hotel, found her during Saturday errands—and in the refusal of anyone to speak with her after church. *I see no need to attack my child.* She mouthed the words toward the ceiling. Blinking, she switched her mind to the task at hand and returned to the shop. "I apologize, a little matter with my son." She forced a small smile. "Have you decided on the trim?"

"Children, a blessing and trouble at the same time. We raised one boy and two girls. Each child gave Mr. Fox and me a few sleepless nights." The cooper's wife, a mild-mannered woman near twice Polly's age, pointed to the widest ribbon. "One row, to hide the seam—three rows, like the illustration, is too fussy for my taste."

"Have you considered a narrow ribbon on the upper sleeve? A slight change might make the gown feel new." She kept a portion of her attention on sounds from the other side of the drape.

The doorbell tinkled.

Polly sidestepped for a better view. "Welcome back. I trust your errands were a success."

Mrs. Clark darted her gaze into the workroom, nodded to Mrs. Fox, and removed her pale-green cloak. "Enlightening—we shall talk."

"Indeed." She would welcome a private moment with Abigail. Returning her attention to Mrs. Fox, Polly kept the conversation on the topics of length, price, and completion date. She jotted a note and pinned the information to the damaged portion of the skirt.

The bell still tinkled with Mrs. Fox's departure when Polly opened the curtain and peeked into the apartment.

Joseph, wearing his magic shoes, sat on the bottom step and hid his face in his arms. Swifty batted a paw at his thigh.

My son is not in the habit of ignoring his pet. Aware of her heart crumbling at the sight of her young son faced with adult difficulties, she held her tears.

"I think"—Abigail thumped a bolt of cloth on a shelf—"we will close now. Polly, will you be so kind as to make tea?"

"Of course, I'll check the kettle." She glanced at the clock and noted it was only thirty minutes before the usual closing hour. A few minutes later, Abigail entered the living quarters and strode directly to Joseph. "Young man—look at me."

Moving his head the minimum to comply, he blinked at Mrs. Clark. "I am sorry, ma'am. I do not mean to cause trouble."

"Accepted. What did your schoolmates do?" The shop owner held her gaze on his face.

Wiping evidence of tears away with the back of one hand, he straightened. "They called Mama names...bad names. I-I thought Thomas was my friend...but he laughed at me. He called my foot a curse."

"Not a good business." Abigail set both hands on her hips and leaned close. "You had a hard lesson today. I think you need to prepare for more to come."

He directed his gaze toward his mother. "Can…may I stay home? You can teach me to spell and read…from the storybook."

Polly added two pinches of tea to the empty pot. "No…you must attend school. You need to be brave. The knights in your favorite stories won the battle only when they faced the enemy."

"Brave is hard." He gathered the cat in both arms and held her against his chest.

"I know, son. Time to do your chores. I will save you a ginger cookie from our tea." *Brave—I fear my display of courage to Mr. Rush is responsible for a large portion of today's troubles.*

The instant the door closed behind Joseph, Abigail sighed.

Polly selected two cups and saucers from the cupboard. "Are the shops full of gossip?"

"Yes, do you know the start of it?"

"I suspect Mr. Rush is at the root. He was not pleased when I left the table at the hotel." If she closed her eyes and recalled the evening, she found herself listening for his footsteps to follow her home. "I told you of my difficulties in the shops during Saturday errands."

"The man wields a lot of influence in Elm Ridge." Abigail collected the sugar bowl.

Polly swallowed and arranged cookies on a white plate. "Do you want us to leave?"

Joseph entered with the first armload of wood.

Abigail shook her head and assisted setting the table in silence until the back door closed behind the boy. "Would you give Mr. Rush a victory so easy? No, instead of fleeing to St. Louis, or moving in with your friends over the bakery, I want you to live here and continue your work in the shop. You are a talented dressmaker. Slander, if unfed, shrivels and dies."

"The rumors might taint your reputation." Polly lifted the kettle from the stove. As she poured the hot water over the tea leaves, she nodded toward Joseph.

He carried the second portion of wood and dropped it into the tin pail. As if a gust of north wind found a hole in her invisible cloak, she shivered. A moment later, she checked to ensure he took the water bucket.

"I have lived in Elm Ridge a year for each of the months since you arrived." Abigail glanced through the window by the sewing chair. "Most of the American women have stepped into my shop at one time or another."

"How can I defend my son when some of the accusations will be true? I took him to Bernard's grave a little more than a week ago. I wanted him to learn his father's name from me. I feared rumors—but not the close timing. Mr. Rush did not delay." Polly gestured Abigail to sit.

"Have you spoken to the man since the shortened dinner at the hotel?"

Polly swallowed. "We exchanged brief greetings at church. He was on the steps, giving the appearance of waiting for us to arrive. As he often does, *Herr* Tafel accompanied Joseph and me to the edge of the property." She hesitated, remembered migrating geese overhead, and the cobbler's brief kiss on her glove. She promptly closed her lips as Joseph entered with the water.

"Chores are all done, Mama. Can…May I have my cookie?" He brushed his hands across his trousers.

"Yes, you may." She handed him the dark, sweet treat. "Go and eat on the back step. Mrs. Clark and I need to have an adult conversation."

"Can...May I visit *Herr* Tafel?" He pleaded with his eyes.

She hesitated only a moment. *Any damage from our friendship is already done.* "Do not pester if he is working."

"I promise." He gave Mrs. Clark a bow before turning and exiting through the back door.

"*Herr* Tafel, the situation becomes a little clearer." Abigail poured the tea.

"He is a friend—a neighbor." *The problem at hand is Mr. Rush and his revenge for my refusing his marriage proposal. I do not see* Herr *Tafel's involvement.* "He would spoil Joseph if I allowed. I did not request the brogans—but I paid him—in coin—plus a supper at our table."

Leaning back in her chair, Abigail smiled. "Friday supper? Your Saturday errands—which took double the usual time—upset you."

"Mr. Winston refused me service...as did Mr. Davis. I purchased from the *Deutsch* grocer on Fifth Street—with many gestures on my part and words I did not understand on his. I doubt an American woman ever set foot in his store before." She bit into a cookie and allowed the spices to bloom in her mouth.

"*Herr* Tafel is a handsome man...vigorous...not married." Abigail straightened. "Or did he leave a wife back East?"

"He speaks of parents and brothers with fondness. He has never mentioned wife or sweetheart. Do you suspect...?"

Ellen Parker

"I believe Mr. Rush is accustomed to getting his way." Abigail sipped tea. "Has Mr. Rush seen you with the cobbler?"

"Several times—*Herr* Tafel often accompanies Joseph and me to church before he continues to the German Lutheran Church." *At parting, he shakes Joseph's hand and brushes his lips across my glove.* "Everything is proper between us."

"The cobbler, with his *Deutsch* language and habits, is viewed with suspicion by George Rush and his friends. Has Pastor Harter called on you?"

Polly stilled. An unrequested visit from the stern preacher implied unacceptable behavior. "Should he?"

"Not in my opinion. However, I do not know what ideas have been planted in his head." Abigail popped the final bite of cookie into her mouth. "Delicious, my compliments to Keil's Bakery."

Polly sighed. "Once more, my son lacks friends. I do hope he does not attempt fisticuffs—most of the boys are larger."

Abigail tapped a finger on the table. "I fear the lad is on his own at school. You are right to make him go back tomorrow. I have an idea for you—and the shop."

"I am willing to listen." Polly set her cup in the saucer and leaned forward.

"How near to finished are the Gordon girls' dresses?"

Polly wrinkled her brow. "The larger one lacks a portion of hem and the ribbons."

"Will you be able to finish tonight?"

"Yes, but why? You told me Mrs. Gordon was returning on Friday." She tilted her head.

"I think," Abigail mused. "Tomorrow, late

morning, you will deliver the frocks and get acquainted with the Gordon ladies. Mrs. Gordon, the elder of the two, is the mayor's wife and influential in her own right."

Polly sipped her final mouthful of tea. "Am I right to picture him as clean-shaven, a hook nose, and old enough to be my father?" She waited for Abigail's nod. "I fail to recall his wife. I hear good comments of the flour mill. Does he own other businesses in town?"

"The family owns several lots and rents the buildings. A married son shares the house and works alongside his father. The other son is away—reading for the law—in Springfield, I think." Abigail stood. "Yes, your task tonight is to finish the dress. I will ask my brother-in-law a few discreet questions this evening. He worked with the Gordons three years ago when the levee was improved. You and I will make final plans in the morning."

Polly left the table and followed her employer to the shop. A portion of her mind looked forward to visiting the Gordon women. *Mr. Gordon is mayor—a position Mr. Rush desires. I do not understand how an acquaintance with the Gordon ladies will change a grocer's mind or stop insults on the schoolyard.* "You have given me much to think on. I will complete the dress while I sort recent events."

"I detest gossip and slander." Abigail fastened her pale green cloak. "I see no profit in humiliating another person."

A few moments later, Polly stood on the shop's front step and watched Mrs. Clark cross the street toward her sister's home.

The foundry whistle dismissed the workers.

She shifted her gaze to the cobbler's shop across the street where soft light shone from the large window. *One tall and one small figure move inside—Joseph sought out his friend.* Herr *Tafel is a good man—patient and kind.* Glancing toward the darkening sky, she moved her lips. *I must seal my heart. The fire in Kurt's touch during the dance should be a warning.*

****

After the final Tuesday foundry whistle faded, and his shop was tidied for the night, Kurt rounded his building with Joseph at his side. "Mrs. Black, are you looking for someone?"

"Mama." Joseph hurried toward her in his magic shoes and awkward gait.

Polly stepped to the sidewalk and welcomed his small form with open arms. "I suspected the two of you would be together."

"He helped me close the shop for the day." Kurt tipped his head to one side and waited.

"Mrs. Clark headed home a few moments ago. I was searching for the first star and debating which door to approach."

He studied her fingers clasping and released her shawl's edge. "I go to the tavern for supper. Joseph tells me school was difficult today. I refused to take him as an apprentice at such a tender age."

"Many thanks." She climbed the dress shop's steps and rested one hand on the doorknob.

He raised his right hand to touch his cap. "I bid you good evening."

"*Herr* Tafel." She paused. "I rest no blame on you…for any current troubles in my household."

"I-I fail to understand." He opened his mouth to

ask specifics but stopped the words. Perhaps, she was not familiar with the frequency at which schoolboys tossed insults at each other.

She opened the door. "Matters are too difficult to explain this minute. Please understand, in any rumor or gossip, I consider you innocent."

For a full minute after the door closed behind the pair, he stood and rubbed his chin. "Which gossip? Is Mr. Rush involved? Joseph's father?" He questioned the deepening dusk and heard only the creak of a passing wagon.

Half an hour later, laughter erupted from a table near the tavern door.

Kurt turned his head toward the group before he spooned a final bite of potato and onion from his bowl. *Foundry workers—I think. After I finish my beer and light my pipe, I must go introduce myself—take a closer look at their shoes.* He sipped the beer and closed his eyes.

"May I join you?"

Kurt snapped open his eyes at the familiar voice. "Welcome, *Herr* Hoffmann. *Bitte,* please, sit and tell me how things go at the stables."

Placing his steaming stew bowl and full beer stein on the table, Hans settled on a stool. In slow motion, he removed his cap, stored it on his lap, and sighed. "Busy…stable work is never done."

"I believe you." He smiled at his friend. "Tell me, why do you eat at the tavern? I thought you would be dining at the bakery."

Hans blew across a spoonful of turnip. "Worked too late—the two new horses—they are slow to settle. Neither of them had heard a steamboat or foundry whistle until we brought them into town this afternoon. However, they drive well when the air is filled with forest sounds or meeting other traffic. They will learn—soon—I pray."

"Is *Herr* Bergmann expanding his business?" He searched for clues in his brief conversation with the stablemaster a week past. *The man spoke of busy times…with merchants receiving large shipments to last while the river is frozen.*

Hans shrugged. "My boss does not confide in me. A man left the levee warehouse. Do you know of anyone in need of steady work?"

Swallowing the final mouthful of beer, Kurt shook his head. "I wonder…I have heard whispers of a man and think you might be able to tell me true."

"I have only been in Elm Ridge since April." Hans tugged a soft bite of bread from the chunk supplied with supper.

"I understand. You know the seamstress, Mrs. Black?" Kurt waited for a nod. "Can you tell me of her brother?"

Hans chewed a sausage slice and swallowed. "Unpleasant man—only English words, but a rough, angry tone the one time I crossed his path. He threatened to take the bakery from *Frau* Keil before she had a full week to mourn her husband."

Kurt clamped his jaw to delay a rude exclamation and clenched a hand below the table. "Only the lowest of scoundrels scheme against a new widow."

"Ja, many failed to hide a smile the day Mr. Black was injured in cyclone." Hans gripped his stein with trembling hands. "Excuse, I am not fond of American storms—the cyclone sounded like the end of the world.

Return as…nightmare."

Kurt searched his pockets and found his smoking supplies. He packed sweet tobacco into the pipe bowl and watched two young men approach their table.

"Guten Abend. Herr Tafel *und Herr* Hoffmann." Christian Giesel smiled and indicated the man beside him. *"Mein Bruder,* Max, arrived from St. Louis."

"Bitte, we have room at this table for two more." Kurt noted a similar build, hair, and nose between the brothers, however, Max's eyes were darker. "Tell us, have you also trained as a stonemason?"

Max claimed a stool, and Christian went to speak with the tavernkeeper. *"Nein.* Less than a month ago, I finished my apprenticeship with a cabinetmaker."

Kurt stifled the question poised at the back of his tongue. The reason for one brother to join another was not his concern. "Have you been in Elm Ridge before?"

Max flashed a smile. "I lived with my brother and worked in a portion of *Herr* Thayer's barn last winter. This year…if I get sufficient orders before spring thaw…I stay longer."

My home lacks furniture. I must be careful of the money. He nodded and lit his pipe. "I have lived here only a short time and find the village lively. Do you speak English?"

"Enough to manage…*Deutsch* community in St. Louis is large…a man can find all he needs with or without English." Max unbuttoned his coat.

"Don't believe him." Christian set a full stein in front of Max. "It is true he will live with me for the weeks before my wedding. Then, he will continue at the boardinghouse and court the fickle Bertha Thayer."

Kurt laughed. "I tell you now…she is only a dance

partner to me."

"Ahhh...then you are the good dancer she chattered about from the time I stepped into the Thayer home until Jacob bid her keep silent." Max smiled with his eyes above the rim of his drink. "She is beautiful."

Hans pushed his empty bowl toward the table's center. "Did you bring a newspaper?"

Max grinned and removed a folded paper from his coat.

Kurt blew a stream of smoke toward the low ceiling. Over the next hour, he smoked, listened, and supplied a few words to the discussion of the articles. *Near as pleasant as talking with Mrs. Black. However, she is more pleasing to the eyes.*

Chapter Seventeen

At a few minutes past ten o'clock Wednesday morning, Polly marched along Apple Street. She noted the frost still lingered in the shade. The mid-November sun, filtered through high clouds, offered scant warmth. She crossed Fifth Street and nodded to a woman sweeping her steps. Stiffening her shoulders, she walked proudly, determined to display courage. She adjusted the basket over her arm and repeated Mrs. Clark's final instructions in silence.

A pair of hogs grunted while they explored a rubbish pile.

Polly sighted the two-story, brick home the moment she reached Seventh Street. Drawing a deep breath, she crossed the street and hurried along the flagstone path toward the front door. She paused on the porch and admired the stained glass fanlight—only the grandest homes in St. Louis bore such a feature. After brushing a hand across her skirt, she lifted the plain, black knocker. *Once…twice…will a servant or the lady of the house respond?*

A pale-haired woman, near Polly's age, with a child on her hip, opened the door. "Are you expected?"

"My name is Polly Black." She clenched the basket handle until her knuckles paled. "I come from Mrs. Clark's dress shop to deliver two children's frocks."

"Oh, I planned to call for the dresses at the end of

the week. No matter, you are here now. Come inside." The stranger retreated enough to allow easy entrance.

Polly stepped into a foyer decorated with polished wood panels. A wide staircase with a generous landing stood on her left. A simple brass chandelier, holding eight short candles, hung from the high, plain ceiling. She heard a phrase of piano music, a pause, and the notes repeated.

"Mother Gordon and my eldest, Suzanne, the reluctant musician, are in the parlor. My name is Martha. My husband is the younger Mr. Gordon." She touched the knob of a door almost concealed in the paneling. "The child staring at you is Lizzie."

"Pleased to make your acquaintance." Polly swallowed a knot of unease.

"Who have you found?"

Polly shifted her attention to the speaker, a stout woman with dark-brown hair shot with gray. *Mrs. Gordon—a woman of influence in her own right.* Mrs. Clark's words circled once before she found her voice. "I am Polly Black. I deliver children's frocks from Mrs. Clark's dress shop."

"Black." The older woman frowned and lifted wire-rimmed spectacles from a small octagonal table. "A former resident of Elm Ridge of the same name was an ignorant, pompous man. My granddaughters know more of milling than he."

Aware all her blood rushed to her feet, Polly stared at the floor. With her legs unable to move at the moment, she managed to erase a scowl before she raised her gaze to the elder Mrs. Gordon. She blinked and found an anger-tinged courage when Mr. Rush's face formed in her imagination. "I agree. Leo Black, my brother, knew nothing of grain. Elm Ridge is better for his departure—though I pray for all honest people when he takes advantage of them in his new residence."

Mother Gordon lifted one side of her mouth into a small, uneven smile. "Brother...you give an interesting description...and maintain my confidence in Mrs. Clark as a judge of character. Show us the dresses, if you please." Mrs. Gordon switched her attention to her daughter-in-law. "Martha, will you please ask cook to prepare tea? Milk and a cookie for the children—in the kitchen."

Suzanne slipped from the piano stool and stood beside her grandmother. "Did she bring our Christmas frocks? Will mine have red ribbons?"

Polly glanced from the settee with deep-red cushions to a green-and-cream upholstered chair. In the next moment, she removed the protective, black cloth from the basket and draped the first dress across the settee's back.

"Mine...mine..." Lizzie extended both arms toward the frocks while her mother carried her from the room. Hesitating with the second gown on her arm, Polly prayed for a steady voice. "Shall I bring them closer?"

"No need." Mrs. Gordon stood and advanced the few steps necessary. Carefully, she lifted the smaller dress and examined a seam. "Very good. Fine stitches. Needlework and I..." She shook her head. "My hands are better at tending flowers, vegetables, and fruit trees than sewing."

"Is this one mine?" The girl pointed toward the rose gown with darker rose ribbons.

"Yes, Suzanne. Now, let the kind, dress shop lady

unbutton your pinafore and day dress so we might see how beautiful you will look on Christmas Day."

Martha, with Lizzie in tow, returned as Polly tied Suzanne's sash into a bow.

"Look, Mama. Ready for the party." The child twirled across the room.

Lizzie clapped. "Me. Dance."

"One moment"—Martha squatted and held her younger daughter's arm—"no dance until we check if your party dress fits."

A short time later, when the dresses had been modeled and examined, Polly knelt and buttoned Suzanne's pinafore over a simple, tan dress.

"Thank you, Jennie."

The elder Mrs. Gordon's words prompted Polly to glance toward the door.

A tall, thin woman holding a dark tray stood one step inside the room. A plain, white, tea service and a plate of tiny ginger cookies were visible over the lacquered rim.

"Jennie, please meet Polly, from Mrs. Clark's dress shop." Martha broke a growing silence.

Rising, Polly concealed her surprise with a small smile. With black hair in a single braid, high cheekbones, and bronzed skin, the woman appeared like a young copy of Madam Robineau, the St. Louis landlady. She glanced at the woman's feet peeking from a calico gown's hem. Releasing a small smile, she noted practical, round toe shoes. "A pleasure to meet you."

"Suzanne, Lizzie, go with cook and eat your treat in the kitchen." Martha moved a book on a round table to make room for the tray. "Jennie, one cookie each…no more."

The door was barely closed behind the trio when the elder Mrs. Gordon motioned Polly to the settee. "Sit…sit…how to you take your tea?"

"No milk…one sugar, if you please." She settled on the thick upholstery and searched for the proper words to open the primary topic.

The elder Mrs. Gordon tapped one finger on her chair's arm. "What is the real reason for your visit? Is it Mrs. Black…or Miss?"

"Most call me Mrs. Black…I have a son." She hid trembling hands in her skirt.

"My name is Geraldine—most call me Mrs. Gordon." She smiled and accepted a cup of tea from her daughter-in-law.

"Tell us of your boy," Martha urged. "You appear too young for him to be more than a wee lad."

"My son, Joseph, started school this term." She alternated her gaze between the Gordon ladies and ignored the cup of tea she held. *Tell more—before they assume worse.* "My son and I arrived in Elm Ridge in May. I had reason to believe Joseph's father lived in the village. My information was correct. However, he died suddenly, without an opportunity to meet his son."

Martha glanced toward her mother-in-law.

Are they searching for a name to fit my description? Do they know many in the Deutsch *community?* Polly took her first taste of the rich, warm tea.

"You tell an interesting story." Geraldine sipped her drink. "Do most assume you are a widow and treat you accordingly?"

Polly warmed under the woman's steady gaze.

"Yes, the merchants and others did so until recently. I fear I have angered a man…an influential man."

"His name?" Geraldine leaned forward.

"Rush…George Rush." She glanced toward the generous, tall window.

Martha raised her right hand to her lips. "Were you…were you the woman at the hotel dining room?"

Closing her eyes, Polly wished to disappear into the floor rather than give details of the humiliating scene. A moment later, she cleared her throat and glanced first to Martha and then Mother Gordon. "I refused his crude marriage proposal and walked home alone."

"I do not mean to cause you embarrassment." Martha hurried her next words. "Stuart, my husband's younger brother, was in Elm Ridge for the court term last week. He was not present at the hotel, but the incident filled the talk between court cases the next day. I have not spoken of it with others."

"All in this house abhor rumors." *Tap-tap-tap.* Geraldine exhibited simmering thought with a finger against the wooden chair arm. "Jane Rush died in childbirth less than two months past. Has he taken liberties?"

"No, ma'am, not in the way you imply. He claims to need a wife to raise his daughter. She is living with relatives on a farm some miles distant. I spoke plain and urged him to hire a housekeeper."

"A sensible man would not need prompting. Within a few minutes' time, I could name several women agreeable to such a position." Geraldine bit into a cookie.

"At present, the merchants, the same I conducted

business with since I set foot in Elm Ridge, refuse me service. The schoolboys follow the example of their parents and torment my son. I managed recent errands with *Deutsch* merchants, but I lack many of the words."

Geraldine set her cup and saucer on the table. "I understand you attend the American church on Sixth Street."

"Correct. Mrs. Clark mentioned her place of worship during our first conversation—the day she hired me. I find the pastor and men of the congregation stricter than the neighborhood church I frequented in St. Louis."

"Sunday, I wish you and your son to attend the Cherry Street Meeting House. Service begins at ten." Geraldine lifted her gaze. "Martha, which day do you think best to invite Mrs. King to tea?"

Polly alternated her gaze between the Gordon women. Evidently, they believed not worshiping under the same roof as Mr. Rush would be the first step away from his current influence. *Cherry Street Meeting House—I have passed the building several times. Opposite direction—no excuse for* Herr *Tafel to accompany.*

"Tomorrow—will you send a note?" Martha waited for a nod, then faced Polly. "Mr. Hopewell, the schoolmaster, currently lodges with Mrs. Chance. Friday, during my regular call on the lady, I will mention your son's difficulties in passing."

Geraldine stared at the dresses displayed across the settee's back. "I will use your name, not Mrs. Clark's, when I compliment the sewing."

A clock in another room chimed the hour.

Standing, Polly savored the kindness of the Gordon

ladies for a long moment. Hope for a resolution to her most immediate problems sprouted as she collected her shawl and basket. "I must return to work in the shop. Joseph and I will see you on Sunday. I look forward to meeting a new group of friends."

Martha and Geraldine escorted her to the front entrance.

Polly placed one foot across the threshold.

"A reputation is a woman's fragile cloak—she needs to keep it well mended."

Polly faced Geraldine. "You repeat a worthy, and familiar, proverb."

During the return walk to the shop, she pondered the state of her reputation. *All rests on a delicate foundation. My skill with a needle means nothing if others do not pay for my work. Should all come crashing down, I would harm my few friends; Abigail...Charlotte...Herr Tafel.*

Chapter Eighteen

A full two weeks later, near the end of the business day, Polly stood beside the dress form and folded Amelia Thayer's wedding dress. She placed the garment into *Frau* Thayer's large, deep basket, tucked the plain, faded-yellow cover into place, and addressed the bride-to-be. "You will be charming—more beautiful than a fashion drawing. I wish you and Christian many happy years."

"*Danke.*" Amelia blushed.

"How much for the green?" Bertha touched a bolt of fine, bright wool.

Polly walked behind the sales counter, consulted the price list, calculated a dress length, and stated a price.

"Oh, dear. For the same price, I can purchase three books." Bertha's voice faded.

"Your winter dress is more than adequate." *Frau* Thayer inspected her second daughter for a moment. "The only item for you today is bonnet ribbons—which you have already selected. Whatever happened—they were not so frayed on Sunday."

Bertha sighed. "I set my bonnet on a chair, and the cat chewed the trim."

Frau Thayer muttered a string of *Deutsch* too rapid and soft for Polly to understand. "Come, girls, we are finished. Hilde…stop gawking at the buttons."

"I…look, the snow has started." Hilde pointed out the door's square window. "Do you think we will get enough to go sledding?"

"Too early in the season." Amelia adjusted her gray cloak.

Hilde tipped her face to stare at her tallest sister. "We went sledding on St. Nicholas Day once. What do you know of snowfall? I shall ask Papa."

"More than a week remains until St. Nicholas Day." *Frau* Thayer adjusted the basket on her arm.

"*Danke, Frau und Frauleins. Bitte,* tell your friends *Deutsch* is welcome in Clark's dress shop." Polly smiled as Bertha opened the door.

"Pardon me." George Rush retreated from the shop step, removed his hat, and nodded.

"*Guten Tag.*" Bertha bobbed her head at George and gestured for Hilde to hurry.

"*Guten Tag. Guten Tag, Herr.*" Hilde and *Frau* Thayer acknowledged George in turn.

"*Danke.*" Amelia turned her face from Polly and toward the door. "*Bitte,* beg pardon, *Herr.*"

George grunted a reply and retreated another step. Leaning forward as if to check for lingering women, he mounted the steps.

"Good—" Polly froze. In a blink, the pleasant day soured like milk left overnight too near the stove. She fought to keep her mouth is a neutral shape and focused on Louisa's advice to show manners and kindness to all—even the most ill-tempered of customers.

"Good afternoon, Miss Black." George spoke loud enough for a person on the sidewalk to hear.

Polly recovered sufficient senses to wind ribbon considered and declined by the Thayer women. "Good afternoon, Mr. Rush. Have you come to purchase ribbon or lace for Hannah?"

"Are you well?" He closed the shop door.

She blinked. "My health is fine, Mr. Rush. You are kind to inquire."

"Two weeks you absent yourself from church service. Pastor Harter claims not to have heard a word from you." Planting his feet shoulder-width apart, he placed both hands behind his back.

Glancing toward the ceiling, she sent a quick prayer of thanks Joseph was visiting *Herr* Tafel and would not overhear if this conversation turned sour. She pressed her lips to prevent a regrettable comment's escape.

"Mr. Rush, what a surprise. We seldom have gentleman customers." Mrs. Clark draped lace on a dress-in-progress. "If you wish to have a new dress made for Hannah, you need to bring her with you. Children need to be measured each time."

"I came to speak to the other seamstress." He tapped one foot.

His tone is worse than I expected. Polly wondered if he was aware she now worshipped at another church by invitation of the Gordons.

"Mrs. Black," Abigail snapped. "My assistant should be addressed as Mrs. Black."

He shifted his gaze from Mrs. Clark to Polly. "Are you going to stand mute all day? Why did you miss worship?"

She hid her trembling hands behind her apron. "If my count is correct, Elm Ridge includes five churches. Two—Papist and Lutheran—conduct their services in *Deutsch*. The remaining three congregations sing,

217

preach, and pray in English to the same God. I have decided to worship within a different building."

Tap-tap-tap. He signaled impatience with his foot against the pine floor at twice the rate of the clock. "You are making a mistake."

"You are entitled to your opinion." She moistened her lips. "Joseph and I have the freedom to worship as we see fit." She reviewed her experiences at the two services she'd attended and her one brief conversation with Pastor King. At each visit, she learned the members at Cherry Street did not hold with all the strict rules Mr. Rush and his friends professed to follow. Suppressing a smile, she remembered the invitation extended by a couple after the most recent service. *They are hosting a party this coming Saturday—with music and dancing. They specifically requested Joseph accompany me—to play games with the other children.* "I see no reason to interfere with where you spend Sunday morning."

"Turning your back on the truest church—you make a grievous error." He advanced toward the counter.

She glanced toward Mrs. Clark and drew courage from the older woman's slight nod. The man in front of her held considerable power in the village. New arrivals, especially among the native-born, tended to give great credit to longtime residents such as the Rush, Franklin, and Gordon families. She mixed her next breath with determination to stay on the proper side of the boundary between brave and foolish. "Mistakes have consequences—a fact I learned early in life. Many times, I have made a private confession and prayed for forgiveness." She lifted her gaze the tiny amount necessary to study his eyes. "I trust you regularly examine your own life in similar regard."

He slapped a palm on the counter. "A woman oversteps to correct a grown man."

Jane Rush seldom smiled. Polly swallowed.

"Last Sunday, Pastor Harter's sermon stressed generosity." George removed his hat and held it against his chest. "I will give you another chance. I renew my marriage proposal."

"No." She braced both hands on the counter and looked him directly in the face. "I will not marry you."

"Why? You could leave working at business behind, live in a fine house, and never lack the necessities."

You omit my treatment would be similar to a lowly servant. My son would suffer from neglect—or worse. "My answer remains a firm *no*."

"Very well, you give me no choice." He clapped his hat onto his head and turned toward Abigail. "Good day, Mrs. Clark."

"Hire a housekeeper—if you can find one," Polly called to his back as the bell tinkled and he slammed the door. She gripped the counter's edge with trembling hands. *What does he have in mind? Already many American merchants refuse my business.*

Tick...tock...tick.

Polly tipped her face toward the ceiling and moved her lips in silence. *What additional trouble have I brought? I wish no harm on another.*

"I will put the kettle on." Abigail scurried into the living quarters.

Polly returned the ribbons to the shelf. In her imagination, the lies and exaggeration sure to cling to the facts appeared as the main obstacle. *I trust too easy. I must guard my heart before my actions damage Joseph.*

****

The next day, as the foundry whistle faded after calling the workers for the afternoon shift, Kurt tugged with the pinchers. *Gute,* Herr *Bergmann's boot settles well on the last. I will attach the new sole when I return from my errand.* He pushed one hand through his thick, shaggy hair. A quarter hour later, Kurt stepped into Andrew Hill's barber shop. He nodded to the proprietor and shrugged out of his coat. Due to the posture and angle, he was unable to recognize the man in the swivel chair.

Mr. Hill paused the razor. "You been in here 'afore. Name slips my mind."

Kurt draped his coat on a peg and added his cap. "Once—name is Tafel—occupation cobbler."

"Tafel?" The customer lifted his head.

Kurt blinked at the deeply-lined face. Sealing his lips, he willed good manners forward. "Good afternoon, Mr. Rush. Does business go well?"

"Tolerable—no concern of yours." George frowned.

Kurt exchanged a glance with the barber. *Is the man always sour?* "This morning, I heard a report of ice on Rumble Creek. Is it true?"

"A few patches...gone well before noon." Mr. Rush averted his gaze.

"Too early for serious ice." Andrew nudged his customer before taking a few more razor strokes. "How far into winter are you able to run the mill, George...late January?"

"Varies—last year was mild. We closed for a week in February and a few days here and there. By mid-March, we worked full-time."

Kurt sat on a plain chair and crossed his legs. "A group at the tavern started taking wagers on the final day of the packet."

"Gambling's a sin." George snorted. "A man needs to work for his living, not risk his future on some roll of the dice."

No dancing...no gambling...no drinking...no smoking. Makes a person wonder what his church allows in way of relaxation. Kurt failed to envision a Sunday afternoon lacking all the things George professed to avoid.

"Gambling does get to be a fever for some." Andrew exchanged the razor for a comb.

"No argument from me." Kurt steadied his breath. With a glance toward the ceiling, he renewed his determination to speak only English—regardless if it reminded him of walking a rail fence—one slip and a man could be bruised for a week. "Much money changes pockets at gaming tables."

Andrew used a towel to brush debris from George's neck. "Last packet—my advice 'twould be to guess later—a week or more into January."

"I decided to sit out and watch." He failed to put a name to the emotions behind George's pursed lips and lowered gaze.

Mr. Hill bobbed his head. "There you go, George"—he gave a final flourish with the towel—"all trim and pretty for the womenfolk."

"Ump." Mr. Rush stood, stepped from the elevated platform, and tossed the barber a coin. "Too many odd notions running in the female community of late. Time some of them were shown their place."

Andrew shrugged. "Speak for yourself. I find life more peaceful when the wife is happy. 'Tis always worth the price of a few pretties and ribbons to me if'n Mrs. Hill stays in a good mood."

George slipped into his coat. "Man needs to be master in his own house."

A few moments later, without a nod to Kurt, Mr. Rush exited and slammed the door.

"Is he always so pleasant?" Kurt settled into the swivel chair.

"George? Today was mild. Last time he was here, he rattled on about an immigrant farmer buying the last of something at Clemons' Dry Goods. If'n a person didn't know his business depended on the town's growth, you'd think he wanted to freeze time at—oh— ten years ago. I dare say, I've noticed a sourer mood since his anti-immigrant ally left town."

"Recently?" Kurt swiveled the chair and studied the barber's face.

Andrew honed the razor on a wide, leather strop. "August—I think. Weather was hot and the nights humming with insects when he departed. He was a younger man. Restless. Bought the smaller of the grain mills. Did a poor job—according to the farmers who spoke about him. Cyclone destroyed the building and busted his leg. A month or two later, he got on the packet."

Kurt recalled *Frau* Keil's comments concerning a miller named Black. "Do you recall the man's name?"

The barber lifted hair with the comb and poised the razor. "Black. Leo Black—full of bluster."

Kurt lapsed into silence. *Polly's brother. Night and day was* Frau *Keil's description.*

"On the other hand"—Andrew nudged Kurt's head forward—"Black's sister remained in town. Speaks her mind, she does. Half the village buzzed with her little scene at the hotel a couple weeks ago."

"Did you witness?" He struggled to sound disinterested. Perhaps the chatty barber would clarify some of the seamstress's recent actions—such as her absence for a casual Sunday morning stroll to church.

"No, not me. My sources, several and reliable, say she refused Mr. Rush's marriage proposal. Understand she walked out—head held high. Left him sitting at the hotel dining table." Andrew trimmed near an ear. "Most men would ask such a thing in private. Guess George figured she would answer the question the other way. Makes a man wonder why—sharp businessman such as he—doesn't hire a housekeeper when his wife dies. Man does best to take his time and find the right lady to marry—never know how long you'll be together."

"Hmm." Kurt muttered into his lap. In a blink, he understood Joseph's comments about attending a different church. *Rush is prominent at the church on Sixth Street. Polly might feel a whole lot more comfortable not seeing him every Sunday.*

Andrew lapsed into a report of crop conditions interspersed with whistling. Replying with an occasional grunt, Kurt created and discarded reasons to call at the dress shop. He remembered the short dance in her apartment. Sighing, he studied his right hand. *One brief reel and a quick kiss on the hand is not enough.*

Chapter Nineteen

Midway through the second week of January, Polly leaned to take better advantage of the afternoon light through the dress shop workroom window. An instant later, she guided the shears between the chalk marks. She caught a whiff of peppermint from Mrs. Clark and moistened her lips. She squinted at the faint marks on cream fabric. "Either the sky clouded or I need to wash the window again."

"A little of both, I believe." Abigail inserted a pin into the dress-in-progress on the form. "The next time we have a mild morning, we should clean the outside of the glass."

Polly nodded. "Please remind me—I can reach from a chair."

The shop bell tinkled.

"One minute." She laid the shears beside the cuff fabric and stepped around the drape to the sales area. "*Guten Abend, Fraulein* Mueller."

"Good afternoon," Louisa replied in slow, careful, accented English.

"What is your pleasure this winter afternoon? Ribbons…buttons…conversation?" Polly lingered her gaze on her friend's face and found cheeks reddened from either cold air or happiness.

"A little of each…do you have time?" Louisa set her basket on the floor and clasped her hands against her blue cloak.

Polly waved an invitation to step forward. "Join us. Today, we have pulled the drape to keep away the draft when the door opens. We do not wish to hide from customers…or friends."

Louisa smiled. "Good afternoon, Mrs. Clark."

"Tell us the news. I have not been on errands since Monday." Polly lifted the shears to resume work.

"*Herr* Rush married today." Louisa lowered her hood to reveal a plain, dark bonnet.

Polly stilled. Determined to stay cautious, she willed her heart to remain steady.

"After I left the bakery, I spied a decorated carriage outside the hotel." Louisa touched a length of narrow lace on the table. "When I inquired of a maid leaving work, she confirmed they served a wedding meal to ten people. She named Mr. Rush as the groom and described the bride as small figured, dark hair, and a large nose."

"The housekeeper"—Polly swallowed quickly. She exchanged a glanced with Abigail. "The rumors were correct. How many weeks has she been in his house—three—four?"

Mrs. Clark pinched a pleat into perfect position. "Four—he brought her from a farm halfway to Springfield a full week before Christmas. She sits stiff as wood in his pew each Sunday. Doesn't speak much—least not to me."

Polly sighed and abandoned the shears. Setting her hands flat on the table, she lifted her gaze to the ceiling for a moment. "A worry has fled from my heart. I pray she is kind to Hannah."

"Don't fret over the girl." Abigail secured a pin.

Louisa alternated her gaze between the two seamstresses.

"I wish all children to be safe." Polly smiled at Louisa. "Will you refresh my memory on a few more sewing words today? Or teach me a few more phrases I can use at the grocer? I find *Herr* Glaus' produce much to my liking."

Louisa lifted a sketch of an evening gown from the corner of the table. Displaying the drawing to Polly, she asked, "Yours?"

"I copied the design from a periodical—sleeves from one dress—neckline from another." She used *Deutsch* when she knew the word and English plus a gesture when she did not.

"One piece?" Louisa raised her brows.

"Two—practical to have bodice separate when you have the deep *V* below the waist." Polly organized her next words. "A lady could have two bodices with different trim—almost as good as two dresses."

Louisa grinned. "I like the idea." An instant later, she frowned and traced the neckline with one finger. "Prefer more…modest…suitable for church."

"Is all well at the bakery? Does *Herr* Hoffmann treat you well?" Polly settled her hand into the shears and made the final cut for Jennie Moon's, the Gordon's cook, new cuffs.

"*Ja, ja, alles gute.*" Louisa moistened her lips. "Mrs. Black…Polly…will you join us for dinner and the afternoon this Sunday?"

Blinking away surprise, she regarded her young, *Deutsch* friend. "At the farm?"

"*Nein,* at the bakery…Joseph invited also." Louisa shook her head. "*Frau* Keil suggested an afternoon party to brighten our winter days. My cousin, Fredrick, and his family will join us. *Herr* Hoffmann…" Louisa blushed. "Perhaps another couple or two."

"Certainly…we will be happy to attend. Joseph will be excited."

Louisa clapped her hands and grinned. "*Gute*— with invitation delivered and accepted—I will shop for a new bonnet ribbon. What do you think if I replace the black with a light color—pale blue—or cream?"

For the next half hour, Polly and Louisa sorted, selected, and measured ribbon. When she ushered a smiling Louisa out the door, Polly faced east, toward the school.

Joseph trudged across Third Street.

He plods like he carries a heavy burden. Perhaps the lessons were difficult. "Come here, Joseph, use the front door today."

He waved. Pausing two steps in front of Louisa, he gave her a deep bow. "*Guten Abend, Fraulein.*"

"*Danke.*" Louisa responded with a slight curtsey. "Shall I request *Frau* Keil to add a sugar cookie to your mother's next order?"

"Yes, please." He gave a hint of a smile and licked his lips.

"Come inside, my little scholar." With a final wave to Louisa, Polly guided her son into the shop. "Did Mr. Hopewell work you hard today?"

Joseph nodded. "Charles was not at school today. Thomas and his sisters were absent, too. I'm thirsty."

"Get a drink of water and do your chores. We are having one of your favorites tonight."

He tipped his head and breathed deep. "Beans with ham hock?"

"Correct." A little shiver raced along her arms as she absorbed Joseph's report of his best friends missing school today. "Now pay respects to Mrs. Clark and go—I will join you when we close the shop."

After a bow and exchange of greetings with Abigail, Joseph clumped and thumped into the living quarters. "Swifty, come here, my kitty. Where are you hiding this afternoon?"

Two hours later, Polly scooped the final spoonful of beans from her bowl. She glanced at Joseph and frowned. "You have eaten only half of your serving. Are the beans too salty?"

"No, Mama. I'm not hungry. My throat hurts." He gave his beans a listless stir.

A quiver scurried across her shoulders. Sunday, Pastor King added special prayers for sick children at the *Deutsch* school. *Which disease? Please Lord— protect my son.* "Take a sip of water. Then join me at the lamp...I want to inspect your throat."

A few minutes later, Joseph closed his mouth and rested one hand on the small table. "Good?"

"Red." She laid the back of her hand on his brow. "Warm." She sighed and stood. "I will make you a cup of special tea and send you to bed."

"No story?" He traced a circle on the cover of the King Arthur tales.

She considered his comment. Evening story time highlighted many days. She crossed the room and inventoried the herbs on hand. *I have no willow bark...a little horehound remains...it will need to do.* "I will read you one story while you sip tea. You must promise to drink the whole cup—no matter the taste."

After Joseph was asleep on his cot in the loft, Polly

sat beside the lamp and worked. Clipping a thread, she secured her needle in the pincushion. "The baker's children want for bread, and the candlemaker sits in the dark." She set aside the repaired petticoat and lifted the next garment from the mending basket. She sighed. "The seamstress and her son possess only one change of clothes—and the lad outgrows his trousers." A short time later, she prepared the fire for the night. The childhood verse of contradictions circled in her brain. "The cobbler walks in bare feet." She stifled her laugh. "No, my cobbler neighbor wears good, sturdy boots. I wonder—are his toes as beautiful as his fingers?"

****

The next morning, Polly knelt beside Joseph's cot and held the back of her hand to his brow. "You have a fever. No school for you today."

He squirmed under the quilt. "Can…May I visit *Herr* Tafel?"

"No…you are staying inside…all day. Put on your magic shoes and come downstairs. I will fix you another cup of special tea."

"Ugh—does it need to taste awful?" He scrunched his brow and perched his tongue on his lower lip.

She smothered a laugh at his reaction. "Hurry and follow directions. I have much to do before I unlock the shop. I will let you test if a dab of honey improves the flavor."

A short time later, Joseph sat at the table and sipped horehound tea.

Polly carried in enough wood and water to last the day. Then she climbed to the loft. She folded Joseph's bedding and brought it to the main room.

"What are you doing?"

229

"Moving your bed nearer the stove." She hurried up the steps before he formed a reply. The cot was soon set where she could keep a close eye on him from her sewing chair. "What do you think?"

"Why did you put my bed under the stairs?" He tossed one of his acorn marbles from hand to hand.

"I want you to take naps—until the fever is gone."

He frowned and shook his head. "Naps are for babies."

"And young boys with fevers." She checked the contents of his mug. "Drink the last two swallows."

He sighed.

She scrubbed a carrot and inventoried her broth ingredients. *Ham bone, with most of the goodness cooked into yesterday's beans, carrot, onion, and parsnip. I will work with what I have on hand.* She glanced toward her shelves. *Extra salt and the last of my rice will improve the taste.*

"Mama, I don't like a fever." He set his mug near the table's center.

After chopping the vegetables, she put them into the cast-iron kettle with the ham bone and covered everything with a generous amount of water. "You and I agree. Fevers in children make mothers unhappy."

He limped toward the lamp table and retrieved his storybook. "Will a story make the fever better? I can read by myself—a little."

"Enjoy the illustrations." She set the kettle onto the stove and wiped her hands on her apron. "If I remember correct, a well-drawn dragon opens chapter four."

As the shop clock chimed nine o'clock, Polly unlocked the door. She wrapped a thick shawl around her shoulders and grabbed the broom. A moment later, she crossed the threshold and removed a light dusting of snow from the steps. Lifting her gaze to the shop across the street, she noticed *Herr* Tafel's stoop swept bare and thin ribbons of gray smoke rising from his chimneys. For a moment, she debated crossing the street to tell him of Joseph's fever. Then, in the next breath, she decided to delay—a fever in a child could signal many things.

"Good morning, Mrs. Black. My goodness, the cold near took my breath away." Abigail approached in her hooded, pale-green cloak and thick, knit gloves. "Is Joseph well this morning? He was not his usual lively self when I closed the shop."

"He has a fever. I used the last of my horehound tea for his breakfast." She followed the owner through the door and removed her shawl.

Mrs. Clark tsked. "Not good. Not good."

The moment she entered the living quarters, Polly smiled. Joseph, the boy who disliked naps, slept on his cot with the open storybook loose in his hands. She leaned to close the book and arrange the quilt over his shoulders.

Meow. Swifty leapt onto the cot.

"I give you an extra job today, Swifty. Watch over your boy," Polly whispered.

"Is he resting?" Abigail opened the workroom curtains to admit pale, winter light and faced Polly.

She studied the work laid out on the table. "He naps. The cat is with him. Will you keep watch while I run a few errands? I need beef bones for proper broth and medicinal tea."

"Joseph is no problem." She pursed her lips. "Do not go to the grocer for your tea—he will sell you worthless weeds. Call on my sister—for her midwife duties, she keeps a good variety. She will sell you willow bark for his fever…better than horehound."

"I have seen willow bark work wonders." Polly remembered Madam Robineau in St. Louis brewing tea for her ill boarders. "I will not delay by visiting with the merchants today." She organized the necessary stops. *Abigail's sister first, then* Deutsch *grocer, Hebing the butcher, and* Frau *Keil. I will purchase for three days— or more.*

An hour after the foundry whistle summoned the workers from their lunch, Polly sat in the living quarters and stitched a fine seam on Jennie Moon's new, cream cuffs. Under her breath, she hummed "O for a Thousand Tongues to Sing." Every few moments, she glanced toward her son.

Joseph sat on the edge of his cot with a blanket draped over his shoulders. Balancing the King Arthur book on his knees, he started reading. "Chapter one. The stone and the sword. One fine spring morning…"

"Your voice is fading…take a sip of water." She took a stitch to fasten the lace.

"Mama, will I be well tomorrow?" He raised his gaze from his book.

"I don't know." He looked a little better after willow bark tea and buttered bread crust an hour ago. "Do you miss the schoolroom?"

He set the water glass on the floor. "A little…I like to toss the ball with Charles and Thomas."

The book slid out of his grasp. *Thunk.*

"Joseph?" She jumped toward the cot and caught his tipping, feverish body. "Easy…easy…let me help settle you under the covers proper. Shall I tuck you in tight?"

Shivering under the bedding, he stared.

She startled at his dull eyes.

"I...cold. You said a fever was hot," he muttered.

"Sometimes, the devil gives a person the chills and fever together." She pressed her lips and hoped he saw a smile. Behind her brave act for her son, she recalled *Herr* Hebing saying scarlet fever was in the *Deutsch* school.

"Where...where is...Swifty?"

"The last I saw her, she slept in a sunbeam in the shop."

"May she sleep with me?"

She leaned close, gave him a genuine smile, and matched his whisper. "Swifty, our dear little employee, sleeps when and where she pleases. You must be grateful she does not catch you a mouse for a present."

"Mama." He yawned. "I'm glad you cook my supper. I do not think I would like raw animal."

His shivers have eased. "I want you to sleep a little. When you wake, you must drink some nice broth." She retrieved his book and water glass.

"Mama?"

She turned and tilted her head at the whispered word.

"Will *Herr* Tafel come to visit?"

Swallowing surprise, she gripped the book so hard her knuckles whitened. She closed her eyes for a moment and failed to imagine inviting a neighbor—a male neighbor—to a sickbed. "I don't know. Do you want me to invite him?"

"I like *Herr* Tafel. He always smells of leather and...and..."

Tobacco. She recalled the faint, comforting scent of pipe tobacco from the few times he leaned close. Stooping, she dotted a kiss on Joseph's brow. "Rest. Sleep. Find your strength." A few moments later, she settled into her sewing chair and resumed stitching. She forced her concentration on the task at hand. When customers allowed, she would discuss the situation with Abigail. She placed three more stitches and removed a pin.

"How does he sleep?" Abigail's words from the curtained doorway broke the soft sounds of bubbling kettle and sleeping boy.

Polly stood and walked to within a pace of her employer. "Have the customers told you more news?"

"According to Mrs. Winston, who left less than five minutes ago, the Samuel Franklin household is quarantined. Dr. Alexander diagnosed scarlet fever. Mr. Franklin took a note to the grocer and requested a delivery to be left on the porch. He plans to sleep at the sawmill and take his meals with Mr. Rush."

Polly schooled her features to appear calm. "The Franklin boy is one of Joseph's fast friends. Perhaps I should summon the doctor."

"Has he suffered chills? Does he show the rash?" Abigail lowered her voice.

"Chills—yes. Rash—not the last I checked." She switched her gaze to Joseph and then back to Abigail. "If…if…we are under quarantine…will you be allowed to keep the shop open? Dare I handle fabric?"

"One trouble at a time." Abigail glanced over her shoulder toward the door.

"Yes, I must remain sensible. If I write a note, will you take it to the doctor?"

"Certainly." Abigail drew a deep breath. "I will keep the shop open, if possible—but I think you should remain in the living quarters. As to the fabric…I suggest we hang everything you sew or handle in sunshine…after any quarantine is lifted."

Polly sighed. "A sound plan…my mother aired bedding each time someone recovered from the grippe."

Abigail removed a peppermint from the folded paper in her pocket and retreated into the shop.

Half an hour later, to the familiar sounds of Abigail closing the shop, Polly started Joseph's evening chores. First, she brought in two buckets of water. Soon, she stood in front of her wood supply and shook her head. With the distraction of Joseph's illness, she had not split a day's supply during the best light. Mixing determination with necessity, she lifted a thick, short log from the top of the stack and upended it on her splitting base—a large round of hard oak. She stepped inside the back porch and lifted the axe from the pegs. Next, she fetched her lantern, lit it at the stove, and hung it on a sturdy hook outside the back door. *I will chop enough to last into tomorrow's good daylight.*

****

Kurt wiped and inspected the edge of his best knife in the glow of the lantern hung above his worktable. A satisfied warmth spread in his body at the close of the workday—a day with two new customers. He glanced toward the shelf where three pair of repaired shoes waited for their owners. Sliding the knife into its leather sheath, he stood and gazed through the window.

Mrs. Clark locked the dress shop door and walked in the opposite direction from her home.

I wonder where she is going—all the stores are

closed. Moving around his workspace, Kurt remained busy, doing routine tidying. When he realized Joseph had not visited since Monday, he frowned. "Have I grown fond of the boy?" He swept the day's debris together. "My young helper seldom misses a short visit two days in a row—never three."

The instant Kurt stepped into the cool, evening air, he shifted his thoughts to the warm meal and male companionship of the tavern. "Much talk of illness last night—scarlet fever at the *Deutsch* school," he whispered and shivered from memories. Forcing his mind to happier topics, he remembered the most recent letter, received a day before packet service paused due to ice. "All my family is well, according to the letter written two days past Christmas."

Thud-thud-clunk.

"What?" He stopped at the rear of the dress shop.

"Have you not seen anyone split wood before?" Polly raised the axe and swung the blade into the short, upright log.

Thud. The axe head remained in the wood.

"*Nein. Ja.* I see many use an axe. But none swing the tool so fierce. Will you accept help?" He strode toward her, shed his coat, and hung it on the pump.

She worried her lower lip.

Words stalled and clogged in his throat. The lantern light cast a halo and made the fine hair escaped from her bun appear as a soft frame around her face. He noticed how her plain gown and tied apron flattered her shape. He advanced another step and extended one arm. "Allow me."

"Joseph lies ill." She tipped her face toward the ground.

A chill, from more than winter air, rippled up his arms. "All the more reason to accept help from a neighbor…and friend."

She stepped away from the axe and squatted to collect several pieces of wood. "I-I…have split wood before."

"I believe you." He kicked several small pieces aside and worked the axe free.

"We wait for the doctor. Joseph's best friend is under quarantine." She hesitated and rubbed her left hand on her apron before adding another piece of kindling to her arms.

"The new American doctor? The man on Second Street who keeps a bay carriage horse?"

"The same." She stood and hurried into the building.

He raised the axe and remembered conversation at yesterday's supper. Bitte Gott, *keep all in the village, especially the children, safe and well.*

Thud-crack-thud.

Polly returned and gathered another armful of fuel. "When she closed the shop, Mrs. Clark took a note."

"Has Joseph a fever?" He waited for her nod. "I hear of first child ill when I took Saturday supper in the tavern."

"Helpless"—she stacked another piece of kindling onto her arm—"a mother feels helpless when her child lies ill."

A pain darting from his heart to his brain reminded him of small, fair Greta. He swallowed hard to prevent speech. *My sister, save for my neglect, would be a young woman now.* "You must let me know what the doctor decides. Will the shop remain open?"

Ellen Parker

"Mrs. Clark intends to keep regular hours. I will beg to have our quarantine, if any, confine only Joseph and me to our living quarters…and yard for water and wood."

Kurt assessed her tidy wood supply and selected another piece. He estimated enough wood to keep a good fire two weeks—perhaps a few days more.

Thud-crack-thud.

He swung the axe at a steady tempo.

"You have done enough—we will be fine." She stood and paused with her arms laden with wood.

"When illness is in the house, it is more important than ever to keep your stove going." He inspected the short logs of small and medium diameter scattered at his feet. "I agree this is enough for tonight. I will split more tomorrow, in good daylight. No argument."

"Joseph and I are not in need of charity." She turned toward the door.

He leaned the axe against the end of the stacked wood. "Friends help each other. Perhaps, when your son is well, you will do a kindness for me." He lifted several scattered pieces and set them on top of the unsplit wood. "Go to your son—do not worry about your fuel." Keeping his hands busy, he managed to prevent himself from gathering her into his arms. He ached with the desire to comfort her, console her, and hearten her. "Tell Joseph I will finish the tale of the trolls when he is strong again."

She returned from taking her armload inside.

He handed her the lantern and retrieved his coat. "If you are in need—day or night—fetch me."

"We will be fine." She blinked and held the light high.

The tremble in your voice betrays you. He sealed his mouth, nodded, and stepped toward the sidewalk. *Never have I seen a woman so worried—save* Mutter *as Greta lay dying. Please God—let Joseph live. Elm Ridge needs a smart, red-haired boy. His mother loves him. I-I...* An ache formed around his heart and stayed even after he entered the tavern.

Chapter Twenty

Saturday evening, Kurt hiked along Third Street, carrying a candle lantern. Snowflakes swirled in a faint breeze during their downward journey to the thin, white layer deposited earlier in the day. He exhaled and ignored the thin cloud formed by his breath. Restless—unsatisfied—he was unable to settle his mind. For the first time in months, the tavern musicians failed to lift his spirits. Tonight, the trio of accordion, violin, and clarinet did not relax him or cause him to tap a foot in the familiar rhythms.

He switched his attention to his left and settled his gaze on the dress shop. A pale light shone in the single side window. *Does she sew by the light of her lamp? Why does she not send me word? Not a sound since Thursday evening.* He tipped his face toward the sky and blinked against the snowflakes. "I will talk to her—tonight. I must learn how Joseph fares," he spoke to the winter air. His breath made tiny clouds as he strode toward the back porch. Inside the first door, he inventoried the wood he had split and carried under shelter earlier today. He pursed his lips and wrinkled his brow at the tidy stack—little or none had been taken inside. *Rap-rap-rap.* He pounded on the interior door. "Mrs. Black—is all well?"

"Go away," her faint voice replied.

"*Nein.*" He tilted his head and listened.

"Illness here—no visitor."

He hesitated, unable to determine if the door muffled her voice, or if she had taken ill. Drawing a breath, he tested the knob.

The latch yielded.

Stepping over the threshold, he lifted his lantern high to supplement the single lamp with a soot-streaked chimney.

A mass of red hair peeking from quilts on a cot was the only sign of Joseph.

Polly, more than half her hair escaped from the bun, slumped in a chair beside the boy's cot. Lifting her head, she frowned. "Go away."

"*Nein*—a blind man could see you are in need." A dart of cold fear for her well-being pricked his chest. "When did you last eat, Mrs. Black?" He set his lantern on the table and noted dirty, empty cups, bowls, and spoons. Walking the few steps to the stove, he opened the firebox. "Your fire is scant coals. Soon, the room will cool, and you will catch a chill."

"You must go—quarantine." She lifted a cup from the floor and struggled to stand. In the next instant, she set the back of her hand on her son's brow. "Joseph's fever remains. He refused the last tea."

Kurt banged the stove door. "You—Mrs. Black—when did you last eat?"

"Yesterday—I think." She remained still beside Joesph's cot and sighed.

He glared at her on his way to the porch. With more noise than necessary, he filled her kindling bucket. *Foolish woman—she needs food—and sleep. One person cannot tend the sick, keep a house, and stay healthy.*

"I told you to leave." She moved slower than a turtle toward the table.

Returning to the stove, he added first one and then a second slender stick of fuel. "How do you expect to nurse your son if you do not eat or sleep?"

"I sleep." She gestured toward the chair beside the cot.

"In a bed—proper." He grunted satisfaction at the cooperative fire. *Has fatigue made her deaf to reason?*

She failed to stifle a yawn. "Impossible. Should Joseph wake and not find me near, he will be frightened."

Lifting the teakettle, Kurt shook his head. He carried the container to the water pail and filled the tin kettle. "Do you know the day? Hour?"

"What are you doing?" Polly stiffened. "'Tis late— I did not count the clock the last it chimed."

"I begin to tend the little things. You must eat— and rest." He set the kettle onto the stove, lifted the Dutch oven's lid, and frowned. "This…this…remains of charred vegetables is not fit for a wolf to eat."

"Go—you will catch the fever."

He shook his head and scraped the remains of some stew or other from the cast-iron kettle. "Passing out from exhaustion in your chair is not restful sleep. I will stay a few hours—while you eat and rest."

"You are a stubborn man."

He sealed his lips against the retort climbing his throat. Arguing while she struggled to stand would gain nothing. He scraped blackened food into the slops bucket, added a dipper of water to the kettle, and continued to loosen stuck bits. Scrape, discard, add water, scrape again. Finally, he grunted and set the kettle on the table. "I go now to empty this ruined food into your yard. When I return, I want you to eat bread with butter and drink water. I will fix you a fried potato with egg to give a little warmth to your stomach."

She stared from dull eyes.

Several minutes later, he returned from the yard with the empty slops bucket in one hand and a pail of fresh water in the other.

Polly stood at the table with her hands flat on the surface and her head bowed.

He dropped his burdens the final inches to the floor and strode toward her.

She crumpled toward the floor before he could join his arms in a full circle.

"Pigheaded woman," he whispered. Shifting his body, he slid one arm under her knees and drew her torso close to his chest. He glanced around the room. Neither the sleeping boy, nor watchful cat, offered a solution to the current situation. At the top of the steep stairs, he paused to allow his eyes to adjust to the scant light from the gable windows. With each slow blink, another shape or two resolved into a recognizable object. He identified small crates and one narrow, iron bedstead. Easing beside the bed, he laid her on top of the quilt. He placed the back of his hand on her brow. "*Gute*—no fever. First, you sleep, then I make sure you eat."

"Mama—warm peppermint," Polly mumbled. A moment later, she lay limp and silent.

"Easy…move your arm…a little more." He loosened the tucked quilt and covered her body. Securing the thick cloth around her dress, he realized the garment was not comfortable for sleeping. For one instant, he thought to undress her. Then better sense, in the form of his father's warning not to take advantage of a lady, guided him. Drawing a deep breath, he reached under the covers and unfastened the top dress button. After releasing four, he withdrew his hand. He stood stiff, opening and clenching his right fist. An unfamiliar tingle wove up his arm and circled his heart. He held his breath and willed the desire to caress her soft skin to pass. "Polly Black deserves a better man than me," he whispered toward the rafters. "Joseph is entitled to an attentive, not distracted, father. I must guard my heart and remain a neighbor. No matter the struggle, I will stay a friend who keeps proper distance." The moment he returned downstairs, Kurt checked on the sleeping Joseph.

The boy breathed light and even.

Removing the damp cloth from the boy's brow, he checked for fever and shook his head. He closed his eyes for a moment and visualized his mother tending him or one of his brothers through an illness. After refreshing the cool rag on Joseph's forehead, Kurt spent several minutes checking shelves and crocks. He found a beef neck bone and placed it into the Dutch oven with several ladles of water. He added a sliced onion, a sprinkle of salt, and several bruised peppercorns. When the kettle was warming on the stove, he returned to Joseph's bedside.

The child's pale skin wore blotches of the signature scarlet fever rash. In a few places, the damaged skin sloughed off to expose a fragile layer. Dry, cracked lips twitched to release a nonsense syllable. The youngster wriggled his shoulder.

"A fever is difficult, my young friend. You must be

strong. Your mama loves you very much. She is sleeping now. I doubt she left your side more than a few moments at a time since the fever took hold." He eased into the chair and noticed a book half under the cot. Bending, he retrieved the volume. He opened the book at random and made no attempt to read the English words. After turning a few pages, he found an illustration of a knight on a horse. *Adventure stories— this explains why Joseph asked questions about armor and squires last week.* He stood and placed the book onto the round sewing table. A few minutes later, he selected a small piece of wood from the kindling bucket and studied the material. He claimed the chair beside the cot and collected his thoughts.

Swifty emerged from a hiding place, hopped on the bed, and sniffed her boy's exposed hand. A moment later, the cat settled on the third step to the loft and assumed sentry duty.

Kurt bathed Joseph's face, arms, and hands from a fresh basin of cool water. "Pardon my large hands— your mama has a tender touch. I am clumsy if you compare." He tucked the quilt against the boy's chin and pulled a folding knife from his pocket. Holding the wood in one hand, he made the first bold whittling strokes. "Do you know the fable of the seven goats and the wolf?" He glanced toward Joseph. "No? Then you shall hear the tale for the first time." He moistened his lips. "Once upon a time, in a house at the edge of the magical forest…"

Each time the clock chimed the hour, or the half hour, Kurt bathed the child's face with cool water. At the conclusion of the second fairy tale, he stood and studied Joseph's labored breathing. "Fight, my little friend. You are precious—to your mama—and me. Your constant questions as you sweep my shop make me think and use much English."

After he checked the progress of the broth, Kurt resumed his seat and continued to shape a slender figure with his knife. "One day, my friend, when you are grown, you will understand the difficulties your mother faced. She is a brave lady—strong against narrow-minded people." He lapsed into memories of his two encounters with Mr. Rush—at his own shop and with the barber. "Why did an established businessman fear my friendship with Polly? She is a grown, sensible woman—capable of deciding who she will marry. He is not the first man to have a marriage proposal denied." Smiling, he studied the form of a sitting cat with an elongated neck in his hand. *Mr. Rush, you claim to love your daughter. I will not call you a liar. But do you want her close for a point of pride? Do you wish to control her?* He glanced to Joseph. *I am sorry you suffered insults due to the actions of adults.*

The clock chimed seven times.

Kurt set aside his small knife and the wooden figure, stood, and freshened the cloth. "When you are well," he whispered, "I will ask permission to take you to the bakery for a treat. Have you tasted *Fraulein* Mueller's excellent cherry *Kuchen?* It is delicious—sweet fruit atop a thin, fine-textured, yeast dough. Makes my mouth water to speak of it."

Joseph stirred.

"Ahhh—good timing—dawn is near." He removed the cloth from the boy's forehead, paused, and checked for fever. He glanced heavenward. "Praise God, the fever is broken. The boy will live."

"Mama…Mama," Joseph mumbled.

"She is sleeping. A broth is ready for you." He waited for Joseph to open his eyes.

The boy squinted. "*Herr* Tafel?"

"*Ja.* Now be a good patient and drink a little of the broth I fetch from the kettle. You need to get strong." With a new lightness in his heart, Kurt put a ladle of broth into a cup and selected a spoon from the cupboard. He gazed toward the stairs. *Wake, Polly—your dear son asks for you.*

****

Polly wriggled her shoulders against the mattress. For a brief moment, she imagined she floated, safe and protected, above sharp rocks.

Clink-clink.

She blinked out of the dream. Pushing to half-sitting, she turned her head from side to side. With the identification of each familiar shape in the loft, she eased her breathing. Facing the window, she studied the pale light. *Dawn? I must hurry to do all the morning chores.* "Jo—" She felt her lungs stall and forced a swallow breath. *My son is ill—downstairs.* Kicking her way out of the bedding, she swung her feet to the floor. She glanced down and frowned. With her brain still tinged with sleep, she puzzled why she wore her dress. *How did I get in this state? I never lay to rest with half my buttons undone.* Standing, she silenced the questions appearing like toadstools after a spring rain. She stood at the peak of the roof, fastened her dress, and caught a whiff of beef broth in the air.

Clink-rap-rap.

She forced another button through the proper hole and searched for a weapon. *An intruder? A thief?* She uttered a quick prayer a stranger didn't harm a sick, defenseless child. Lifting the sturdy stick used to prop the window open in fine weather, she turned for the stairs.

"Eat…drink…soon, you will run fast as your cat." A low, male voice drifted toward her.

Polly trembled. Gathering courage in her next breath, she placing her stockinged feet on the first of the steep steps. She gripped the stout stick with both hands.

"Ahh." Kurt stood at her table. "See, Joseph, your mama is rested now and will give you the broth."

"Joseph, Joseph, my darling." From the second-to-last tread, she focused on her son and dropped the worthless weapon. In two heartbeats, she was at Joseph's side and gathered his slim frame into her arms. "You are safe?" She slid one hand to his brow. "You are better?"

He nodded and lifted one hand to hide a yawn.

With each breath, the past days, and present situation, clarified. *I dozed beside Joseph. Kurt arrived and…and…* The next events blurred in her memory. She remembered the quarantine rules and faced Kurt. "*Herr* Tafel, you must leave."

"*Nein,* I stay until Joseph drinks broth and you eat a meal." He extinguished the lamp.

Tick…tock…tick.

She drew strength from an unknown source and straightened. "You must leave now…the illness…the quarantine…the rumors." *Reputation is a woman's fragile cloak—she needs to keep it well mended.* She studied the floor. *My cloak is in tatters—not yet fully repaired from Mr. Rush's harsh tongue.*

Kurt lifted the cup and advanced two large steps. "Here, tend your son. He woke within the hour and asked for you."

Accepting the mug, she wrapped both hands around the warm china and perched on the edge of her son's cot. "Thank you, my manners evidently are still asleep. I do not remember starting a new soup."

"After you were in bed, I found what I needed."

Hiding embarrassment with an intent look at her hands, she switched full attention to Joseph and presented a spoonful of broth. "You must drink warm broth and tea to get well."

He accepted spoon after spoon of the salty liquid. "Mama," he whispered. "How long did I sleep?"

She thought for a moment. *He took no liquid after Saturday's noon foundry whistle.* "Most of a day...does the warmth feel good on your throat?"

"A whole day?" He stared from wide eyes.

She smiled. "When the fever visits, a person sleeps a lot."

"Today is Sunday." Kurt gathered items from her shelves and opened a small crock.

"What are you doing? I told you to leave." She interrupted spooning broth to glare in his direction. Did men not understand how to follow directions? The longer he stayed, he put himself at greater risk of the illness.

"I prepare a proper meal for you—bread, butter, potato, and egg. Have you bacon grease?" He inspected the contents of another container. "You must eat—or you will faint again."

She snorted. While she did not recall last night's events well, she doubted his words. "I don't succumb after a missed meal."

"Perhaps I use the wrong English word. Last night, when you were half-sick with exhaustion, you collapsed. I intended for you to eat before sleep." He shrugged and carried a round potato and small crock to the stove. "Your body chose a different order."

A flash of heat bathed her neck. With one hand, she rechecked her dress buttons. She glanced toward the man standing calmly near her stove, holding her lard supply in one hand. She shook her head and allowed silence to fall between them. Closing her eyes for a moment, she failed to picture him taking advantage of an exhausted woman.

He set the frying pan onto the stove and added a spoonful of lard. "You did not send me word of how Joseph fared. Since Thursday, I did not know if he lived or died. When I left the tavern early Saturday night, I stopped to learn how my neighbors managed. You told me nonsense when I knocked on your *unlocked* door."

Searching her memory, she found a blank after Abigail closed the shop. She recalled lighting the lamp and reading Joseph a story. Then…snatches like pieces of a torn sketch swirled. "I do not remember."

"No surprise. Did you sleep well?" He opened his folding knife and sliced potato into the sizzling grease.

"I dreamt…of floating…a burned meal…snow on boots…a red-haired knight."

"A red-haired knight," he chuckled. "I think you have been reading Joseph tales from his book."

She leaned and guided her son to take a sip. "Every day—they are his favorite stories." *I am not the only person to tell him fables. Last week, he returned from your shop talking of an ogre and a lady.* Focusing on

Joseph and the last of the broth, she attempted to ignore the man and the familiar sounds of a meal-in-progress. However, she remained aware of his every move. Drawing a deep breath, she caught a trace of leather, tobacco, and sawdust in the air. Glancing toward her feet, she frowned. "How did wood shavings appear on my floor?"

Kurt cleared his throat. "I apologize. I whittled while your son slept. I have not swept the debris."

"Mama."

"What is it, Joseph?" She leaned close to catch his soft words.

"I itch." He wriggled his shoulders.

She smiled and touched his nose with one finger. "I will give you a good wash—and a clean nightshirt. But first, I think you need to rest again."

The cat leapt onto the cot and stretched.

"With Swifty?" He turned his head but failed to hide a yawn.

"Perhaps. I think your pet will decide for herself." Polly stood and watched the calico settle beside his hip.

"Bread and butter are waiting." Kurt stirred the frying pan's contents.

After setting the empty cup onto the table, Polly paused in front of the mirror above the washstand. "You need to leave. I can finish—I know when to add the egg." She removed hairpins and set them beside the basin. Frowning, she remembered the hairbrush and comb remained in the loft, on the shelf where she set them each evening.

"Why do you chase me from your home? I mind manners."

She stalled her fingers in the midst of doing a

rough combing and faced him. Seeing kindness and friendship on his features and in his stance, she grasped for proper words. "I know. You know. Others will be neither kind nor generous should they see you leave my apartment in the early morning. I will lose what little respect I hold."

"Do you think the people of Elm Ridge evil?" He paused a spoon above the pan.

"I believe them human—no better or worse than residents in other towns." She thought of the delicate new friendships at the Cherry Street Meeting House. She doubted even the Gordon women, or Mrs. King, would risk defending her a second time.

Cracking the egg on the side of the pan, he lifted his gaze. "I will defend you. I speak truth to those who ask or repeat a rumor."

She sighed and glanced toward Joseph. The boy slept, in a true—not fevered—rest.

Bernard tried to defend me—before he knew I carried his child. She hesitated and recalled the words of two sober witnesses to her brother threatening Bernard's life.

"Do you trust me?" Kurt steadied his gaze on her.

"I want to trust you." She added tea to the round, china pot. Memories of her father and brother—untrustworthy men charged with her protection—competed with shopkeepers and neighbors—honest men of more recent acquaintance. "Three months after Bernard abandoned me—wrong word—sorry. I found singed paper—scraps of a letter—in my landlady's parlor fireplace. I knew in my heart the message was from Bernard. But I only had a hint of the town." She sighed. "It is dangerous for me to trust you."

"Do I lie to you? Do I spread tales?" He stirred the frying food.

"You tricked me." She joined him at the stove and lifted the tea kettle. "You tempted me to dance—in this room."

He shook his head. "I invited you to dance. I was plain, not deceptive, with my words. I remember you smiled at the end."

Filling the teapot and settling the kettle on a trivet, she delayed a response. For several nights after the dance, she dreamt of happy, lively music. An instant later, she frowned at memories of Mr. Rush spreading rumors. "I worry for Joseph. His turned foot and lack of a father cause him problems making friends. The schoolchildren insult him with adult words—language not fit for dock or tavern."

"He will thrive despite cruel schoolchildren. He has the most important thing."

She lifted an eyebrow and met his gaze.

"A mother who loves him." He answered her silent question.

Turning toward the window, she blinked at the first bright rays of sunshine reflecting off new snow. "Don't discount a friend who puts magic in shoes." She buttered a slice of bread. "The day promises to be fine."

"*Ja.*"

She looked toward her sleeping son and sorted a dozen necessary tasks. Warmth in her chest reminded her how great a blessing the boy brought her. Chewing flavorful bread, she regarded the man standing at her stove. Herr *Tafel—are you a blessing for me—or a trial?*

Chapter Twenty-One

Tuesday morning, bright light entered the window near Polly's sewing chair and illuminated the entire room. The steady *tick-tock* of the shop clock noted the passage of time.

Dressed in a recently brushed gown and fresh apron, Polly stood at the stove and poured a thin stream of milk into porridge. "A good, warm breakfast will help make you strong again."

Joseph sat at the table and adjusted her warmest shawl around his body. Wrapping both hands around a cup of herbal tea, he swung his magic-shoe-clad feet. "Can...May we have noodles today?"

She gave the pot a final stir and ladled a small portion into his bowl. "You speak like a boy who is feeling better. Today, I make a new soup. I think a few noodles with the beef and vegetables will aid your recovery."

After another sip, he set the tea aside and moved the whittled cat figurine closer to the covered jam jar.

A moment later, Polly set two bowls of porridge onto the table. She waited for Joseph to take a small mouthful.

He swallowed and frowned. "Tastes bitter."

"One moment, I will test." She sampled a spoonful. *Strong flavor in this bag—more barley than wheat.* "I know how to made porridge taste better for recovering boys." She went to the shelf and returned with the honey pot. As she drizzled a spiral pattern of the treat on his porridge, she cautioned. "Only one portion of sweetener."

"Thank you." He ate several spoonsful in silence before pausing. "Mama?"

She halted the growing mental list of work to accomplish today and gave him her full attention. "What is your question?"

"Do I need to go to school today?" He touched his spoon to the remaining portion of breakfast.

"Not today—or tomorrow. The busy doctor said our quarantine remains for several days after the fever breaks Do you miss the lessons?"

He shrugged. "My friends and I built a snow fort. Will it melt?"

"Not today—the air is very cold this morning." She shivered at the memory of the first step into the yard. A moment later, she swallowed a bite of her breakfast. "A fresh layer of snow arrived during the night."

"Did we have any rabbit tracks in the yard?" He brightened.

"I did not see signs of rabbit." She noted the droop to his mouth at the statement and contained a laugh. "A dog passed between the pump and the woodpile."

"A big dog?" He paused with his spoon in the air.

She delayed an answer with another bite of porridge. "A dog with large feet."

"I want to think it is Pastor King's dog. Do you know Stormy?" He abandoned the half-eaten porridge and lifted his tea.

"Yes, I have met Stormy. He is a large dog with much hair." She intersected his gaze and put authority in her voice. "We have a cat. We do not have room for a dog."

"He could sleep on the porch." Joseph placed a hand in front of his mouth. But the delayed gesture only partially hid his yawn.

She took her final bite of breakfast. "I think you have eaten enough for now—wash your hands and face before you lay on your cot."

"The fever is gone. I don't have to sleep in the daytime." He tipped his face to the floor during his next yawn.

"Did I tell you to sleep? You may read—or tell me a story while I start the soup and wash the dishes." She stood and motioned for him to follow her directions. In the next moments, she began to make the soup and clean the kitchen area.

The shop clock chimed nine times. Polly wiped the final dish and set it into the cupboard.

Tinkle-tinkle. The shop bell announced Abigail's arrival.

Polly smiled at her sleeping son, walked to the drape over the shop entrance, and pushed it open a few inches. "Good morning, Mrs. Clark. Are all well in your household?"

"Fine as a clear sunrise. I detoured to the bakery and purchased you a loaf of wheat bread—and four sugar cookies. My sister sent another packet of herbs. She says this mixture aids sleep and suggested both mother and son drink a cup in the evening." Abigail set a basket within reach at the base of the thick curtain. "How is Joseph this morning?"

"Better—he sat at the table and ate a small breakfast." She squatted and inspected the basket's contents. "I am grateful to your sister for the herbs. I credit both the willow bark—which Joseph struggled to drink—and the lavender mixed with mint for much of his recovery." She held the bread in one hand and the paper of herbs in the other. "If I write a note to the doctor, then will you deliver it at noon?"

"Certainly." Abigail stepped to the corner and grasped the broom. "Another child died during the night—the Winstons' grandson—age three."

Polly tallied the recent deaths. "Six new graves—the parents—the entire village—endures a difficult winter." She glanced toward her son and breathed a prayer of thanks. "Do you have word of the Franklin children? Joseph mumbled Thomas' name before he drifted to sleep after breakfast."

"Thomas and Sarah are recovering. The baby took ill three days ago—so they will stay under quarantine longer. Mr. Franklin appears worn. Every afternoon, he goes to the porch and visits through the window."

Polly sealed her lips. *Mr. Franklin is so different from his business partner, Mr. Rush. I do not understand how they can work together at the sawmill.* "I will keep the Franklin household in my prayers. Tell me, is all well at the bakery?"

"The young baker, *Fraulein* Mueller, sang happy tunes this morning. She flitted about the workroom like a songbird in spring." Abigail swayed as if dancing with the broom in her hands.

Polly chuckled. "Let me guess—at the afternoon party Sunday—they announced her betrothal to *Herr* Hoffmann."

"Correct—a spring wedding—I think." Abigail faced her. "Most of the chatter between laughter and song was in *Deutsch*. I did not understand well."

"Good news. I believe *Fraulein* Mueller and *Herr* Hoffmann are well suited." She started to turn away and then changed her mind. "I do hope she allows us to make her a new dress for the wedding." She recalled illustrations from the newest issue of *Godey's Lady's Book* and imagined Louisa wearing a bodice with the most fashionable pleat arrangement.

"Plenty of time for you and Miss Mueller to discuss a dress. A large fabric order will arrive when the river opens. I suggest something light and cheerful." Abigail stepped outside to sweep the new snow from the entrance and sidewalk.

After putting the bread and tea in their proper places, Polly set a clean piece of paper on the table. She removed the battered tin from the high shelf and smiled. Joseph called the container the *treasure box*. She danced her fingers over the scorched, embossed design and remembered her mother using the tin to store sewing supplies and a few coins. Now, in the only keepsake from the lady, she safeguarded mementos of Bernard—a pressed yellow flower and a scrap of singed letter—plus her pen and ink. Moments later, she wrote her request to Dr. Alexander in a bold script.

The shop bell and Abigail's greeting to a customer punctuated the quiet.

Polly reviewed her note, signed her name, and sighed. From the corner of her eye, she spied the wooden figurine sitting beside the tin box. She extended a finger and caressed the sitting cat with an elongated neck. *Kurt whittled and carved while he tended my sick child. Joseph has the most important thing—a mother who loves him.* Kurt's words circled twice in her mind before she sighed. "*Herr* Tafel," she whispered. "Your family lives far away. What—or who—gladdens your heart and gives you courage to face each day's tasks and trials?"

****

Later the same day, Kurt tapped the final peg to secure the new sole on *Herr* Widder's boot. After attaching the new heel, a routine task, Kurt would have another order finished. He stood and stretched as the foundry whistle called the men for the Tuesday afternoon hours. After one glance out the large, workroom windows, he smiled. *Gute.* He firmed his resolve to have a word with Mrs. Clark before splitting more wood for Mrs. Black. A few moments later, wearing his wool coat and leather cap, Kurt entered the dress shop. "Good afternoon, are you and your family well?"

"Aye, we are. Have you come for linen thread—or conversation?" Abigail tied her apron.

He noted a twinkle in the shop owner's eye and relaxed. "I seek a little information, if you will be so kind. How do Mrs. Black and Joseph fare? Does my young friend continue to improve?"

"He does." She rested her arms on the smooth sales counter. "I understand you have been splitting the stove wood. I am grateful. At times, Mrs. Black is slow to admit her limits…or ask for assistance."

Aware heat climbed his neck, Kurt tipped his face to study the floor. "I am a neighbor helping a neighbor in need. In fact, I go now to chop more—while the light is good."

"*Herr* Tafel"—she beckoned him to lean close. "Will you accept a jar of blackberry jam at your door tomorrow—as a token?"

"You are a good woman, Mrs. Clark." He swallowed sudden moisture prompted by the mention of one of his favorite sweets. "I go now—work—eat my humble lunch."

"Bless you." Abigail's words mixed with the bell's tinkle.

When he arrived at the rear of the building, Kurt smiled. A line was strung from the corner of the building, past the pump, and secured to a tall post. Blankets, sheets, shirts, and one thin pillow hung limp in the cold, still sunshine.

He skirted the new obstacle and hung his coat on the post. Pleased at the sight of airing bedding on a crisp, sunny day, he wondered if Mrs. Black followed advice from *Deutsch* friends. He positioned the first thick log on the splitting block and retrieved the axe.

Thud-crack-thud-clatter.

Follow your heart. Frau Keil's words from weeks ago surfaced as he split log after log. "My heart is unreliable," he muttered into the winter air. "At nine and twenty, I burned for Irish Kathleen. Parents, priest, and pastor objected. Within a few months, she proved fickle and showed the others correct." He propped the axe against the end of the wood rack and bent to collect the fresh-split kindling. He puzzled over why none of the *Frauen* from the Sunday dances warmed his heart as much as one smile or laugh from Mrs. Black.

The porch door creaked.

"*Guten Abend, Frau* Black."

Polly, with two empty buckets in one hand and the teakettle in the other, paused. "Good afternoon. I heard you working. I want to thank you for your labor."

"How many more days of quarantine?" Since he departed her apartment Sunday morning, he'd been careful to go no farther than the porch.

"I do not know. I sent a note to the doctor today. He is busy, but I trust he will send me word at first opportunity." She stepped beside the pump, set one bucket under the spout, and worked the handle. Frowning, she dribbled water from the teakettle down the pump's shaft.

"I go to the butcher and baker after I finish with your wood." He kept his smile small when her third stroke of the pump handle resulted in a thin stream of water from the spout. "Do you want me to bring you something?"

"Mrs. Clark keeps us supplied. I thank you for the offer." She moved the pump handle slow and smooth.

Kurt deposited one armful of wood inside the porch. Returning to the yard, he assessed the remaining supply. "Your fuel dwindles. Which wood seller do you favor?"

"Old Mr. Adams." She swapped the two buckets. "I sent a note Friday...no...Saturday. How many days to you think remain?"

The wood dealer's name caused a cloud to vanish from his mind. According to talk at the barber shop and the post office, Adams sold dry wood and minded his own business. "A week—perhaps a little more, if the weather moderates."

She turned toward the river. "Clouds are coming. 'Tis January...I expect snow tonight...and for winter to continue. Joseph will want to sit at the window and watch the snow."

Switching his attention to the western sky, he

confirmed a line of clouds approaching. "I think I will be quick about my errands." He brushed bits of bark and debris from his shirt. "Tell Joseph I will come and tell him the entire story of the goats and the wolf when your quarantine is over."

"He will look forward to your visit."

And you? Will you welcome me? Or do you continue to fear the gossip of others? He kept his distance and shrugged into his coat. Pushing his hands into his pockets, he resisted the urge to tuck a wayward curl behind her ear. *Colors are brighter, smells sharper, and sounds clearer when she is near.*

Chapter Twenty-Two

Friday, February 20, 1852

A quarter hour before nine o'clock, Polly unlocked the shop door and stepped into mild air. A dirty mark on the unpainted siding indicated the recent height of the snowdrift against the building. She filled her lungs with a hint of spring. In the next breath, she reminded herself pleasant days in February were called *false spring* for a good reason. "Joseph"—she faced the shop—"time to leave for school."

"I can't find my cap," he replied in a high, soft voice.

"Look on both pegs." She tipped her face toward the sky and requested an extra drop of patience. On mornings when her son wanted to avoid school, he acted half-blind. "Hurry."

Clump-thump-clump-thump. The distinctive sound of his special brogans announced his progress toward the front door.

"I found it on a chair." He tugged the gray, flat cap over recently trimmed hair.

She touched his shoulder when he paused on the sidewalk. "Be a good little scholar today. Obey Mr. Hopewell."

"Yes, Mama." He nodded and pushed one hand into the coat pocket holding his lunchtime apple.

Resisting the urge to give him a kiss, she withdrew

her hand. "Go. I will watch only a minute." She stood in place while he crossed Third Street. Rubbing her hands on her upper arms, she shivered under her dress' sturdy fabric. She drew a deep breath, expecting the usual scents of wood and coal smoke, but something was not right...not the same as a few moments ago. She pivoted, making a slow circle.

Thin, white-and-light-gray ribbons of smoke rose from chimneys at the dress shop, the cooper, and across the street.

Polly turned her attention toward the north, toward Cherry Street. In an instant, she raised both hands over her mouth.

A ball of black smoke rose above the roofs."Fire—fire." She dashed across the street, pounded on the cobbler's shop door, and yelled again. A moment later, she ran toward the cooper's shop, and then across the street, pounding and yelling at every door on her way. "Fire—fire."

The instant she turned the corner at Second Street, she heard the foundry whistle blow—loud, long, and out of ordinary time.

Men, women, a few children, and one brown dog exited houses and shops, following in Polly's wake. Shouting and pointing, the residents hurried toward a billow of dark smoke. Several people, even in their haste, snatched a bucket or two.

"Fire—fire." Polly continued to shout the alarm and pound on doors under the foundry whistle's blast. With her lungs feeling close to bursting, she dashed between two houses. She could see the meeting house did not burn, but the smoke poured from Pastor King's home. One fear replaced another as she noticed sparks shower onto the roof. *The children—please Lord—save the people.*

Two men sprinted past her and battered open the home's back door.

A surge of thick, black smoke escaped. A flicker of flame appeared.

"Water—water—save the church," a strong male voice commanded.

Polly jerked to her senses. She stood a few steps from a pump. Stepping forward, she studied the crank and chain design and breathed relief at the bucket under the spout. She inched into position and turned the handle clockwise. The apparatus groaned, hesitated, and moved. Careful to mind the chain, she turned the handle steady, not rapid. Water, precious water, dribbled from the spout. "Good...thank God," she muttered, "for false spring."

The moment the bucket was nearly full, an unknown person swapped it for an empty tin pail.

Polly focused on drawing her next breath and cranking the handle. Bucket after bucket was removed and set in place by others. Shouts directing people to form a line or pour the water faded to a mumble. *I must turn the handle—pump the water.* She did not release her grip on the crank to wipe the tears spilling down her face. *Breathe...turn the handle.* She commanded her body to continue the work. But memories of the terrible summer day when Joseph slept in the loft and flames escaped the stove insisted on circling.

****

After opening the shop before nine o'clock, Kurt unrolled a hide on his worktable. He inspected the cowskin in the strong, morning light and glided his hands over the leather. As he examined the material, he imagined various arrangements of his pattern for sturdy boots. When creating a new pair of boots, he attempted to cut all the uppers from the same animal for a more uniform thickness and color. He selected chalk from his work apron and marked a blemish he wished to avoid.

Thud-thud. His shop door shuddered.

He glanced toward the entrance. *The curtain is open. Why not turn the knob and enter?* A dozen steps later, he opened the door and leaned outside. The only person in sight, a woman without bonnet or cloak, hurried toward Second Street with a pause to pound on another door.

The foundry whistle cut the morning air.

He jerked and glanced to check the time on his clock. *Whistle has no reason to sound.* A second, longer blast demanded Elm Ridge residents pay attention.

Kurt stepped into the street and looked toward the river. As soon as he shifted his gaze north, rather than west, he gasped. Black smoke, not confined to the size and shape of a chimney, rose above the buildings.

Kurt dashed into his shop, grabbed two buckets from the apartment, and exited the side door. Hurrying through slushy yards, he aimed for a point on Cherry Street near the river. He became aware, but did not sort, voices of several men and a few women sprinting in the same direction.

A ball of black smoke cleared the roofline of a small church.

"*Wasser—Wasser.*" Kurt looked for a pump.

"Come on, man—children inside." A stranger in workman's clothes tugged on Kurt's arm.

Tossing his buckets in the general direction of the

backyard pumps, Kurt followed the man to the street. *Children?* He felt his heart skip a beat with terror. *Not a second to waste.*

In the middle of the road, one woman placed a shawl around the shoulders of another. An elderly lady and two small children hurried to join the pair.

"Get back"—Kurt waved his arms at the women. "Go—now." He followed the workman up three steps, across a narrow porch, and through an open door releasing whisps of smoke.

"On the stairs"—a stranger commanded—"form a line."

"Hand them down." A voice from the second story demanded attention.

Kurt planted his feet on two adjacent treads and turned his face upward. *What are they handing?*

"How many?" A voice above Kurt broke into a cough.

A few moments later, the man on the steps above Kurt twisted and handed him a small, startled child. Kurt grasped the sleepy toddler around the waist, turned, and presented the child to the next man.

"Another—stay alert, men." The voice faded.

A blanket-wrapped bundle was thrust into Kurt's hands. For one moment, he cradled the infant, then passed the precious parcel to the next man.

"One more—"

Crack-crash. The entire building shuddered.

The man above Kurt collapsed in a coughing fit.

"Get out, man—save yourself." He climbed one step. "We will get them." A moment later, he accepted a squirming, blanket-wrapped baby from a man up the line. He twisted and discovered the man below him kneeling and coughing. Leaning to shield the infant with his body, he descended one step...then another. Half-blinded by smoke and tears, he brushed against the banister. *Careful—precious bundle—remember Greta.* He forced each breath to stay shallow and managed the final steps. Moving his lips in a prayer, he crossed the small foyer and half-stumbled out the front door.

"I'll take him." A stranger's voice offered.

Kurt shook his head and drew fresh air. "*Mutter*— where is the mother?"

"Come with me." A strong hand grasped his elbow. "She waits across the street."

"My darling." A dark-haired woman wearing a nightgown and shawl gathered the infant from his arms.

Sinking to his knees, Kurt alternated coughs and deep breaths. *Saved—children were saved.* A weight, present around his heart since the day Greta died, lightened to a handful of chaff discarded by the wind. Each breath came easier than the one before. "Are you injured?" a stranger with smoke-scented trousers asked.

"*Nein*...no...weary." He struggled to his feet and blinked the man into focus. "Are all saved?"

"Every one—close for the second twin. The infant was not across the room's threshold when the ceiling collapsed into the cradle."

Kurt nodded and plodded across the street. Soon, he was among an aimless throng. He lifted his gaze and spied three men dousing the church roof. Watching them pass buckets, he remembered he brought two pails. He changed direction and walked between the damaged home and the next house. At the rear of the building, he paused and drew a sharp breath. *My God.*

The home's entire back porch, and a good portion

of the kitchen, lay blackened and shattered. A busted bed rested against a corner cupboard with broken glass. Bits of bedding dangled from a fractured second-floor joist.

"I hear the children are safe," a woman spoke from his right.

He broke out of his daze and faced Polly. "*Ja—drei Kinder.*" He extended three fingers. "A glad reunion."

"Prayers of thanks and joy—the twins are but a few weeks old." She shivered.

"Walk you home?" He skimmed his gaze over her wet skirt, red cheeks, and untidy hair. "You look chilled." Reaching for his coat to lend her, he realized he wore shirt and cobbler's apron—nothing to loan. He clenched his fist to prevent him from extending a hand to warm her cheek. Swallowing, he found the manners to offer his arm.

"I will accept." She stepped to his side and set reddened fingers on his smoke-drenched shirt.

With a slight pause near the church's pump, Kurt retrieved his buckets, or two very similar. "Did you bring one?"

"No, I did not think beyond spreading the alarm." She glanced toward the muddy ground.

"You did well—got my attention." He guided her past patches of shrinking snow and dormant gardens behind buildings. "Where is Mrs. Clark? I did not see her among the others."

"Abigail planned to do errands before coming to the shop. When she finds the door unlocked, she will have questions." Polly halted.

Kurt paused beside her and puzzled at concern over an unlocked door when children's lives had been in danger. In the next instant, he doubled over in a coughing fit and released blobs of dark mucus.

"You have swallowed smoke. Come to the shop, and I will make you an herbal tea." She touched his upper arm.

"No need." He swiped a sleeve across his mouth and adjusted his hold on the buckets. "I will manage to brew myself a cup." He slid his gaze toward the woman beside him. *Much stands between us—language—customs—religion.* A tremble in his fingers ascended his arm. *During recent weeks, I have lost my desire to search for a bride among the immigrants.* Each and every dance partner faded to a shadow beside the American woman standing within arm's reach. He struggled to breathe, not from smoke, but at the realization he desired Polly to be more than a friend and neighbor.

She lifted one hand and touched her hair. "Oh, my, I must look like a witch from one of the tales you tell Joseph. I need to wash—and find a clean apron when I get home."

He clenched his teeth to keep hasty words inside. Darting his gaze to her profile, he admired her beauty and strength. He shook his head, but the advice to follow his heart, voiced by *Frau* Keil many weeks past, remained. Instead of telling Polly he thought her beautiful—regardless of hair in disarray or soot-stained apron, he steadied his gaze on the path ahead. Soon, he spied Mrs. Clark standing in front of the dress shop. After a quick lift of an arm to acknowledge the older woman, he faced Polly. "I think we part here."

"You do not wish to tell your story to Mrs. Clark?" She placed a tease in her tone.

"Every person who steps into your shop today will tell a different version. I go to wash, make tea, and listen to my own customers." He reached to tip his cap and realized his head was bare. Several hours later, after the whistle dismissed the factory workers for the day, Kurt guided his knife around the pattern on the leather. He pushed aside the memories from the morning, which attempted to overwhelm his thoughts. Again, he renewed his focus on the work at hand. Each order was important. He was well aware a satisfied customer told his workmates.

Jingle-jingle. The bell on his door signaled a visitor.

He finished the final inch of the cut and lifted his gaze. "*Guten Abend, Fraulein* Thayer." He smiled at the pleasant, young woman.

Bertha beamed. "I count it good fortune your door is unlocked."

"My work held my attention so well I did not lock it at the usual time. How may I help you today?" He sauntered from the far end of his work table to the sales counter.

"Are we friends?" She clasped gloved hands at her waist.

"*Ja*—I count your family among my friends." He added a nod for emphasis. Jacob Thayer was generous with friendship and filled a portion of the hollow left by the distance from family in Pennsylvania.

"You did not dance with me but once all of Sunday afternoon." She met his gaze.

He swallowed and studied the beginnings of a pout on her delicate face. "I find it pleasing to dance with many during an afternoon. Did you lack for partners?"

"Well…no…but few polka as well as you."

"You flatter me." *Max Giesel courts her. Is she blind to him?* "I believe the younger *Herr* Giesel sought your company on the dance floor. Did he accompany you home?"

She blushed and tipped her face toward the floor.

Pressing his lips, Kurt delayed a response. He silently reviewed the virtues of the young cabinetmaker before deciding to speak plain. "*Herr* Giesel is a good age for you. He appears to be industrious, serious, and moderate in both drink and speech. I am an old man when I stand near you, *Fraulein.*"

"Will you"—she fingered her bonnet ribbons—"join us for Sunday dinner?"

He glanced toward the exposed rafters before intersecting her gaze. "Why?"

"You are good company. Do not lie and deny you enjoy a conversation with Papa."

He traced a circle on the counter with one finger and arranged words on his tongue. "An afternoon in front of the fire with *Herr* Thayer is a pleasure. The invitation to your home should come from him—not you."

"Why are you playing shy?" She inched toward him.

He added courage to his next breath. "*Fraulein,* you are a charming, intelligent, young woman. You dance well and hold good conversation. But I am uncomfortable with our age difference. You need to open your eyes. A good man, near your age, pays you court."

"I expect you speak of *Herr* Giesel."

He nodded. "Over half the patrons at Althoff's

acknowledge his affection for you. He is a good man—not a spendthrift."

"I want…"

" 'If wishes were horses…' " He planted the old proverb.

"Are you telling me to marry Max?" She backed a step and paused her mouth in a circle.

He drew a deep breath and failed to find an answer in the still, leather-scented air. "Has he offered?"

"Twice. I am…uncertain. Papa approves of the match." She eased to the shelf holding repaired shoes waiting to be claimed. With one finger, she tapped the toe of a lady's half-boot. "I find I enjoy the smell of leather equal to the scent of wood shavings."

He stilled his tongue until the harsh response in his throat retreated. "I think you seek adventure. You read many books…I expect they tell of wonders in all parts of the world." He waited for her nod. "I urge you to accept the difference between ordinary life and grand stories. Please consider *Herr* Giesel's offer. Do I seek a wife?" He shrugged away an image of Polly priming her pump with a dribble of warm water. "At present, none of the dancers at Althoff's stir my interest—including you. Therefore, I must learn patience."

"Sunday—shall I tell *Mutter* to set a place for you?" She tipped her head enough to gaze directly into his eyes.

"*Nein,* I decline the kind invitation." In a blink, his mind replaced Bertha's petite form with a memory of Polly several hours ago, including a smudge of soot on her face. However, the practical portion of his mind saw the chasm between himself and an American seamstress as impossible to bridge.

Bertha sighed. "You will disappoint Hilde."

"Your younger sister will find greater frustrations in life. Tell Hilde I will seek her out for a set of schottische the next time we are both at the dances." He flicked his gaze over Bertha's face and knew he desired a more mature woman to better fit his age and nature.

"I expect the promise of a dance will satisfy her." Bertha eased to the door, set her hand on the knob, and studied him. "Do you really think *Herr* Giesel is a good man?"

"I know nothing to the contrary." He focused on the wall behind her.

With a swish of skirts and a jingle of the bell, she exited the shop.

Snatching the key from the hook, he stepped to the door. *Max and Bertha—I wish them happiness.* He sighed and visualized his favorite dance partners. *Fraulein* Thayer knew the most complicated steps. *Fraulein* Mueller, betrothed to *Herr* Hoffmann, smiled with joy when dancing, regardless of her partner. *Fraulein* Widder danced the simple steps with much energy.

As he pulled the curtain closed for the day, he noticed movement at the window across the street. He failed to rid his mind of Polly—a good woman—a loving mother—a fine seamstress. His arms ached with desire to hold her in a proper dance—in public. He compared the impromptu reel in her home to a nibble. He yearned for a feast.

Chapter Twenty-Three

Monday afternoon, Kurt lifted the scraps from a freshly cut welt. In silence, he reviewed the business day and sighed contentment. Before lunch, a farmer and a roustabout each left shoes for new soles and heels. Mrs. Cook called for her repaired half-boots less than an hour ago. He glanced at the teamster's boots-in-progress on his worktable. Selecting the proper last, he hummed "*Grossvatertanz,*" a happy folk song.

A tap on the door preceded the bell.

Stepping to the side, he glanced toward the door and smiled at Joseph.

"*Guten Abend, Herr* Tafel." The boy snatched off his cap and bowed.

"*Guten Abend.*" Kurt chuckled and paused his words as the foundry whistle signaled the end of the workday. He had been honored to have the boy resume his visits to the shop two weeks ago. "Does your mother know you speak *Deutsch*?"

"She allows *Fraulein* Mueller to teach me a few words." Joseph squatted, peered behind the round heating stove, and then past the half-open door to the apartment. "Why do I not see your cats when I visit?"

"Smoke and Coal find hiding places to sleep during the day. It is official closing time, according to the foundry. Do you want to help me put away tools and sweep the floor?"

Joseph straightened to his full height and held his cap against his chest. "Mama sent me to invite you to share supper. Please accept. Mama's cooking smells especially good tonight...and she visited the bakery."

"Today...supper in your home?" He paused his hand over a knife sheath. Aside from a brief exchange of greetings when he walked to the tavern Saturday, he'd not spoken to Polly since the Friday morning fire.

"Yes...*ja*...I invite you, also." Joseph continued to clutch his cap.

Kurt studied the boy's face and almost laughed at the youngster's losing struggle to keep his mouth straight while his eyes twinkled. "You give a kind invitation, which is difficult to refuse." Tucking the blade into the protective pouch, he pursed his lips. He sneaked a peek at Joseph and ceased his teasing. "If you start sweeping, then we will finish cleaning and be ready to eat sooner."

"Yes, *Herr* Tafel." He plopped his cap onto his head and set to work.

For the next quarter hour, Kurt hung tools on pegs and stored patterns on shelves. Between tasks, he glanced toward his helper.

Joseph swept dirt and debris into a compact pile between the worktable and sales counter. "*Herr* Tafel."

"What do you need, my young assistant?" He retrieved the shaped tin to gather the sweepings.

Joseph clutched the broom and leaned toward Kurt. "Will you live with Mama and me?"

Kurt changed a sudden choke into a cough. "I think we have much dust today. Do you understand what you ask?"

Nodding, Joseph inspected him with serious eyes.

"You will be my new papa. Together, Mama, you, and I will be a whole family."

A whole family—sharing life—and a bed—with Polly. As the image circled, he feared the boy would hear his heart thundering. Many nights, his dreams were filled with a similar fantasy. In daylight, he found it easier to be practical. "You are my friend. Your mama is my friend. That is good—no?"

"Good—yes." Joseph frowned and glanced at his shoes. "New papa is better." He met Kurt's gaze. "A girl at school is getting a new mother. Her first mother was buried a year ago—not so different from *Herr* Keil in the cemetery."

Kurt contained a sigh at the display of child logic. "New papa, as you call it, is a decision for your mama." He glanced through the window and envisioned more than a street separating the seamstress and the cobbler. Often, since the day the King family had the fire, he listed reasons to keep Polly as a friend—nothing more. At the top of his invisible paper was the fact she was native-born and he…born in Pennsylvania…appeared as an immigrant to many. *What makes an American? Language? Food? Customs? How many generations to shed suspicion?*

"Come here, Smoke, I will not harm you." Joseph squatted and extended a hand toward the young cat. The gray-and-white feline stood in one spot and twitched her tail.

"She is not as familiar with young boys as Swifty." Kurt walked into the living quarters and poured water into a basin. As he washed today's dust and grime from his face and hands, he considered Joseph's words. The phrase, new papa, did not leave as he soaped and rinsed. The words circled again while he blotted his face and wiped his hands. Joseph abandoned coaxing the kitten and waited beside the kitchen door.

"Come, Joseph, we will go see what smells so good in your mama's kitchen." With each step toward the dress shop, he thought of Polly as wife—and lover. He felt his heart speeding as if he ran to catch a horse.

****

Half an hour later, Polly faced Kurt over steaming plates of beef stew. The entire room smelled of biscuits, meat, peppercorns, onion, and garlic. However, the conversation sagged after exchanging accounts of business and weather. She chewed butter-coated biscuit, swallowed, and found courage to address a new topic. "Pastor King and his family are staying with generous people across the street from the church. Mrs. Clark and I are altering donated clothes."

"I observe the people of Elm Ridge to be charitable." Kurt speared a piece of carrot with his fork.

"Very much." She glanced toward Joseph and gave silent thanks to *Herr* Hoffmann for saving her son, the most precious person in her world, from the fire last summer. "Tomorrow, I will deliver a dress and two aprons for Mrs. King, plus a gown for the eldest child. Mrs. Gordon called at the shop today and ordered a dress length to make an Easter frock for Mrs. King."

"I spoke with *Herr* Thayer yesterday. He estimates two more days with his crew to make the structure tight against the weather."

"They did not need to knock down the building?" She shivered at the memory of men with poles tipping the burning shop wall away from the cooperage. Kurt gestured with a spoon in his hand. "The damage was limited to the back porch, kitchen, and one bedroom. According to the carpenter, a few stout timbers and new roofing will allow use of the rest of the rooms. A little good fortune mixed with the tragedy."

"Mama—"

She sent Joseph a silent warning to stay quiet during adult conversation. When only the two of them ate a meal, he had permission to speak of school and similar things. But tonight, with a guest at the table, he needed to remember his manners. She returned her gaze to Kurt. "Did you hear the cause?"

"The family burned green wood."

Polly swallowed a bite of parsnip and surprise. "A person needs to be careful. Two farmers attempted to sell me the same. I am grateful Mr. Adams is an honest woodcutter. Dry wood is worth the extra cost."

"*Ja,* a man…or woman…needs to be watchful in many situations." He placed a morsel of meat into his mouth.

Tick-tock-tick. The clock marked time while Polly and Kurt pretended great interest in the meal.

"False spring." Kurt popped a final bite of biscuit into his mouth.

"Pardon me…what did you say?" Polly jerked out of musings including fires, green wood, and children saved, to the present.

"Mild weather in February—*mein Mutter* calls the situation *false spring.* She always insisted we split extra wood—too often, the mild days ended with a storm."

Polly envisioned the amount of stove wood on her back porch and on the stack. Both grateful and humbled by Kurt's insistence on continuing the heaviest work of splitting the thickest logs, she studied her plate's rim for an elongated moment. "Have you been to the river?" She kept her voice level. "Do you have a guess when the first packet will arrive?"

"Are you eager? Do you miss the steamboat whistles?" He met her gaze.

"I miss the letters—I wait for news from St. Louis friends." *Madam Robineau was ill with a lung fever the last I heard. I pray she recovered.* "We have many supplies—lace, fabric, and thread—ordered for the shop." She remembered the scant quantity of pale thread remaining in the sewing box. Frowning, she imagined spools of thread at Mr. Clemons' store—the only merchant who continued to refuse service to both Polly and Abigail. "Are you anxious for letters from your family?"

"Letters from family would be most welcome. I think of them every day and wonder how they fare."

Keeping her smile internal, she admired the way his eyes softened when he spoke of his family. She tamped down envy at obvious love between parents and children and equal affection of brothers for each other. Facing reality, she prayed often for her brother, her only close relative, to stay far away from Elm Ridge. "Tell me of the dances in the new hall. Do you waltz with many pretty girls?"

He paused his spoon filled with rich gravy and met her gaze. "The Sunday afternoon dances are a good place to meet many people. I polka and waltz with both old women and young girls. But none of the *Frauen* grab my heart."

"No special partner—a handsome man such as you?" She laid one hand on the side of her neck, certain she would feel heat.

"None of the ladies at Althoff's are as charming as a certain lady who dances only in her kitchen—after much coaxing."

"You danced with Mama once," Joseph spoke in a rush.

"Quiet—children do not speak at table unless spoken to." *I cannot help the fact he listens to every word.* She sent a stern glance toward her son before again directing her attention to Kurt. "Please excuse my son's poor manners. We seldom have a guest for a meal."

"I understand." He scooped a final piece of onion from his dish.

She abandoned eating. "You and I"—she pointed first to Kurt and then herself. An instant later, ashamed of her own manners, she clasped her hands into her lap. Memories of the dance—his touch—his kiss—threatened to overwhelm good sense. She swallowed and searched for proper phrasing for her son to hear. "Are we friends…or do you dream of more?"

"I imagine a great many things. However, I see great obstacles to more than friendship." He leaned against his chair's back.

"Language?"

He nodded.

"Do you know how I learned my first *Deutsch* words?" She waited for his slight head shake. "The spring I was seventeen, my brother, Leo, installed me at Madam Robineau's boardinghouse. He paid the fee for six months and went to do business up the Missouri River. A week after he left, three *Deutsch* boarders approached me in the parlor as I sewed. With many gestures and a few accented English words, they invited me to join them. They sewed for one of the city's many shirt factories. I discovered I enjoyed the work—and the small wages I earned. The ladies taught me both *Deutsch* and fine stitching. Leo returned, and I stayed in contact with them—despite his grumbling. During his next trip to Fort Benton, I again lived in the boardinghouse." *Bernard arrived during early summer. He rented a room on the third floor.* She glanced toward Joseph. *The best and worst of my life are knitted together in those months However, I must not dwell on the past.*

"Religion is another obstacle." He set knife, fork, and spoon onto his empty plate. "Before my brothers married, the pastor asked them a great many questions. I was not in the room, but I heard much muttering and complaining from them during those weeks."

"You speak of a great difficulty. She glanced toward Joseph—"Bernard spoke to at least ten pastors before he found one willing to perform a marriage such as ours. I count but five clergymen in Elm Ridge."

He drew a circle on the tabletop with one finger. "Religion is too important for me to change."

Blinking slowly, she considered her side of the religion difference. "I do not think I could worship in *Deutsch.* I find myself able to conduct a little business and mix the languages in conversation with *Frau* Keil and you, but I cannot imagine praying in anything except English." She experienced a tug on her sleeve and jerked her attention to her son.

"May we have *Kuchen?*"

She checked Joseph's plate. Seeing the dish empty and the flatware positioned similar to Kurt's, she gave him a soft smile. "Soon…today the bakery had plum.

Fraulein Mueller claims it is her favorite—I have not eaten it before." She intersected Kurt's gaze. "Have you?"

"*Ja*—often—a plum tree grew at the edge of the apple orchard at home. It is important to add the right amount of sweetener to the fruit."

She stood and gathered the dirty dishes from the table. While preparing for dessert, she puzzled over the emotion present in Kurt's eyes. She hesitated to label it *mischief*—perhaps *longing* fit better. She glanced toward Joseph and smiled at his open expression—her son desired *Kuchen*. She lifted the dessert from the shelf, removed the linen cloth, and cut three slices—generous for Kurt, modest for Joseph, and a mere taste for herself.

"Why so small a piece?" Kurt pointed toward her tiny portion.

"I am full with the meal." She suspected he was aware of the lie; however, the serious turn in the conversation caused the fine meal to feel like rocks in her stomach. She reminded herself patience was a virtue. Hurrying events, instead of letting life unfold at a sedate pace, caused previous problems in her life. "Do you want me to make tea?"

"Not necessary." He took a bite of dessert, closed his eyes, and smiled. "*Gute—wunderbar*—even better than her cherry *Kuchen.*"

Polly pursued a familiar debate. The widow persona gave her more freedom than either spinster or wife. She needed to guard against foolish notions. Friendship contained great value—a fact she needed to remember. In the next moment, she sampled the sweetened plums on yeast dough. "Delicious—what do you think, Joseph? Have you found a new favorite?"

"I like plum *Kuchen*...and apple...and cinnamon buns..." He took another bite.

Kurt grinned. After his next swallow, he tapped the table with one finger. "Tonight, I dry dishes. A few minutes labor is small payment for a grand meal. No objections permitted."

She flicked a crumb from her lips. Repeating the words *friend* and *neighbor* in silence, she closed her eyes for a long moment and listened to her traitorous heart patter faster than raindrops during a spring storm.

Chapter Twenty-Four

Kurt waited beside the water trough in the stable yard. With a glance toward the western sky, he sought assurance. "Today is second Sunday in March," he whispered toward heaven. "My time in Elm Ridge is a little shy of six months—am I letting my heart run ahead of a practical mind?"

Clop-clop-clop. The mare's iron shoes struck the cobbles.

"All ready, *Herr* Tafel. Sal will do you well, she is mild-mannered." *Herr* Hoffmann, gripping the bridle strap, halted the harnessed mare.

"*Danke*, I return both horse and vehicle before dark." He paused long enough to allow the animal to sniff his hands.

Hans chuckled. "I wish you good fortune. Do you take the South Road?"

Nodding, Kurt stepped into the gig. "I promised a friend an adventure today." A few minutes later, he halted Sal in front of the bakery. He climbed down, secured the reins at the rail, and sighed. "I will not be long," he addressed the horse. "Soon, you will be able to stretch your legs. I believe the road will be solid under the thin layer of mud."

The mare shifted her weight and released a soft snort.

Kurt hurried around the building and climbed the

Ellen Parker

apartment steps. Pausing on the landing, he heard two female voices. He listened for twenty seconds before he determined the women were joking, not having a dispute. He raised one hand and rapped his knuckles against the door.

"Goodness—I didn't expect to see you." Polly stood in the opening with the slops bucket in one hand.

"May I enter?" He removed his cap.

She stepped aside and gestured. "Welcome to *Frau* Keil's home."

Three steps across the threshold, he turned in a slow circle. "*Guten Abend, Frau* Keil, Mrs. Black, Joseph. Please, I ask you to delay your errand, Mrs. Black. I invite you for an afternoon drive. A reliable source tells me the river view is exceptional from a point on the South Road."

"A drive—with a horse?" Joseph slid from his chair and clumped and thumped across the large room to the front window. "It's Sal, Mama, my favorite. Do we have carrot? May I go and give her a treat?"

Kurt pressed tight his lips. According to *Herr* Bergmann, the gentle mare was the only horse rented with the gig. "What do you say, Mrs. Black?" He pointed first to her and then to his chest to make his invitation clear. "You and I?"

"I-I am not sure." She clutched the slop bucket's handle with both hands.

"I like drives." Joseph looked to Kurt with hopeful eyes.

"Sorry, Joseph." He watched the boy's smile fade. "Today, I ask you to stay with *Frau* Keil."

Charlotte set a clean dish into the cupboard. "Joseph and I will have a delightful afternoon. I think he is a good age to learn a *Deutsch* table game."

Alternating her gaze between the cobbler and the bakery owner, Polly moistened her lips. "Have you plotted together?"

"The plan is my doing." Kurt remained in place and listened to his heart's increasing volume and speed each second of delay. "I will confess, *Frau* Keil did not hesitate when I asked for her cooperation. Please, Mrs. Black, the weather is fine."

Joseph left the window and paused by the settee. "I will obey *Frau* Keil."

"I am sure you will." She set the bucket under the coat pegs and sidestepped until she rested her hands on her son's slim shoulders. Worrying her lower lip, she maintained her gaze on Kurt's face. "You sound quite confident...as if you have made a great decision."

He forced a shrug. Fisting the hand hidden by his cap, he managed to avoid stating his purpose. No matter the difficulty to hold his tongue, he would voice his request in private. "I would be pleased if you gathered your bonnet and shawl and accompanied me." He studied her appearance, including light-brown hair in a smooth bun, blushing cheeks, and a mouth able to go from serious to laughter in a blink. He struggled to remain still while his feet wanted to cross the room and his arms ached to hold her in a close embrace.

Polly dabbed a kiss on the top of Joseph's head. "Mind your manners, son. *Herr* Tafel and I will not be gone long."

"Do not hurry." Charlotte walked to a shelf and lifted a small, wooden box. "The young man and I get along. Perhaps, on your return, I will find the remains of a *Kuchen* to share."

"Plum?" Joseph widened his eyes.

Kurt chuckled.

"A surprise," Charlotte replied.

A few moments later, Kurt handed Polly into the gig. "Your appearance is charming, Mrs. Black."

"Today's invitation makes me feel sympathy for the mouse the instant before Swifty pounces." She fussed with her skirts.

"My intentions are pure. I will go to great lengths to never harm you—or Joseph." He adjusted the reins in his hands and ordered the horse into motion.

"Have you driven on the South Road?" She turned toward him a tiny amount.

"*Nein,* but I hear of one or two lookouts. Perhaps you can tell me the proper place to turn from the main road." He guided the mare onto Fourth Street and allowed Sal to set the pace past homes, a few closed shops, and Althoff's Dance and Assembly Hall. Moments after crossing the plank bridge on Skunk Creek, the character of the scenery changed to untamed, scrub forest.

"The streams are running low." She interrupted the quiet.

"*Ja,* until the next rain." He cleared his throat, glanced toward her, and focused his gaze on the road. "Since you are settled now in Elm Ridge…have you thought to marry?"

She glared and slid another inch away on the bench seat.

"Apologies—I spoke blunt. My tongue and my brain do not always move at the same speed when you are near." *My heart gallops ahead of either of them. In my dreams, I hold you, caress you, kiss you—I fear some days I long to sleep my life away.* "I enjoy your company, Mrs. Black. I desired to have a conversation none but songbirds will overhear."

"You do not fear the busy tongues of those who glimpsed us pass on the street?"

He shook his head. "Are we near the first overlook?"

"We need to pass one more farmhouse. When the main road turns left, we go right past a clump of cedar."

"Thank you. You are a special person, Mrs. Black. You—and your son—are always welcome in my modest home." He forced a deep breath of mild air filled with scents of damp earth, new growth, and spring promise. "I believe you are aware of my age—past the years when many find a wife. During my months in Elm Ridge, I have become acquainted with many people in the *Deutsch* community. They are good, kind people—for the most part. However, my heart—an undependable organ—yearns to be in your company instead of any *Fraulein.* Have you advice?"

****

For a moment, Polly feared her lungs would remain stalled. She concentrated on his exact words and organized a reply. "I agree with your description of the heart." Polly switched her focus from the intriguing man beside her to the landmarks along the road. "You ask if I have thought of marriage. I beg to remind you, at my age, the topic is never far from a woman's mind." She hid her hands in her skirt and reviewed the men in Elm Ridge, other than George Rush, who approached her with the intention of courting. *The farmer and the blacksmith are too old—near fifty. The teamster from the foundry is nearer my age—but not trustworthy.* "I do not have a direct answer to your question."

"Do you welcome the affections of another?" He tightened his hold on the reins.

She stiffened. "My life is full with work and motherhood. I have little time for courtship." She glanced toward his face and labeled his pursed lips and lowered gaze as disappointment. "We turn here—see the three cedars and the stump."

A few minutes later, the mare stepped from a narrow path into a small glade.

Kurt tugged the reins. "This is a beautiful place."

"In late summer and early fall, *Frau* Keil, Joseph, and I picnicked here." She waited while he tethered the horse to a small tree and continued to the gig's side.

"My lady." He bowed and extended his right hand.

She giggled. "Has Joseph been telling you the stories from his book?"

"*Nein,* we *Deutsch* have our own tales of valiant knights and beautiful damsels in danger." He guided her toward several flat rocks prominent near the bluff's edge.

Standing beside him, she gazed across the water toward the Missouri shore. Within the river, large pieces of ice, some half the size of a steamboat, drifted and bumped each other. "If the weather stays mild, the first boats will arrive in a week or two."

"Ahh…letters and supplies. I am getting eager for both." His voice took on a lighter tone.

The mention of letters carried thoughts of Madam Robineau and her other St. Louis friends. In recent days, when stitching a straight seam or washing supper dishes, she imagined the landlady's opinion of the

Deutsch friend beside her. Did the intelligent widow have advice for untangling the multitude of problems present in an attempt to follow her heart? She surveyed the river and held her breath as a large bird swooped low over the water.

"Splendid," he whispered.

She slid her gaze from the majestic bird to his intriguing profile. For a long moment, she held her gaze on his open, honest face. A familiar comfort warmed her chest as she regarded his blue eyes, ruddy cheeks, and generous mouth. Questions without answers danced in the air between them, begging for consideration. She blinked slowly and imagined seeing him across the supper table each evening.

"What are your dreams for the future, Mrs. Black?" He slid his gaze toward her.

She warmed at the intimacy in his voice. "Polly— please call me by my Christian name when we are in private." She skipped a breath. "Dreams…I need to think on your question."

"Very well—I shall call you Polly when we are alone. But only if you agree to use Kurt in return." He clasped his hands behind his back. "Do you dream of one day buying the shop from Mrs. Clark? Do you intend to stay in Elm Ridge? Will you train a young seamstress or two?"

"You list grand ideas." She grasped her skirts and stepped onto one of the large rocks for a better river view. "I do plan to remain in Elm Ridge. I believe I told you of all the times we moved during my childhood. I want Joseph to have less turmoil—be able to tell a new acquaintance where he is from in a simple phrase or two. Buy the shop?" She turned her face from the river and met his gaze. "My dreams of the future do not extend very far. Mrs. Clark…God willing…shall continue for many years."

He stepped nearer and encircled her with his arms. "Polly," he whispered near her ear, "will you marry me? I have fallen for your charms."

She eased her head and upper body away enough to assess his face. She studied his generous mouth in a straight line and clear eyes devoid of mischief. Pressing her lips, she waited for her heart to settle into a steady beat.

"I think you and I could be happy together." He continued to gaze at her as soft, forest sounds swirled in the air.

"Obstacles"—she swallowed—"I see so many, so large."

He adjusted his stance and arms until he faced her and held her gloved hands. "I am aware you worry for Joseph. I will treat him as my own…even if other children follow."

"You voice but one of many concerns." Never, in the months of their acquaintance, had she sensed any harm to her son at Kurt's hand.

"Yesterday, I called on Pastor King. He speaks like a good man, concerned with the welfare of all, not only his congregation." He released her left hand and rubbed his chin. "If we go together and talk to him, he is open to performing a marriage ceremony."

She breathed deep and sampled the stimulating scent of plants ready to grow. "Your question…is a surprise. However, you speak as if you have given the situation much thought—and taken important steps." *This is* Herr…*Kurt Tafel.* In a blink, she recalled his consistent kindness. A shiver crossed her shoulders when she considered his touch—a touch which caused her body to plead for more. She glanced toward her feet, balanced on the flat rock, and his boots, planted on dull, brown grass. *Why does God put another* Deutschman *in my heart? Why not a Scotsman, or an Englishman, or a man with deep French roots in America?* "I must think."

"How long?" He tilted his head.

His question, soft and clear, gave the impression of great distance. However, when she raised her gaze, he stood with less than a foot's separation. "A few powerful people in town refuse to associate with me."

"Time will silence all but a handful."

A memory of Mr. Clemons standing at the door of his dry goods store on Wednesday clarified in her brain. The merchant had glared when she passed his door. She blinked away the image and drew courage with her next breath. "The schoolchildren call me a harlot."

"You...I...the people who really matter...know the truth." He pointed one finger at her chest and then his own.

In simple words, he identifies the basic matter. She relaxed and allowed his calm words to soothe the edges of her worry and shifted her gaze toward the river. Her body's reaction in his presence was impossible to deny. She felt an odd combination of weakness and power each time he touched her. "You do have one advantage—compared to Bernard."

He raised his brows.

"My brother is unlikely to return and threaten you with his pistol." She steadied her gaze and curved her lips. *Does my smile reflect the desire in my heart?*

"I view that portion of the story as a worse reflection on your brother than *Herr* Keil."

She laughed and stepped from flat rock to damp ground. A moment later, he snaked one arm around her waist. She shivered with excitement and anticipation. "I see...difficulties...great obstacles."

"*Ja*—I also see great reward." He nodded and gazed from his greater height.

She rested her head against his tall, strong form and drew a portion of quiet courage. *Reputation is a woman's thin cloak—she best keep it in good repair.* She closed her eyes and listened to his strong heartbeat. Each gentle *thump* sent her a drop of confidence and determination to face the bigots, no matter their position or influence in Elm Ridge. *Together...together, we will be stronger than either alone.*

"Come, Polly the seamstress, we will return to town." He adjusted his arm to circle her shoulder.

"Wait," she muttered. Focusing on the budding trees behind him, she pictured joining pieces of fabric together with fine stitches to create an entire garment. At the moment, she viewed the fragments of her life as irregular swatches of cloth scattered across a table before a skilled person arranged and sewed them into a warm, beautiful quilt. She trembled at the invisible task. "Before I answer your question, I want you to kiss me."

Kurt widened his smile, lowered his head, and touched her lips.

Tiny, imaginary wings fluttered in her stomach. One, or both, deepened the kiss.

She clung to his arms as the fluttering bird within her breast multiplied into a flock taking flight. *Never before have I felt so light.* She ignored the welcoming glade, the mighty river, and the patient horse. Kurt's lips, and the magic within them, became her entire world.

He broke the kiss.

Cool air bathed her face.

"You give me great joy." He panted. "Dare I call you the future Polly Tafel?"

"Yes." She placed a quick, bold kiss at the corner of his smile. "Mrs. Tafel...*Frau* Tafel...both names sound lovely."

Chapter Twenty-Five

Early September afternoon sunshine illuminated the living quarters behind the cobbler shop through small, clean windows. The open kitchen door allowed entrance of the sounds of end-of-work-day traffic on Third Street. The scent of vinegar escaped the lidded kettle on the stove.

Polly frowned. In the next moment, she scooped a cup of salt and added the seasoning to the simmering brine. She gave the pot of water, vinegar, salt, and sugar a quick stir and replaced the lid. *I must have fresh air. The kitchen is too warm, and vinegar turns my stomach worse than coffee.*

"Sixteen…seventeen…eighteen cucumbers makes two layers in the crock." Joseph lifted a thick onion slice. "I'm glad we are making pickles, Mama."

"I am thankful for *Frau* Keil's advice." She stood in the open doorway and cleansed her lungs. She sneaked a glance at her son and compared the youngster who enjoyed reading stories, playing marbles, and telling jokes with his friends, to the shy child of a year ago.

"Shop is closed for the day." Kurt stepped into the large room and shut the door behind him. "How goes the pickling?"

"Well." Polly fastened her gaze on her husband. Drawing another deep breath, she regarded the kind, capable man. *My husband. How can I be so fortunate?* For a moment, she allowed herself to recall the small wedding ceremony on a mild May morning. Often, she paused in amazement at the joy and laughter sprinkled in the long hours of work which made her life richer than she had ever dreamed.

"More dill." Kurt peeked into the crock and directed Joseph before he joined Polly. "I want to finish the letter to Pennsylvania tonight. Do you have any special words to add?"

She glanced toward the sky before meeting his gaze. "Have you told them of the garden crops?"

"*Ja,* do you want me to read the page aloud before you decide what to say?"

Allowing a smile to grow, she shook her head. Her husband was talented at many things, but his reading and writing were limited to *Deutsch*—in a script she found baffling. "I need a moment or two to organize my thoughts. The warm kitchen has muddled my mind."

Kurt tipped his head. "Today, the weather is fine— not near the heat of three days ago. Are you ill? According to my customers, two are sick at the Clemons' household."

"I don't want to hear of the Clemonses." As recently as two weeks ago, the elderly dry goods proprietor chased her from his store with a string of insults. Included in his tirade were remarks on her character, Joseph's parentage, and *filthy Deutsch.* Straightening from the door frame, she marveled. Her Bible did not condemn a married couple who attended separate Christian churches or spoke different languages since birth. Evidently, Mr. Clemons...and Mr. Rush...studied a different translation. She stepped to the woodpile and petted Smoke, the gray cat perched on the logs. "Joseph."

"Yes, Mama."

"Go to the garden and get two more onions and wash them at the pump. Do not hurry."

"More onion? We have enough on the plate to finish this crock." He stared with wide eyes and an open mouth.

"Go, do as I say." She returned to the kitchen and surveyed the table.

Kurt followed her and added two more heads to the dill layer. "Now, you have me curious. Are you keeping a secret?"

"I...I want you to add news to the letter...tell your parents and the others...another Tafel will join the family in the spring." She studied him as his eyes reflected first questions, then confusion, and finally widened with joy.

Grinning, he opened his arms for her to step close. "A baby...our baby. In spring...Joseph will be a big brother. When?"

Our baby... She closed her eyes for a moment and savored the phrase. "April...early in the month...if I have counted the weeks correct."

"You are well...no problems?" He studied her face.

Polly forbade her smile to grow. "I am well...aside from certain smells. Will you...ladle the brine over the cucumbers?"

"With joy in my heart." Adjusting his hold, he positioned her for a dance and hummed "*Tauberin-Walzer*, Little Doves Waltz."

One...two...three. She counted the still-unfamiliar

steps in silence and followed his lead around the furniture. Completing the second circle, she spied Joseph in the doorway.

Her son stood perfectly still, his mouth half-open and water dripping off a plump onion in each hand.

"A celebration...private...Your mama and I will tell you family business...not to leave the household. Do you understand?" Kurt addressed Joseph.

He nodded. "I can keep secrets."

A few minutes later, the pregnancy news told, Polly hugged Joseph. "You will make a good, big brother. I am certain."

"This baby"—Joseph glanced from Polly to Kurt and back again—"will he speak English or *Deutsch?*"

Polly laughed and slid her gaze toward Kurt. "We teach both, I think."

"Yes, good to teach from a young age." Kurt kissed her on the cheek. "You are an excellent mother, a fine wife, and a talented seamstress. You stitch dreams into a life."

Dreams. She closed her eyes for a long moment. An image of her hands, stitching a fine seam joining different fabrics, formed. She imagined her life, her new family, as an excellent quilt—not made of cotton, or wool, or leather, but dreams.

A word about the author...

Raised in a household full of books, it was only natural Ellen Parker grew up with a book in her hand. She turned to writing as a second career and enjoys spinning the type of story which appeals to more than one generation. She encourages readers to share her work with mother or daughter—or both. When not guiding characters to their "happily ever after" she's likely reading, tending her postage stamp size garden, or walking in the neighborhood. She currently lives in St. Louis. You can find her on the web at: www.ellen-parker-writes.com or on Facebook at: www.facebook.com/ellenparkerwrites.

Other Titles by this Author
Comfort Zone
Morning Tryst
New Dreams
Stare Down

Thank you for purchasing
this publication of The Wild Rose Press, Inc.

For questions or more information
contact us at
info@thewildrosepress.com.

The Wild Rose Press, Inc.
www.thewildrosepress.com